HEIR'S AFFAIR

SCARLETT FINN

Also by Scarlett Finn

ROMANTIC SUSPENSE

GO NOVELS
GO WITH IT
GO IT ALONE
GO ALL OUT
GO ALL IN
GO FULL CIRCLE

TO DIE FOR...
TO DIE FOR TRUTH
TO DIE FOR HONOR
TO DIE FOR VIRTUE
TO DIE FOR DUTY
TO DIE FOR LOVE

KINDRED SERIES
RAVEN
SWALLOW
CUCKOO
SWIFT
FALCON
FINCH

MCDADE BROTHERS NOVELS
ALL. ONLY.
ONLY YOURS

THE EXPLICIT SERIES
EXPLICIT INSTRUCTION
EXPLICIT DETAIL
EXPLICIT MEMORY

WRECK & RUIN
RUIN ME
RUIN HIM

LOVE AGAINST THE ODDS STANDALONE COLLECTION
SWEET SEAS
HEIR'S AFFAIR
RESCUED
MAESTRO'S MUSE
GETTING TRICKY
THIRTEEN
REMEMBER WHEN...
RELUCTANT SUSPICION
XY FACTOR

HARROW DUET
FIGHTING FATE
FIGHTING BACK

THE BRANDED SERIES
BRANDED
SCARRED
MARKED

RISQUÉ SERIES
TAKE A RISK
RISK IT ALL
GAME OF RISK

EXILE
HIDE & SEEK
KISS CHASE

MISTAKE DUET
MISTAKE ME NOT
SLEIGHT MISTAKE

CONTEMPORARY ROMANCE

NOTHING TO...
NOTHING TO HIDE
NOTHING TO LOSE
NOTHING TO DECLARE
NOTHING TO US

LOST & FOUND
LOST
FOUND

ONE

TALLULAH TAYLOR HAD KNOCKED on the apartment door when she arrived, but no one had answered it. She'd been told not to return to work until she confirmed they'd found the man they'd been searching for over the last three months and this was where he was supposed to be.

Tally had worked for the Stretton family since leaving college and knew their official story almost as well as she knew the unofficial one. Staff at the Stretton Estate, and those at the corporation of Stretton Chemicals, loved to share gossip and rumors. Patriarch and CEO Theodore Stretton had been married only once and believed above almost everything else that it was important to keep up the appearance of respectability. Teddy was good at it. But he prided himself on being good at everything he did.

In her role as the family liaison, Tally worked mostly at the Stretton Estate, and had been asked to do all sorts of unusual tasks for the family.

But this mission was a first.

It all started three-and-a-half-months ago when Teddy and his wife, Laura, were involved in a vehicular accident. The limo they were traveling in was hit at high speed and Laura was killed. Her death changed a bunch of perspectives.

The couple had a daughter together, Kimmy. But because of his old-fashioned views, Teddy had made sure that his daughter was raised as a spoiled princess. Kimmy grated on her father, but a lot of people did, he wasn't a patient man.

Though Tally did recognize that Teddy was proud of his daughter, not because of any immense achievements on Kimmy's part, but because she was exactly what she was supposed to be: shallow, materialistic, and subservient.

But there was one thing Teddy Stretton lacked… he had no male heir.

Teddy Stretton liked to rule whatever room he walked into and didn't like to take second chair to anyone. Ever. Although there were people at the company who were capable, Teddy didn't trust them enough to pass his life's work to them. He wanted to hand down the company to family, male family, meaning there was a gaping hole in his will.

And that's what had brought Tally here. To this apartment.

A thirty-two-year-old rumor that Teddy had never spoken of was proven to be true in the form of Max Flynn. It turned out that the illegitimate son of Teddy Stretton was a real person and not just conjured up by gossipmongers.

At least, she'd been told that the rumor was true by the PI who'd been on the case, chasing up leads, for three months. That rumor was supposed to live in the apartment that she'd been standing outside of for two hours. But the longer she stood there, the less hopeful she became that this night was going to end well for her.

It had been her role to stay on top of the PI, to bring his reports back to an impatient Teddy who was not likely to take bad news well. Tallulah was only there because she'd been tasked with putting the proposition to Max. She wasn't the most persuasive person, but she'd been called unthreatening, so she guessed it made sense that she should explain what was going on to the man who may, or may not, even know his father's identity.

In other circumstances, a person may be nervous to

approach a stranger about the father who'd abandoned him. But Tally was confident that she had nothing to worry about. She was inviting this Max guy to meet a father who was going to bequeath him a multibillion-dollar company and make all his dreams come true. Who would argue with that?

Since arriving at the rundown apartment block, Tally had begun to build an impression of the man she was here to retrieve. The light in the corridor at the top of the stairs was broken and the one at this end was blinking. There was a weird smell too, and enough suspect stains on the floor that there was no way she was going to sit on it even though her shoes were starting to sting her feet.

Teddy didn't accept failure and she didn't feel like being reamed out, as she would be if she went back to the estate to say she'd given up for the night. Her boss had been known to reduce assistants to tears. But because she was a personal assistant to the family rather than the company, she usually avoided facing his intense wrath. Tally wasn't involved with the big bucks deals done by Stretton Chemicals. Those deals had a tendency of stressing Teddy out; the assistants who were part of those negotiations were the ones who really had to be on their toes.

Tally couldn't go back or call and say she hadn't pinned this guy down. But she was beginning to worry that he might have no intention of coming back tonight. Maybe he was spending the night with a girlfriend or maybe he'd moved. This place did suggest he might be a bit of a nomad, he sure didn't seem to care about curb appeal. And according to the PI reports, Max had gone through a phase in his twenties of moving around all the time, as revealed by his several previous addresses. Could it be that he'd moved on again?

What else could she do? How could she salvage this night? Just as she was beginning to think of contingencies, Tally heard heavy footsteps coming up the stairs.

A masculine cough.

A grumble.

"Yeah, dude," a deep husky voice said. "Yeah, man, I'm there. Don't worry about it."

In the darkness at the far end of the corridor, a broad

man measuring approximately six-four emerged at the top of the stairs, but Tally couldn't decipher his features.

His long strides ate up the floor. She only got flashes of his dark eyes and scruffy jaw in the flickers of distorted illumination pulsing from the broken light. Tallulah hadn't expected her heart rate to jump up, or to feel intimidated by her boss' son. She worked around powerful men every day and didn't blink when they walked into the room. But something about this guy was different... more oppressive... dangerous.

The phone at his ear wasn't his focus anymore. When he was within ten feet, there was no denying that his attention was on her.

"Yo, dude, I gotta go, there's a hot little brunette at my door." The guy on the other end of the line must have said something funny because the stranger smiled, and the sight of its sinister glow dazzled her. "Nah, I don't think so, Rob, I'd remember banging this one... yeah, see ya."

He hung up the phone and stopped in her personal space, crowding her against his door. "Am I wrong?" he asked. "You're not here to tell me I knocked you up, are you?"

Oh God, this guy couldn't be any less like Teddy Stretton if he sprouted wings and horns. Maybe this wouldn't be as simple as they'd all thought it would be. Why hadn't it occurred to Teddy that maybe his illegitimate son wasn't going to be easily moldable?

"Uh, no," she said, having to clear her throat twice when her voice cracked. "You are Max Flynn... aren't you?"

Intrigue lit his keen eyes. "Yep."

Relief. Good, at least she knew she was in the right place and had already managed to do half her job. "I have a proposition for you."

Taking a half step back, his brow rose as he examined her body. "Oh, yeah? For a babe like you, I'll listen," he said, leaning past her to unlock the door. "But we better make it quick. I've got somewhere to be tonight."

He gave the door a hard push, forcing it open, and she spun around. Max squeezed past her, forcing her to inhale when his jacket made contact with her shoulder.

Tally scanned inside.

The apartment was a mess.

There were dirty clothes on the couch. Empty beer bottles on the coffee table were punctuated by open pizza boxes and Chinese food containers. As she tiptoed over the threshold, she was assaulted by the scents of stale food and rugged man.

Minding her manners, Tallulah tried not to cringe when he reached over her to shove the stiff door hard, closing it with a startling thud. On the plus side, she got the chance to note that he didn't smell bad. In fact, he was wearing an intoxicating deodorant that she wouldn't mind smelling more of. For some weird reason, Tally was pleased to learn that his slobbish ways didn't extend into his personal hygiene.

He lumbered to the right into the open-plan kitchen and pulled a beer from the fridge. Holding one toward her, he only shrugged when she shook her head.

"I don't drink," she said.

He looked her over again, which he seemed to do a lot. "Alcoholic?"

She didn't want to be outraged, but he smiled and she guessed he'd read her reaction and found it funny.

Holding on to her composure, Tally remembered her manners and explained. "No… my employer doesn't allow it."

There was a bottle opener attached to the side of the fridge with a bucket beneath it. He used it to pop open the bottle and slugged down some beer. "Bummer," he said, propping himself up against the fridge on one broad arm. "Guess you're here on the clock… you don't look like one of Tony's girls. But if you are, you trot back and tell him he owes me cash not barter." He moseyed over, entering her space to whisper just above her ear. "If you wanna come back when you're off duty, I'll leave the door open for ya."

Taking another hit from his scent, Tally was dazed. "I… I thought you had a prior engagement tonight," she said and was immediately shocked by her words.

Whatever that was she could smell on him had to be a solvent or some other mind-altering substance. She was usually demure and almost meek, especially when on Stretton business. Respect, that was what it was all about, and women were supposed to be modest. Except she'd just spoken out like she was a hussy who'd take him up on his lurid offer if it wasn't for his alternative plans.

His lips twisted. He examined her body again. "Want me to cancel, sugarlips? We can get right down to it. Bedroom door's on the other side of the TV over there."

He slid a fingertip down her jawline and began to bend down like he might be going to kiss her.

Regaining her senses, she stumbled as she retreated. "No," Tally stuttered. "I... I came here to... Your father sent me."

His whole demeanor changed in a snap. He tensed, and took his own step away from her. "What the fuck? I never had a father. Never knew the bastard."

Okay, yes, she could do this. Business. "We know," she said, having not considered what she'd do if he got angry because it was such an unlikely scenario. "It took us quite a while to track you down."

His scowl was intense. "What the fuck?" he said again.

It was a surprise to find that Teddy's son was so coarse and that he lived in this squalor when the Strettons were multibillionaires. But the why wasn't her business; she had a job to do.

"Your father wants to meet you. He wants to build a relationship with you."

She expected a positive response. Instead, his frown deepened. "And who the fuck are you? His old lady?"

Uh, she'd swear herself if it wasn't against another of Teddy's rules. "Your father is sixty-five," she said. "I'm twenty-eight."

"And that fucking matters? My mom said my father was some rich fuck who ditched her. That true?"

"Oh." She blushed and tucked a loose strand of hair behind her ear. "I'm sorry, I don't know anything about their relationship. I was sent here to retrieve you."

His brow went up. "Yeah? Well come on, Sugar, retrieve me." When she said nothing, he lunged forward, pinning her to a post that stood between the kitchen and living room, his hand landed on it high above her head. "What kind of fuck sends a little thing like you to a place like this? You know we had a murder in this building last week?"

Tally inhaled through her nose because she feared if she opened her mouth that her heart would leap out of her throat. "No, I… I didn't know that."

His anger was aimed at her, at Teddy, at everything. "Do your research before you walk into any place, little thing. If you thought I was like him, you're wrong. I'm nothing like him."

"How do you know that if you don't know him?" she asked, adrenaline giving her gumption. "Your father is a serious man, he's thorough, and intelligent… you could do worse than be like him… He also just lost his wife; he could've lost his life too. You could've lost him. But you have a chance to get to know him."

"Thanks," he sneered. "But no thanks." Dropping his attention, he grumbled at the floor before making eye contact again. "I'd love to toss your butt into the hallway and slam the door in your face, but your skinny ass won't see the street if I don't walk you out." Seizing her arm, he slammed his beer onto the kitchen counter, then dragged her to the door. "You parked somewhere around here?"

Pulling back, Tally wasn't ready to give up. "Mr. Flynn, please," she said, trying to free herself, but he got her out of the apartment and tugged her down the hallway. "Please, hear me out. I have so much to tell you! Please! Let me explain!"

"Where's your car, kid?"

Fighting him was as effective as the fly fighting the spider. Tally was powerless and weak in comparison to this predator who was on a mission. Throughout their descent of the stairs, she kept trying to pull away. But when he did stop, it wasn't because of her efforts, it was because of what they came across at the bottom of the stairs. Between them and the door were a group of guys wearing gang colors. Max's grip got even more serious… she'd thought it was serious before, but she'd been wrong.

"Flynn!" The guy at the head of the group said while checking her out. "Nice bitch."

"Bored of her now," Max said in a deep grumble. "I'm getting rid of her, Strap."

The guy laughed and ran his tongue along his upper teeth. "She looks high class."

"Out of your price range," Max said and tried to keep going, but the group closed in.

"You hand her over and the first time is free, right?"

With one step, Max put a forearm on Strap's chest and thrust him to the wall. "You don't put your hands on this bitch, none of you, get it?"

"It like that?" Strap asked. "She yours?"

"Yeah, that's it," Max said. "Now get your asses out of my way."

Strap held up his hands. "We don't want no trouble with you, homie. You say she's yours, she's it."

The guys parted like the Red Sea. Tally staggered along beside Max when he strode through the leering group. And though she tried her best not to look at the men who were curious about her, she couldn't believe Max had just stood up to what had to be ten men in that narrow space.

"Mr. Flynn," she said when they got to the street. It took her that long to be able to breathe again. "Oh, my God, if I'd run into those men alone—"

"Yeah, Tiny, think about that next time you rock up to strange guy's places."

"Thank you," she said because he'd stepped up for her.

Tally was still in a daze, stumbling as she trotted along behind him until he came to an abrupt halt.

"Where's your car?" he asked and she looked around to see they were on the corner of the block.

If that's what he was looking for, he'd be looking for a long time. "I don't have a car," she said. "I was dropped off by a company driver."

Pierre lived in the same section of staff quarters that she did at the Stretton Estate. He helped her out whenever he could, but tonight he had other places to be and couldn't hang around.

"Company car? Nice. My old man must make out all right."

That answered her question about whether Max knew who his father was. "More than all right," she said, thinking his attitude would change when he learned the scope of what she was presenting to him. "Theodore Stretton is worth a few billion…" For the first time since she'd identified herself, Max lost his scowl. "And he wants to bequeath it to you."

A second later he laughed a short, sinister sound that had no resemblance to amusement. "Not interested." What? Tally didn't even know how to… What? Stepping into the road, Max stopped a cab and opened the back door. "Hop it, girlie, don't come back."

Casting off her surprise, Tally refused to get into the back of the car. "Please let me explain," she said. "Let me tell you what he wants."

"No," Max said, trying to wrestle her into the car.

This was her job. Panic was making her fingers shake. All she was supposed to do was identify that he was Max Flynn and bring him to his father. If she couldn't do that…

She couldn't keep fighting him, he was stronger than she was, but she tried her best to resist. Already her muscles were aching as she battled his attempts to push her down, and he wasn't even really trying.

"Please!"

"No!"

Desperation was making her frantic. The Stretton's were all she knew, if Teddy got mad, that was it, he'd fire her and life as she knew it would be over. "Please!"

"Get in the damn cab!" he demanded.

"Just let me explain!" she begged.

"Get the fuck outta here!"

"He'll fire me, Max!" she exclaimed. The words just tumbled out of her. She didn't know what she'd do if she didn't have the Strettons. Max stopped pushing her and frowned again, but this one wasn't angry so much as it was curious. "I'm sorry but… this means a lot to him. A lot of time has gone into finding you and… Teddy's not the most patient man. If I go back there and tell him we talked, but I didn't tell you everything… he'll fire me and… I live at the house, Mr. Flynn. I'll be homeless, jobless, and he'll never give me a reference. Please… you have to hear me out. I've worked for your family for years. I've never seen it like this. Please…" Taking a breath, she tried to find a thread of composure. "How bad can one conversation be? Will it kill you?"

His jaw worked side to side as he ground his teeth. "Fine. Tomorrow night, meet me at Fitzpatrick's a block over… I'm buying you a drink."

Shaking her head, Tally had to refuse. She'd been teetotal for years. The idea of picking up a glass scared her. "No, my employer—"

"Yeah, you gave me that line upstairs. 'Cept now I know who your employer is, I don't give a fuck. How'd you like that? Drink with me or no conversation."

Max liked to be in control, just like his father. Which was the lesser of the evils? Agree to have a drink or get fired from the only respectable job she'd ever had?

To get what she needed, Tally had to acquiesce. "What time?"

TWO

WHAT WAS SHE DOING HERE? Tally shouldn't have dressed up like this was a date. Though to be fair, she'd worn this dress to the last SC event. A professional event. It wasn't a dress designed to allure, it was meant to be worn on a social occasion… and this was, technically, a social occasion.

Except she'd forgotten that a social occasion with a billionaire wasn't the same as one in a dive bar in a crappy neighborhood.

God, she was out of practice.

To say she was drawing attention to herself was an understatement and she'd only gotten out of the car ten seconds ago. The gang on the corner were loitering, whispering as they checked her out. It was too dark to read their expressions, but she'd bet they weren't simply speculating on who'd designed what she was wearing.

Tally had no choice but to cross the sidewalk and go into Fitzpatrick's.

Keeping her head down, she moved past the curve of the bar and picked a central spot on the straight edge. It wasn't busy, only a few tables were occupied, but the back of the room was gloomy, meaning she couldn't pick out any features.

There could be a whole football team back there and she wouldn't be able to tell.

The floor, the walls, the ceiling, everywhere was painted black. Furniture was sparse and shabby. This wasn't just a ramshackle place, it was ominous.

The curious bartender was almost mocking her with his sneer when he came over. Examining her sequined clutch and the diamonds dangling from her ears, he couldn't hide his smile.

"Uh…" she said, trying to hold her posture. "Club soda, please."

"Fuck that," Max's booming voice vibrated behind her and she turned to see him striding over. He tossed some words to a table he passed, then laughed, and came to her at the bar. He must have been here already, sitting at a table somewhere, and she hadn't even noticed him. "Usual, Trey."

Tally was almost afraid to ask. "Wha…? What's the usual?"

Max didn't even look at her, he just rested an expectant hand on the bar. "Tequila."

"Oh no," she said as the bartender nodded and disappeared. "I couldn't—"

"Leave us the bottle, Trey," Max called to the bartender who sauntered back over while pouring out a measure. "Put it on my tab."

"Oh, yeah?" Trey sniggered. "And when you think you'll pay that tab, buddy? Huh?"

There was a smile on Trey's face, but it wasn't one of humor. This guy had to have a store of smiles and she'd yet to see one that was happy.

Max took her by surprise when he turned and unhooked her earring to slap it onto the bar. "That should cover me for a while."

The bartender's intrigue made him pick up the jewel to scrutinize it. The diamond must have passed inspection because Trey slid the bottle onto the bar in front of them.

"Oh no, wait," she said, but the bartender was already walking away.

Max ignored her too. He stood up and leaned over

the bar to snag another glass from a lowered shelf. Straightening again, he poured out the second drink that Trey had neglected.

"Okay, sweetheart," Max said, picking up his glass to toss back the shot before refilling it with a more generous measure. "You're out of your comfort zone here, so let me give you a few tips."

"Tips?"

He shoved her glass to her. Tally touched it with her fingertips, but didn't want to drink. "First, drink," he said, picking up the glass to put it in her hand. She sipped, but he sniggered. "Drink it all."

Oh, God, she hadn't had a drink in years and he was asking her to down this potent liquid all at once? Closing her eyes, Tally took the biggest mouthful she could and tried not to choke as the liquor scorched her throat. She covered her mouth with the back of her fingers to stifle a cough.

"Good, now lose the sparkle," he said, turning her hand to unclip her tennis bracelet. "I'm surprised you didn't get mugged on the street out there."

She unhooked her other earring and opened her clutch to slide the jewelry inside, not that keeping it safe mattered; she wouldn't be able to wear those earrings again since Max had just bartered the other one for their drinks.

"I was dropped off by—"

"A company driver, sure," he said. "How come they drop you off but never pick you up or wait? Take your hair down."

Pulling the slide from her chignon, Tally put the accessory in her clutch too, then pulled the pins from her locks. His question was probably rhetorical, but she answered it anyway for lack of anything better to say.

"Pierre is nice to me, he drops me off when he's on his way to official jobs… he's not really supposed to drive me," she said. "I'm just an assistant, I don't warrant official attention. Your father and Kimmy are going to the ballet tonight and she—"

"Yeah, yeah."

Tally gasped when he grabbed her dress at her waist

and tugged it down with such force it almost ripped. "Mr. Flynn!" she exclaimed, looking down to see that her breasts were now heaving over her neckline with the lace of her bra cups peeking over the top of the conservative fabric.

But he didn't slow down, he licked each of his thumbs in turn and cradled her head to smudge the make-up at the corners of her eyes. She was still stuttering when he slid one of her dress straps off the ball of her shoulder.

"Sit up on your stool, baby, nice and straight," he said, putting his arms around her to direct the seat under her ass and closer to him. "Cross your legs toward me."

Without much of a choice given his proximity and actions, Tally perched herself on the high stool and did as he said. He pulled her even closer so that her crossed legs were nestled between his wide thighs.

"What are you—"

"Good girl," he said and drove his fingers into her hair. Tally wasn't used to any man being so rough and brazen with her. His hands were so big, his wide fingers tangled and tugged as they rumpled and messed her hair. He tilted his head. "Hmm..." If she was reading his scrutiny right, something still wasn't meeting his standard. Max landed on some idea and leaned forward with her chin pinched between his curled forefinger and thumb. "Open up for me, sweetness."

Tally did open her mouth, because she was going to ask what he was planning. But that opening gave him the opportunity to slip his tongue between her lips. She was too shocked to even respond; he forced his mouth over hers to kiss her more thoroughly than she'd ever been kissed.

He tasted of bitter liquor and dangerous man. Max was powerful and his lack of propriety proved how he felt entitled to dominate her, even though they were still practically strangers and sitting in public.

Tally was still in shock when he leaned back and picked up his glass to toss back his tequila. "That's better," he said, rubbing a thumb over the corner of her mouth before sliding two large hands up the front of her thigh and under her skirt. His brows rose when he touched lace. "You wearing something fancy for me, babygirl?" No, she wore thigh-high stockings every day. They weren't for him. "Show me."

But he didn't wait for her to do anything, he gathered up her skirt, bunching it above her stockings, exposing a line of flesh on her thighs and he grumbled something that sounded like appreciation.

"Mr. Flynn," she said, trying to push his hands away when he began to stroke the bared skin of her legs. "Please."

"Listen, baby," he murmured, sliding his elbow along the bar so he could cup her face under her hair and stroke her cheek. "The only way you get out of here without trouble is if you fit in. And the only way you fit in is if you belong to me, got it?"

"Belong to—"

"That's right," he said, the corner of his mouth tilting as his eyes fell to her lips. "Now show me you understand."

How was she supposed to do that? This was beyond out of her element. Tally touched her naked earlobe and cleared her throat. Suddenly she was aware of the other patrons, and how they might view her as a stranger coming in here wearing diamonds and designer clothes, and then she remembered those men in the entryway of Max's building and those on the corner outside. The necessity of fear made her play along.

She wasn't usually forward and hadn't been on a real date in… forever. Tally was too busy to date. Yeah, she often went to social functions, but she was only there to be on hand for her employer.

The men who accompanied her were usually other Stretton employees who had their own reasons for being present. She was a good cover for security or for lawyers who wanted to be close to Teddy. For men who didn't necessarily want to declare themselves as anything other than the innocuous date of an insignificant assistant.

When she dropped her hand onto Max's knee, he smiled. "Gotta give me more than that," he murmured.

More, okay, pushing her shoulders back, she arched into him like she wanted him to notice her cleavage and, with a sly smile, he did.

"Nice," he muttered. "More… make them really believe it, Sugar."

Geez, how far was she going to have to go with this guy for appearances? Leaning in, Tally touched her lips to his and that was when she noticed it. Here in these close quarters, she saw the light of interest in his eyes. She couldn't usually read men, but this guy was more unashamed than others and it was there. Definitely there. He was attracted to her, without a doubt.

Instead of worrying her, a heat clenched in Tally's belly and her constricted breasts grew heavy. Awareness tingled through her. Why did it kick her hormones into overdrive to know she'd caught the attention of this uncivilized animal?

Skimming her lips over his stubble, she kissed his jaw then parted her lips to rasp her teeth against him. If he wanted more, she was going to give it to him. Did he have a limit? How far would he let her go?

Her hands moved higher up his legs and Tally used that point of contact as a lever to rise. Pushing her body into his, she ran her tongue along his lower lip and then opened to give him the kiss she'd been too shocked to give him before.

It started slow and sped up until they reached a kind of fever pitch. Grabbing her hair in an unyielding fist, Max gripped her so tight that her scalp burned, but it was enlivening. The sheer possession of that masculine hand lost in her mass of loose hair made her feel primal.

Holding her head back at a sharp angle, he forced her to stay under his mouth, under his domination, beneath his need.

Her hands skimmed to the top of his thighs and her thumbs trailed up each side of the thick erection pulsing in his jeans. God, she shouldn't be touching him like this, this wasn't "more," this was beyond the line, far beyond the line. But the next time her thumbs pushed down, they were more insistent, rubbing harder, making it clear she had found his arousal and wasn't afraid of it.

The hand that wasn't in her hair left her thigh and closed around her breast. Tally gasped when Max squeezed her hard, but the sharp inhale just drew his tongue deeper into her mouth, intensifying their kiss.

An abrupt whistle to her left interrupted their mouths and both of them turned to see that the bartender was right there. "Yo, that's what the alley out back is for," Trey said, glaring at them both with mischief. "Cool it or split."

Oh God, what had she done? She'd been making out with Max Flynn in public! More than making out! She'd touched his…

Twisting away from him, Tally put both elbows on the bar and grabbed up her glass to down the last of her tequila. This time the burn of the liquor was welcome. She needed that cleansing wash in her mouth, to slide over her tongue and down her throat to the want that was still softening her core in preparation for slaking her surprising desire.

The bottle came into view. She was so happy to see that the next measure Max poured for her was more liberal than the last and she was grateful to gulp it down.

Max leaned in at her side, losing his mouth in her hair until it was pressed against her ear. "Now you're getting it, baby," he murmured and slid his hand to her inner thigh, massaging the flesh between the top of her thigh-high and her panties.

It went higher until the edge of his finger touched the lace of her crotch and that was when she grabbed his wrist to pull it back down to her knee.

"Don't," she whispered. Lowering her glass to the bar, she turned her head toward his, which was only an inch away. "I'm sorry I touched you, that was… rude."

But his heavy eyes weren't offended; he leaned in to kiss the corner of her mouth. "You're good at being rude, angel," he said and picked up her hand to put it back on his thigh. Pressing his palm against her knuckles, he slid her hand all the way up until it was covering the bulge behind his fly. "And you got my attention in all the right places."

"I don't want that attention from you," she whispered.

The most shameful part of that statement was its dishonesty, because some secret, naughty part of her did want it.

"Too bad, gorgeous, 'cause you've got it… and it ain't going anywhere."

"Can you just pick a pet name and stick with it?" she snapped in an uncharacteristic burst of anger.

Every time he used a different one it made her think that he did this with every woman; tossing out different names, showing no commitment to any, like their identities were interchangeable. It was insulting to be lumped in with every other female who'd ever crossed his path.

Except, she shouldn't care, didn't care before they'd kissed and now…

Tally felt off-balance and sick. Not disgusted, just confused, and aroused, and angry at herself. The impatience itching under her skin wanted to grab his hand and drag him out to that alley the bartender had mentioned, proving what a disappointment she was to her employer and to her gender.

He eased back a little. "Okay, Boss, you got it… I've got no problem following your orders. You like to be in charge, baby? Like to keep your guy in line?"

She hated the way his hand was stroking her lower back. It was making her relax in all the wrong ways. Her lungs were getting tighter as her sense began to dwindle.

"You're not my guy," she whispered.

"Okay, casual, you got it, Boss… whatever you want."

Gulping more liquor, Tally surprised herself by being the one to pick up the bottle this time. "You said I had to belong to you to survive. It's a show, right?"

Marginalizing what had happened was supposed to ensure that it didn't happen again.

"Sure, baby," he murmured and pushed her hair away from her shoulder, but he didn't get the message. He used her locks to force her head aside so he could close his lips over the side of her neck.

She was supposed to be here to talk business, to tell him about his father, and put the proposition to him. She wasn't supposed to be here to seduce him or be seduced.

"Mr. Flynn," she said, struggling to find her voice as

his lips caressed her neck and found her shoulder to follow her collarbone. "Please, we have… business."

"We sure do," he said and his hand tried to move higher again. "You tell me what you want, Boss. Where do you wanna be touched?"

She yelped and had to brace when he suddenly spun the seat of her stool. Tally found herself facing away from him. He yanked her back, pulling her between his legs again. One powerful arm curved around her and he slid her to the back edge of her stool, pulling her ass into his erection and her back to his chest.

He kept on kissing her neck, and she exhaled when he sucked lightly and sent a skitter of needles from her throat to her breasts that weren't neglected of his attention. When Max grazed his hands over her chest, she quickly combed her fingers through the ends of her hair to cover up the action.

The bartender had threatened to throw them out the last time he'd touched her there and she didn't want to get into trouble. But Max took her action as encouragement.

His warm laugh on her shoulder loosened her further. "Nice," he grumbled into her. "You like that, Boss? Like it when I play with your cans? You've got some set, they feel real good. I bet they taste even better."

His squeeze got more insistent. In an involuntary move, she pushed her hips back hard, showing her appreciation by wriggling against him. But he liked it and anchored himself to give her security in her grinding.

Tally curled her fingers into his thighs, digging her nails into him through his jeans. "God, you're good at this," she whispered without meaning to say anything.

But her senses weren't working on full capacity. For some reason, her entire being had been reduced to her erogenous zones. Tally had become little more than a raw, eager hormone. But she was struggling to fight his appeal. It had been so long since she'd had any male attention, and the intensity of Max's attention was unique in her experience.

Lifting her arm, Tally coiled it around his head and clenched her fingers in his hair. Max curled further around her to kiss her throat and upper chest, and when she couldn't take it anymore, she used her tight grip to pull him up so she could fumble her mouth over his.

Kissing him was the end of her resolve.

Something about the way his tongue took control of hers made her forget everything about who she was and how she was supposed to behave.

"Get a room!" someone hollered.

Blinking open her dazed eyes, Tally turned to see she was in prime, central view of the whole room. Everyone in the place was watching her and Max here at the bar acting worse than a couple of horny teenagers.

Shit.

This was bad.

Except…

She wasn't as self-conscious as she should be. In fact, she smiled.

Oh, God, this was one of those crazy moments in life. Those once in a life time opportunities to say to hell with consequences. Tally hadn't been crazy in a long time. In truth, she'd never been this crazy.

Man, she wanted to be crazy.

Insane, crazy.

Right now.

Leaping from her stool, out of Max's arms, she picked up her glass and tossed back the last of her drink before grabbing her clutch in one hand and Max's wrist in the other. Pulling him toward the back of the bar, she sought the exit sign and laughed when a chorus of whoops and cheers followed them out of the room and down a corridor past the restrooms.

Shoving the metal bar on the rear fire exit door, they burst into the cold air of the dark, shadowy alley. But she didn't slow down, she pulled him across it and into a doorway before dropping her clutch to the ground.

Hitching up her skirt, Tally caught the elastic of her underwear and drew it down her legs. "Boss—"

"Shut up and do what you're told," she said, more alive than she'd ever been as she stuffed her panties into his jacket pocket and grabbed his buckle to loosen his jeans.

"Yes, mam," he said and bent to pick her up.

This was insane.

There was still time to tell him she didn't want to go all the way. But he kissed her and that was it, decision made. Of all the times she could choose to be crazy, this probably wasn't the best one. But she'd never felt so base, so in need, so wanted.

The head of his dick stretched her to her limit and she hissed, but he was on a mission and pushed in hard.

"Oh, fuck," she yelped in pain and smacked his shoulder in reflex. "Ow!"

"Fuck," he ground out in a groan from the back of his throat. "I thought you were prepped."

She was, she'd never been so wet, as evidenced by the dampness she'd felt in her panties as she drew them down.

"Go hard," she said and he surged forward, but she cried out and he swore again.

His head bumped on the door behind her as he slapped the steel with the side of his fist. "Shit! You're so fucking tight. You have done this before, right?"

Panting, she reassured herself by rubbing his shoulders. "In an alley with a stranger? No."

"Sex," he said. "You have been fucked before, right?"

The last thing she wanted was for her inadequacies to make him withdraw, so she smiled and kissed him. "Not by a real man."

That compliment made him groan again. She smiled so wide that he almost smiled back before pushing his forehead onto hers. He took a slow breath then slid his hands to her hips and held her tightly as he worked himself back and forth, taking a gentler approach to easing his way inside.

Kissing her jaw, he rubbed his cheek on hers. "How's that feel, Boss?"

Biting her lip, she whimpered and nodded. "Amazing."

"Good," he purred out and drew back to push in harder.

"Yes," she exhaled. "Fuck me." She didn't usually swear and using the primitive words sent a frisson of arousal zipping through her. "Please, fuck me hard." Turning her face against him, she kissed and rubbed her mouth on his angular jaw. "Do me fast and hard. Right here."

Now that he was all the way inside her, he could pick up the pace and she got what she wanted; he surged in deep making her call out in delight at their achievement. But he didn't slow down, he pumped hard, his dick loosening her passage with every thrust.

Tally clenched hard and dug her teeth into his jaw when orgasm hit her like a freight train. His climax wasn't far behind and she bucked against him to meet that final thrust though his pelvis slammed hers so hard it smashed into the solid steel door behind her.

They both took a second to recover. His panting frizzed her hair and she breathed against his throat while coming to terms with the shame of what she'd just done.

This was bad.

She felt amazing.

But this was bad.

Oh, so very bad.

Max shifted his mouth down to her hairline. "I've always heard the classiest chicks like it dirtiest," he said and inched back to put her on her feet. Tally pulled her skirt back down as he fastened his jeans. When he'd put himself together, he ducked to grab her clutch from the concrete. She took her purse in one hand, Max took the other and linked their fingers to lead her down the alley. "Come on, my place is just a block over."

His place where they'd probably drink more and would definitely have more sex. If they hadn't been able to contain themselves in a public bar, she'd never be able to resist him in his private apartment.

"No," she said, taking her hand back when they hit the street. "I…" She couldn't even look at him now and the alcohol was beginning to make her feel sick. "I have to go."

"Go?" he asked. "Where the fuck do you have to go?"

Stepping off the sidewalk, Tally saw a cab driving toward them and held out a hand to hail it. "I'm sorry, Mr.

Flynn, I… someone will be in touch." The cab stopped and she opened the door. She put one foot in and then felt that she should say something else, but what the hell should she say? "I, uh… I had a good time, thanks." Slipping into the cab, Tally gave her address and then clenched her fists and punched the seat beneath her thighs while she bounced her head off the backrest. "Shit! Shit! Shit!"

"Good night?" the driver asked.

Taking a long breath, she narrowed her eyes on the dark street whizzing past. "Oh, yeah. I just fucked my entire life in one night."

"Sorry to hear that," the driver said. "But, hey, your boyfriend looked pretty upset that you cut out on him."

Sure he did, she'd just pulled the plug on a night of debauchery. He'd probably go back into that bar and everyone would jeer and cheer, but they'd paid for the liquor, he might as well drink it. Hell, that one stone would keep him in liquor for the rest of the year.

"He's not my boyfriend," she said. "He's my boss' son."

The driver wasn't so quick to respond this time. "Oh, yeah, huh… that might not have been smart."

"Tell me about it," she muttered and closed her eyes as her head fell back again.

Good going, Tally, well-fucking-done.

THREE

IF TALLY COULD CHOOSE to never face her embarrassment again, she would. Unfortunately, Teddy was losing his patience with her. He'd threatened to put someone else on the case and Tally couldn't let that happen, not before she spoke to Max and asked him to keep their indiscretion a secret.

He owed her nothing and might tell her to go to hell. And if he did, she'd deserve it. Her stupidity would hang over their heads forever. Max was going to take his place in the family and at the company, so their encounter would become another secret, another thing for the rumor-mill to chew on.

But if Teddy found out about it, he'd fire her for sure and her life was the Strettons. Tally didn't know who she was without them.

But, God, facing Max was going to be embarrassing.

Deliberately choosing to come to his apartment in the afternoon, she figured there was no way he could try to coerce her into having a drink. So she should be able to keep her head. Tally kept her purse on her shoulder and her chin in the air, reminding herself to be professional and not skanky.

The idea of returning to this apartment building on

her own was a bit scary. Her heart was pounding when she stepped into the entryway because she feared finding the gangbangers who had been here before. Luckily, it was empty. She hurried up the stairs and along the hallway to Max's door.

Lifting her fist to knock, Tally tried to figure out what she should do if he didn't answer, like he hadn't last time. Before, when they'd been strangers, waiting was frustrating, but no big deal. But hanging around on his doorstep now might come across wrong, like she was a needy stalker.

Trouble was, she couldn't put this off any longer. It had been more than a week since their Fitzpatrick's encounter and she'd fed Teddy every excuse she could think of to delay coming back to Max's.

The door opened fast, but swung to an abrupt stop when Max registered it was her. His surprise faded to a frown. "Boss Lady," he said. "Here for another session? 'Cause the rates for slumming it have gone up."

Snarky, okay, she deserved that. But she couldn't care about their personal relationship, she had to steel herself against her feelings on that subject. This was her. Professional.

"No, Mr. Flynn, I came here to talk."

" 'Kay," he said. "Come in."

"No," she said when he took half a step back.

His smirk mocked her. "Don't trust yourself?"

Actually, yeah, that was the exact reason she didn't want to go in there, but Tally didn't admit it. "This won't take long," she said and retrieved a card from the front of her purse. "Your presence is required at this address tomorrow night."

"That right?" he asked, moving his hand from the door to take the card from her.

As he read it, he took a beer bottle to his lips; she hadn't even noticed it was there. What was he doing drinking in the afternoon? Yeah, okay, it was the weekend, but still, it was daylight outside! Maybe she wouldn't be so worried about his alcohol consumption if she wasn't also worried about his hands… his mouth… his tongue… his…

Damn.

She knew he had a job; he and his friends ran a garage

just a couple of blocks from here. But from everything the PI had told her, they didn't keep regular hours and the shop was closed as often as it was open. Tally had considered going to the garage to find him but had been reluctant to announce his family business in front of his friends and colleagues… especially if they were anything like him.

"Yes," she said. "Dinner will be served at eight."

"Yeah, I don't think I'll show," he said, tucking the card into the front of her purse again. "But if you want to grab a burger sometime, gimme a call."

He started to close the door and she stuttered, she couldn't let him shut her out, she'd have no way back in.

Stepping forward, Tally planted her hand on the door. "Please, Mr. Flynn."

"Why'd you call me that?" he asked, narrowing his eyes on her. "What do you have to do with a guy before you'll use his first name?"

She hadn't thought about how ridiculous it was until he pointed it out. Now her thoughts were a mess again and it took a minute for her to pull them back.

"That's… irrelevant. I really would urge you to reconsider dinner at the Stretton Estate. I think you'll find the visit worth your while."

His eyes scanned her figure. "You gonna be there?"

That question was unexpected; he'd thrown her off-kilter again. "In the building? Probably. At Mr. Stretton's dining table? No." Imagine that, her seated at the family dinner table. Tally's smirk hid a laugh, but Max didn't like that she was so amused by the idea because he scowled at her. "But uh… you'll meet your sister, Kimmy."

"Sister?" he asked.

She nodded. "Yes, she's… eager to meet you." *Please say yes'* was all she could think while he looked at her. "Your father will send a car—"

"That will ditch me."

"Oh no," she said, worrying that her comments might have given him the wrong idea. "You will be taken care of in every way. Your father has already hired a full staff for you. You'll have your own suite and a full fleet of cars at your disposal."

"A full fleet, huh?" he asked, leaning on the doorframe.

Being that his main trade was working on cars, she figured that would be a good way to get through to him.

This was going well, he was getting it, she was making progress. "And you'll have access to the corporate jet and accounts with all major retailers and entertainment venues."

"Entertainment venues?" he asked. "Like for baseball?"

She nodded. Could sports be what persuaded him? It didn't matter, she'd take it. "Tickets for the best seats."

He tipped his head and clucked his tongue. "Shame, I already have those."

Reversing, he turned into the apartment. Throwing the door wide, Max walked away from her to continue on into the kitchen. Tally was shocked to find that the television above the fireplace to the left was displaying a baseball game right now and there were four guys seated around his living room watching it. Seeing beer bottles on the table and a pizza box next to a couple of open packs of chips, she realized she'd stumbled on a party.

The guys glanced over at her one at a time but didn't say anything. Another guy came into the apartment behind her, forcing her inside. While she'd been ignored, the new guy got a cheer and conversation. As he answered his friends, he urged her deeper inside to shut the front door.

That was it. She was in the apartment where Max was entertaining. It didn't matter that she couldn't have picked a worse time, Tally couldn't leave without convincing him to go to the dinner tomorrow night. But she didn't know how complete his focus would be while he was having this get together.

Instead of standing gaping at the guys in the living room who were ignoring her in deference to the game, she chose to head into the kitchen after Max. Tally found him leaning against the counter, typing something into his phone.

He did a double take and kept typing. "You want a beer?" he asked and opened the fridge, leaving the door swinging on its hinges, implying she should help herself.

"No, thank you," she said, pushing the door closed.

"Why is it he tells you not to drink?" Max asked, locking his phone and sticking it in his pocket. "He must be a controlling fucker."

"No," she said, because it was her job to make Teddy sound appealing. "Technically, I'm always on duty. He likes to know he can call on me any time and I'll always be sober, you know? Ready for him. For whatever he needs."

He swiped his beer from the counter and slugged some down, peering at her so intently that she squirmed under the scrutiny. "Do you fuck him?"

Shocked, Tally was struck dumb for a minute. "Wha…? Excuse me?"

"Stretton, that's his name, right? Do you have sex with him?"

"No!" she exclaimed and glanced back at the living room beyond the breakfast bar before going to him to murmur, "I don't make a habit of doing… what we did. Before that, I hadn't had sex for… months."

More like years, but she wasn't going to admit to that. Any guy she'd be interested in having a relationship with wouldn't understand her commitment to Theodore Stretton.

Max pushed away from the counter, swinging his beer down from his lips as he started toward the living room.

En route, he twisted to whisper in her ear, "Figured. You're too tight to be a whore."

Oh God, her heart sank into her guts as her eyes closed. He wasn't making this easy for her and what was worse, every reminder of that night aroused her as much as it mortified her.

When Tally shook herself back to reality, she spun around to find him in the living room, sitting in the armchair nearest the bedroom door, the one with its back to the window, perpendicular to the TV.

Taking a fortifying breath, she went into the living room and tried to block out the other men, who were chatting, eating, and commenting on the game. She went over to stand right in front of Max, but instead of acknowledging her, he curled his fingers around the inside of her knee and looked past her at the TV to comment on the latest play.

"We have to—"

"Relax, Boss," Max said and sank back in his chair. "I'm not having any conversation while the game's on."

Catching her off-guard, he pulled her down into his lap. "I can't—"

"Sure you can," he said, and bent to hook her legs with one forearm. Twisting her around, he draped her legs over the arm of his chair and then slid a hand between her thighs, just to rest it there while the other arm stayed around her back, holding his beer on the arm of the chair. "Relax." He kissed the side of her neck and she tried to get up, but he snaked his arm all the way around her to hold the beer up to her mouth. "Drink."

Their eyes locked. She had a decision to make, stay and play along until she got a chance to talk, or fight to get away and leave. But if she did that, she'd never have a chance to convince him to come to dinner, and she'd have to psyche herself up to come back here or be prepared to lose her job.

So she took the beer and as his satisfaction almost curved his lips, Max whistled at one of the guys and held up a hand. His friend tossed him a beer and his arms tightened around her when he twisted off the cap, which he tossed to the table.

Tally hadn't meant to take over the beer, but now she had her own she'd have to nurse it; she couldn't get drunk, she just couldn't.

TALLY HAD BEEN THERE for over an hour and she was learning a lot about his friends. Tomas was a bit slow on the uptake, and the others liked to jeer him for always being behind the curve. Robbie and Mark were brothers, but they didn't seem to like each other much because they were always making snarky comments at the other's expense.

Bobby was the joker, he had a great sense of humor; she'd never laughed so much in her life. Ryan was the flirt, too cool for school in a lot of ways. It was obvious he was the preener of the gang, though he had nothing on the vain men she was used to having around her.

Right now, Tally was sitting on the floor between Max's open legs, carefully opening the newest packet of chips.

"You just never learned?" Robbie asked her while the others were still intent on the TV.

Robbie was at the end of the couch closest to the chair she'd been sharing with Max throughout the game. But Robbie was less interested in the game and more interested in leaning over to talk to her.

Tally wasn't much of a sports buff, so she was okay with talking. "Nope," she said, opening both ends of the chip packet.

"Why not? I thought everyone knew how to drive? Cars are Max's whole life, he takes them apart, puts them back together. He grew up jacking them and chopping them with us to put food on his mom's table."

She shrugged. "My mom didn't drive either," she said. "We were living on food stamps in section eight housing. We couldn't afford heat let alone driving lessons."

Robbie opened another beer and handed it to her. She'd managed to nurse the last one for long enough, apparently it hadn't gone unnoticed that she was sans drink. "But you said you went to college?"

She nodded. "My dad died when I was seventeen, he had a life insurance policy. My mom said it just made sense to use the money to get me an education."

"Wow, that's… cool."

She smiled. "It is. She was a good mom."

"You still close, do you see her a lot?"

She shook her head. "She lives in France now with an art professor who swept her off her feet. He's twenty years older than her, but it works for them."

"Cool," Robbie said and turned to hit Ryan's chest. "You hear this?"

"Hear what?" Ryan asked, sliding closer to his friend to focus on her. "She's something to look at, huh?"

Tally wondered if he ever stopped flirting, but she wasn't threatened by his words. The flirtation felt more polite than calculated.

"Yeah," Robbie said, like he hadn't really been listening to his friend. "Her mom lives in France."

"Wow," Ryan said, looking impressed. "France, huh? In Paris?"

"Burgundy," she said.

"Cool, like the wine," Robbie said.

She laughed. "Yes, like the wine."

Max was behind her, talking to the other guys who were still focused on the TV. He leaned forward, sliding his hand over her shoulder, down her chest to inside her shirt, where he curved his hand around her breast and gave her a squeeze. It was such an absent move that she didn't want to draw attention to it thinking that would make it a big deal. He was still talking to his friends and probably didn't even notice that he'd done it. But it was making her heat in all the right… or rather, wrong… places.

Max reached for the chips with his empty hand, but she hadn't finished opening out the packet because she'd been too busy talking.

Catching his hand before he accidentally pushed all the chips out the bottom, Tally turned it over and scooped a few chips out onto his palm. There. No mess. Easy. His lips disappeared into her hair. He kissed her head then sat back to eat the chips she'd given him.

"You coming to The Lounge tonight?" Ryan asked her as she tore the edge of the pack from top to bottom in a makeshift plate for the chips.

She flattened the pack, leaving the chips on top. "The Lounge? No."

"You should, it'll be fun," Robbie said. "Aaron's band is starting to go places. They're headlining after open mic night. Max probably told you, but it's like their favorite venue. The Lounge gave them a chance when no one else would."

"His band, Horizon, are big in the city now," Ryan said. "They're booked every week."

"Lucky them," she said, sipping her beer.

"Yeah, they worked hard," Robbie said. "Do you play an instrument?"

"Some piano," she said, "but I'm awful. A friend taught me a couple of years ago."

"Mark plays piano," Robbie said, pointing past Ryan. "Hey, Mark, you can play with Max's girl."

Mark stopped drinking to look at them. "Excuse me?" she asked and laughed at how naughty that sounded. "Play with me?"

Max sat up straight behind her. "What the fuck?" he asked, with enough anger in his voice that she felt the need to rest her head against his thigh for reassurance. He put a possessive hand on her hair. "Listen, you fuckers, she's hands off. You get within three feet of her without my supervision and I'll break your fucking face, get me?"

All the guys held up their hands or nodded as they conveyed their agreement. Great, why was Max putting his mark on her? They weren't together, could never be together. Tally seemed to have forgotten why she was here.

As if the universe had prepared a perfectly timed reminder, her cell phone burst to life. The shrill ring was set on maximum; she had to be able to hear it at all times, no matter where she was or what she was doing. Crawling around Max's leg, she unzipped her purse and pulled out the phone.

Clearing her throat before she answered, she used the support of Max's leg to help her scramble to her feet. "Tally!" Teddy snapped before she'd said a word.

"Yes, sir," she said, trying to use her body as a shield for the noise of the TV.

Max tapped her leg and she glanced down. He pointed over the back of the chair to the door in the corner. "Use the bedroom," he whispered.

Climbing over his leg, she was surprised when he smacked her ass, but couldn't say anything because her boss was talking in her ear. "Where are you? Have you got confirmation yet?"

"No," she said, going into the bedroom. The bed was a mess and there were clothes strewn on the only chair in the room while a towel was on the floor, trailing out of the open bathroom door. "I'm working on it now."

There was a complete weight rack in the corner next

to a bench, it seemed that Max worked out right here in his bedroom. His whole life was in this apartment. Moving to the Stretton Estate was going to be a huge adjustment for him. There was a full gym and swimming pool at the estate, everything Max could ever want or need.

"This is a disappointment," Teddy said. The coolness of his voice made her feel shame. "I don't understand what is so difficult about this task. If you are incapable—"

"Incapable? No, sir, I... I'm working on it. I promise."

"You've been saying that for days," he said. She went over to sit on the other side of the bed. "I wasn't sure you were up to this task. Perhaps I should move you to Kimmy's detail permanently."

"No," she said because she couldn't think of anything worse than trotting around after the perfect princess who spent her day lunching and melting plastic.

Tally could only spend so many hours watching Kimmy in the spa with her friends before she began to consider self-harm.

"Maybe I should send Ken," he muttered.

"No!" she exclaimed, though he probably hadn't expected her input. Silently cursing herself for raising her voice, she closed her eyes. "Mr. Flynn won't respond to intimidation. He just won't."

"Apparently, he doesn't respond to you either. This is your last chance, Miss Taylor. If my son does not attend dinner at the house tomorrow, I will reconsider your employment."

"I understand," she said because what else could she say.

He softened a little. "I like you, Miss Taylor, it would pain me to reprimand you. Don't disappoint me."

"Yes, sir."

The line went dead, and she hung up her end. "Damn," she bit out and squeezed the phone.

Max's voice came from behind her, "Sounds like a real charmer."

FOUR

WHIRLING AROUND, TALLY WAS SURPRISED to see Max standing in front of the closed bedroom door. "How… how much of that did you hear?" she asked.

"I won't respond to intimidation?" Her eyes closed, and she bit her lip again. Why was her day going from bad to worse? She just couldn't catch a break. "Lie down."

Why did his voice sound so soft? "What?" she asked, watching him walk to the end of the bed.

"Lie down, on the bed."

"Why?" she asked, looking at the coiled comforter.

At his behest, she'd taken off her shoes in the living room and her thigh-highs too. It was nice, and unusual, to be able to wiggle her toes while there was daylight outside.

"Do you want me to go to this dinner or not?" he asked.

Yes, she did, and she was up for anything that might persuade him it was a good idea. Pushing her fists into the mattress, she slid back and lay down in the middle of the bed, her head sinking into his pillow.

"What now?" she asked.

To her horror, he began to loosen his jeans. "Close

your eyes."

"Mr. Flynn—"

He laughed. "I think it turns you on to call me that, Boss," he said and when his jeans were open he bent to rest his hands on her ankles. "Go on, baby, close those eyes."

If she did, she was consenting to anything he wanted to do. His hands slid up the front of her legs as he crawled onto the mattress between them. When his palms skimmed over her knees, she let her eyelids sink shut.

His hands were rough and entitled when they continued up her thighs, pushing her skirt out of the way so he could grip the lace of her panties. She lifted her hips expecting him to pull them down, instead he used two hands to rip the lace and her eyes opened in shock, no man had ever done that to her underwear before.

"Ah, ah," he said. "Eyes closed."

He was so confident in his control. All Tally could do was comply. Her heart was hammering and her stomach was alive with frantic butterflies, but her fingers curled into his bedsheet in enthralled anticipation. What was he going to do next?

She inhaled a terrified and excited squeak when his tongue skimmed through her folds over her clit. Directing her legs over his shoulders, Max sucked on her, flicking her arousal with the tip of his tongue in a quick motion, sending a vibration through her.

"Oh…" she said as he kissed and tasted her. Lapping her juice, he warmed her with his breath and circled her with his commanding tongue. His next clit kiss made her buck up and the pincer of pleasure formed by his lips made her pant. "Oh, God, Max."

He rose, his whole body sliding up hers as he ascended to kiss her mouth. "That's better, baby," he murmured. "Say it again."

"Max," she exhaled, and her eyes fluttered open to see his just above hers.

Dark and drowsy, he was intent on her though his hand was busy unbuttoning her shirt. "Again."

"Max," she said in that same breathy voice, which was

the best she could muster right now.

"Good girl."

He unclipped the front of her bra and ducked down to suck one nipple into his mouth, then he kissed the other, teasing the very peak with the tip of his tongue.

"Max," she whispered. "You feel amazing." He mumbled in appreciation, his mouth enjoying her breasts while his hand went down to play with her clit. "But we can't."

"Why not?" he asked, sucking her nipple into a proud peak that he admired while she struggled to take a breath.

Glancing to the window, she saw sunshine. "It's the middle of the day."

He smiled and kissed her mouth, sharing with her the alluring taste of herself. Running her fingers over his face, Tally lost them in his hair until he lifted to speak.

"You've never had a little afternoon delight before?"

No, but she'd never been considered adventurous and she didn't want to confess how boring she was, so she moved on to her next excuse.

"There is a gang of men I don't know, right on the other side of that door."

But as she nodded toward the door, he ducked down and kissed her pulse point. "Jealous fucking guys who'd give their left nut to be where I am right now."

"Don't use me as a trophy," she said, but was too boneless to be offended.

Of their own volition, her hands somehow found the hem of his tee-shirt and as they pushed up, they took the garment with them.

He smiled and rose to pull off his shirt. She stopped breathing for a minute. Every muscle was defined, and the hard lines made her knees bend to stroke up his sides. God, she wanted to touch him, everywhere, so she did. Running her hands over his toned torso, she fingered a couple of scars and outlined the black tattoo on his right pec and the one sweeping around his ribs to his back.

"Up to spec?" he asked.

But she was lost in her fascination with him. "Huh?"

He scooped up her chin and came down to kiss her.

"Your tongue's hanging out, babe."

"Sorry," she whispered, but he picked up her hands and skimmed them around his ribs to his back and down again.

"You've got a lot to learn about guys if you think you have to apologize," he said and let his tongue slip into her mouth. "You drool away, Boss… What you've got here is all yours."

All hers. Was he a one-woman man, was that what they were doing? Were they starting something? And if they were, what the hell did that mean for their futures?

She understood what a culture shock he was going to get when he was enveloped by the Stretton machine. When he was a part of it, Tally would have to take orders from him. She'd have to see him on dates with women she couldn't even begin to compete with.

The realization should've made her push him away and explain. But he moved over her and slid both hands down her thighs to hook them up around him. Tally complied with his direction and locked her ankles behind him as he guided himself into her. On her back, it should've been easier, but his initial push didn't get him far.

"Damnit," she said, pissed at herself.

She had to relax and stop thinking.

He smiled and stroked his fingertips down her face from her temple to her jaw. "Look at me, baby."

Her eyes rose to his and he eased forward, pushing without thrusting and although she had to pant through some of the sting, he didn't let up and kept on going until he was all the way inside her; deep, snug, happy.

"Your pussy's my favorite," he murmured. "Of any I've been in, it's definitely the best."

Tally didn't want to be thinking about who else he'd been with. But it was flattering to see him breathe through clenched teeth, trying to control himself. She sensed his tension; that the thread of his restraint was pulled to its absolute limit.

Whimpering, a moan slipped from her and she had to squeeze her lips together to hold it in. She couldn't stop wriggling, trying to move around the thick column occupying her intimate space. Her stomach clenched, and she rocked faster.

Max was braced on both hands and didn't resist when she turned her head to seek one out. He kept himself propped on one taut arm as she pulled the other one to her. From the way his muscles worked, he thought she was going to put his hand on her breast. Instead, she pressed it to her mouth and squashed hers on top.

He laughed and slid it away to kiss her. "You make as much noise as you want to, Boss. Fuck those guys out there. Right here, in this bed, you're at home. This is your castle, baby."

On his next kiss, he pulled out and thrust back into her hard, pulling his mouth away from hers in time to make her squeal.

Tally shoved his shoulder. "Oh, Max," she half-moaned, half-chastised.

"Tell me off, baby. I love it," he said and kissed her again as he fucked her.

Doing it in bed was different to doing it against a door outside with tequila coursing through her. This was more intimate. More permanent. More alluring. She didn't know how many times she said his name, but by the time her orgasm was pulling the oxygen from her lungs, it was the only word she knew.

He thrust hard, driving himself into her so fast that she shunted up the bed and hit her head on the wall. Max braced a hand on the wall and the other on her hip as he shoved up once more and emptied his balls into her.

On one long exhale, he flipped over onto his back beside her. "That's what we should've done the other night."

Okay, once she processed what he'd said, she felt better. That's what this was, they were just finishing the night that they'd started. This wasn't a new encounter; it was a delayed conclusion to their first one.

She was limp when he drove his arm under her shoulders and hauled her over to lie against his side. "You got a boyfriend, Boss?"

Drumming his fingers on her face, Max dragged her hair beneath them.

"Several," she said, rubbing her lips up and down on the solid pec her head was resting on. His fingers stopped moving. She laughed and explained. "I date whoever Mr. Stretton tells me to date."

"I thought you weren't sleeping with him."

"I'm not," she said, cringing at the idea of being intimate with both father and son. "I don't sleep with them. I'm a prop. If he needs me to entertain an associate, or he has to bring someone to a party that he doesn't want to declare to everyone as his guest, they come with me so they're dismissed as insignificant."

"Hmm," he said as his fingers moved through her hair again. "And if I said I didn't want you to do that anymore, would you stop?" So much for post-coital bliss. Tally sat up and his arm fell away. "What? What did I say?"

"Nothing," she said and pulled her bra closed again before starting work on her shirt buttons.

Max stayed on his back but brushed a lazy finger up and down the outside of her sensitive thigh. "Moving too fast? You wanted something casual?"

Any contact messed with her equilibrium, so she picked up his hand and pushed it onto his torso. "I didn't want anything at all," she said, and scooted to the edge of the bed.

"When we fuck you're like putty, then as soon as we're done, you bolt."

They'd only done it twice, but that had been her MO so far.

Sliding off the bed, Tally stood up and turned back to try to locate her phone. "Your life is about to change in ways you can't possibly imagine, Mr. Flynn," she said and held up a hand to silence him before he could object. "And I call you that because it's who you are to me. Right now, we feel like equals because there's no airs, no graces."

"Equals?" he said and rose onto his elbows. "Are you fucking kidding me? You're a goddess and I'm like pond scum."

She smiled because he seemed incredulous. "I'm not

rich, Mr. Flynn."

"Ah," he said, sinking back to link his fingers behind his head. Tally fumbled through the sheets trying to find her cell phone. "And that's what puts us in different leagues?"

"Yes… Forgive me for not making myself clear, let me fix my mistake." Rounding the bed, she crouched next to where he was lying, and his eyes turned down to fix on her. "Theodore Stretton plans to make every one of your dreams come true… Anything you've ever wanted, Max, anything in the world, it's right there for the taking."

"Money."

"Yes," she said, exhaling a laugh. "Money, it will give you security like you've never known. You'll have everything, not just possessions, but possibilities, opportunities. Money opens doors. You go there, meet with him, and you'll see what he can give you. Power. Respect. People will covet your time. They'll fear your reprisal. No one will cross you. You will be king of your own kingdom. And women…" She smiled. "Geez, Max, you'll have any woman you want, they'll do anything to make you happy, anything. Any fantasy you've ever had, they'll beg to make it come true for you. You'll have supermodels on speed dial, women desperate for a second of your time… for a smile, for a kiss. You're going to be a god."

"A god," he said, and his focus rose to the ceiling.

Rising to stand straight, she guessed she'd got through to him. Tally should've given him the sales pitch in Fitzpatrick's instead of being distracted by their attraction. "I'll leave the card," she said. "And the car will be here at seven-thirty tomorrow."

She turned, but he sat up and grabbed her hand, pulling her back. "I gotta go to a thing tonight."

"I know," she said. "Horizon, Aaron's band is topping the bill after open mic night at The Lounge."

He smiled. "Right… You coming?"

"What?" she asked, paling. "No."

"Come on," he said. "If this is my last night as a mere mortal, I deserve to get laid, don't I?"

What a fly boy, she turned and folded her arms. "You just did get laid."

"Did I?" he asked, bouncing up out of the bed. "I forgot." He held up her cell phone proving with a wink that he'd been keeping it deliberately hidden. Handing it over, he took advantage of their proximity and hooked an arm around her. "Let me get you drunk, sweetheart… you'll get your happy ending."

Tally laughed and glanced down at his jeans, which were in disarray. She tucked him away and straightened them up to fasten his buttons. "I'm not wearing panties."

He kissed her. "That's all right, I won't hold it against you." Max pulled her to the bedroom door. Without caring that he wasn't wearing a shirt, he guided her out to the living room again. "We've got another member for our posse tonight," he declared to the guys who cheered, but were fixated on the TV. "We gotta pick up the others and eat first, so we'll be leaving in ten minutes." Tally glanced around at the mess and he stopped before he sat down, noticing the discomfort in her eyes. "Babe?"

"Can we… tidy up some of the mess before we go out?"

All the guys at least had the decency to look at the mess, acknowledging it. She squirmed, hoping they wouldn't be offended. But Max smiled. "Okay, guys, you heard the boss, let's square the mess."

The guys all groaned. "I'm sorry," she said. "I don't mind doing it myself, I just don't want to be distracted by mess when we get back later tonight. I'm guessing it will be after midnight?"

The guys were all smiling at her with various levels of mischief in their eyes. Max's smirk was intense in a unique kind of way. Damn, she was an idiot, and wanted to slap herself. The last thing she had meant to do was confirm that she was going to bed with Max tonight, but she just had.

"After midnight, sure," Max said. "And I don't want you distracted." She went to squeeze into the space between him and the coffee table to begin gathering up empty bottles. He leaned in to murmur at the back of her ear, "I want you naked."

Her eyes flared, and the guys didn't look directly at

them, but their smirks and furtive glances betrayed that they'd heard what he said.

Gathering the bottles between her body and her forearm, Tally grabbed Max's wrist with her other hand and wound around the furniture with him in tow, stopping when they got to the kitchen.

Dumping the bottles on the counter, she spun to take a breath, and had to duck away from his advancing hands that seemed to be trying to find her face or her hair.

"I need a favor," she said.

"Name it."

His hands dropped. Taking her seriously, Max didn't even hesitate to agree. His concentration became absolute, which made it harder for Tally to ask.

"I don't know if… well… your friends… they might…"

"Might what?" he asked, offense contorted his face into a scowl. "What's wrong with my friends?"

"Nothing," she said quickly, resting her hands on his ribs as she stepped into him. "I love them, they're amazing."

"Okay, that's too much," he said, stroking her arms. "I'd have taken 'they're decent guys' or 'not a patch on you, lover.' Amazing is too much. Love is definitely too far."

Relaxing into a smile, she turned her face down to rest it on his chest and he stroked the back of her head. "You smell so good," she murmured.

He kissed her hair and bent to pick her up, hooking her legs over his hips. "Should we take this back to the bedroom?"

The hussy that he brought out in her wanted to say yes, but she held back.

Looping her arms around his neck, she squeezed herself close. "Your friends can see us," she whispered.

The guys had their backs to the kitchen, but there was only a narrow breakfast bar and small bistro table between them and the five other men in the room, so the couple didn't have great cover.

Sucking her bottom lip, he walked her into the corner. "You never done it with an audience?"

Pushing her skirt up over her ass, Max set her down on the cold tile making her gasp and pull him closer.

"You said we only had ten minutes," she murmured, trying not to draw attention to them.

"I can do something with you in ten minutes," he responded and nudged her head aside to kiss her neck.

His mouth was incredible, so wet, and thorough in the way it hit every nerve ending and managed to stimulate her insanity enough that she couldn't hold on to reality.

His finger slid inside her, making her gasp. "Max!" she yelped. Some of the guys turned, Tally buried her face in the crook of his neck, mortified that she'd drawn attention to them and their antics. "Oh, God."

His voice was triumphant and amused. "Bedroom it is then," he said into her hair and curved a hand around her hips to lift her up again.

"No," she said, her ass would still be on show if he turned and walked them past the guys. But Tally had to make eye contact to show she was confident. "We have to tidy up and get out. There will be time for… other stuff, later."

He nodded and put her on her feet, kissing her until she was balanced. She was loose and feeling a bit high when she had to take her own weight. But, if she didn't get away from him, Tally didn't trust her resolve to hold.

Deciding to return to the job of tidying up, she passed him to head for the living room.

"Hey," he said. Tally turned to face him. "What was the favor?"

Would it cause a fight? Could she afford bad feeling now? No.

"Nothing that can't wait," she said and offered a smile before turning to walk away.

Tonight was going to be another adventure, one that would deepen her connection to Max Flynn. But she knew it would be severed quickly enough when he saw what being a billionaire involved.

Tally also knew she'd take way longer to get over their brief affair than he would, but she'd take the crash when the high was this good.

FIVE

ADVENTURE DIDN'T EVEN BEGIN to describe the night she'd shared with Max and his buddies. In a dark, crowded nightclub, there was barely space to move. The music was loud and intense, the flashing lights disorientating, and the liquor free flowing. Max barely took his hands off her for five seconds. When he wasn't fondling or fingering her at the table, he was kissing her mouth, her face, her neck, anywhere he could reach. And after a few shots of tequila, Tally was as free with her hands as he was.

They had sex in the men's room. He got oral in the ladies' room. They screwed in the alley behind the club, and she had three orgasms at the table by his hand, spread throughout the night of course, not all at once, and another on the dancefloor where he loved to dance dirty with her.

It wasn't just the sexual contact that opened her eyes to her need for him. It was the casual way he looked after her that really made her yearn to captivate him. He kept their fingers laced together or his arm around her at all times. When space got tight at the table, he put her on his lap, and still managed to converse with his friends, and take part in the evening, without making it seem like she was in the way.

Tally became an extension of him, she wasn't an obstruction, or a barrier to him connecting with the social occasion. And she was included, which was maybe the most eye-opening part of the night. People wanted to talk to her, they wanted to get to know her and include her. Max put her front and center whenever he thought a random woman was getting too close to him and stuck his tongue in her mouth more than once when guys took too much of an interest in her.

His attentiveness was a surprise.

She expected him to be caught up with the guys or like Stretton society, to have more important things to worry about than entertaining the woman he'd brought. But he didn't mind sharing quiet moments with her at the table or at the bar. He'd cornered her after dancing with her just to check she was okay, and she had a drink in her hand all night. If she put it down or either of them took their eyes from her drink, he removed it, and wouldn't let her touch it again.

Even when she got to a point where she felt she'd had too much alcohol, he didn't push her to drink more liquor, he was happy to switch her to soft drinks. Tally didn't spend a cent and whenever she tried to, he referred to looking after his woman.

She'd never been on a date like it. But then, Max wasn't like any man she'd ever dated.

"DO I GOTTA TIE YOU DOWN?"

Max's hand was still scooped around the back of Tally's head, where he'd left it after the blinding kiss he'd laid on her just a second ago.

They were on their backs, side-by-side in his bed, the buzz of the night still pulsing through their skins that had just been joined in the most intimate way. One thing Max was good at, sober or drunk, was screwing her to within an inch of her life.

"Tie me down?" Tally asked, panting, but managing to twist her head to look at him. "Why would you—"

"We just fucked, this is usually when you split."

Right. Except she'd broken that habit during their trysts at the club. "We've done it a bunch of times tonight and I'm still here… Do you want me to split?"

Bending his fingers, he scrunched her hair with his trapped hand. "Nah, I'd say you've got a few miles left in you."

Gasping, she rolled over, throwing herself on top of him to curve her fingers around his throat. "Miles in me?" she said, laughing.

Tally growled at him and bit his lip.

But he opened his mouth wide and captured her in a kiss as his arms closed around her, holding her body on his. Kissing and kissing, she loved how his mouth varied its demand. Sometimes it just wanted hers to respond in a calm kind of reassuring and intimate way; other times it wanted to drive her wild and pump up her desire.

Just when she was ready to beg for his body again, he slowed it down and let his hands trail over her back. "Oh, hey, what were you and Rob talking about during the game?"

"Why?" she asked, running her tongue across his lip to request access again.

But when he opened for her, she ducked back, teasing the kiss. She should've known better. Max got what he wanted. He rolled her onto her back, keeping her in his arms and forcing his mouth over hers, not that she was particularly reluctant to give it to him.

"I wanna know if I've got anything to worry about," he said.

Oh, oops. On a wave of panic, she forgot about teasing and opened her hands against his shoulders. "I didn't tell anyone who I was, or… who you are."

His jaw clenched, and he huffed. "Worry about like him moving in on you, I don't give a fuck about your boss." Her boss, not his father. "I figure my buddy shouldn't know more about my girl than I do."

Exhaling, she looked up at this guy who'd turned out to be far more than she'd initially thought. He wasn't anything like Teddy. But he wasn't the brute she'd assumed he was after meeting him either. Max was keen and attentive, the kind of decent guy wrapped in a rough exterior that any woman would be lucky to claim.

Pointing her forefingers, she grazed them along his collarbone. "Lover," she hummed, drawing out the word.

Max winced. "Rough start."

"I can't be your girl," she said. "With you, I've… I've done everything I shouldn't. It's my fault we've ended up here. I should've been smarter about this." As he considered her, saying nothing, Tally got self-conscious. "What? What are you thinking?"

"That I'm fucking lucky I'm on top right now," he said. "You're thinking about bailing."

She shook her head but couldn't maintain her innocence and stopped to lick her lips. "It would be easier if I left… Coming back here with you was selfish, of me, not of you. You've done nothing wrong, I… I'm the one who should know better."

His smirk eased some of the tension. "Think you've got more experience than me?"

In sex and relationships? No. But in the politics of elite families and their machinations? Yes. "I think that in a couple of weeks, you'll be avoiding me in the hallways. I'll be embarrassed. I'll blush and stumble over my words and—"

"Blush?" he asked and hummed before kissing her. "You don't gotta blush around me, Boss. But I'll be straight with you, any time you're not naked around me, I'm picturing it."

Groaning, Tally tried to wriggle out from under him, but he shifted to pin her deeper into the mattress. "Max, you're not taking me seriously."

"I get that you have responsibilities," he said. "I know why you came here." Good, that was encouraging, and Tally hoped it meant he was about to let her go. "But can we forget that shit for tonight?" Sighing, she felt so useless, he just didn't get it. But he brought her attention back to his when it drifted by following her mouth with a kiss. "Please, baby, didn't you have fun tonight?"

"I did," she said. Her hands slid around his neck. "You're the best date I ever had."

"Then forget what you think you know and just

spend the night with me," he said, beseeching her with his gaze. "Just be a babe spending the night with a guy she's into… can you do that?"

The damage had already been done. Tally should never have slept with him, but she had. Throwing herself into the fantasy for a night wasn't going to make the situation any worse, not when they were the only ones who'd ever know what happened.

"Okay," she said. "Rob was asking about my family and how I grew up."

"So he does know you better than I do."

Turning her smile upward, she coiled her legs around his hips. "Well, I guess that's a matter of perspective."

But he wasn't biting and instead moved off her to lie on his side. "Rob's always asking questions, he's a nosey fuck."

Shifting onto her side, Tally folded her pillow under her head. "I didn't mind. I don't really have secrets."

At least, she hadn't had secrets until she'd slept with her boss's son.

Lying there, facing each other, they finally took the time to really look at each other, and at what was beyond their physical connection. "Tell me, how did you grow up?"

Rob's questions were more specific, but she'd guess all Max wanted to know was what she'd shared with his friend. "It was tough. My dad was an artist; he never worked a steady job. He'd take off for months at a time. One time he left for a pack of smokes and didn't come back for three years. But I guess my mom loved him because she always took him back. She worked all kinds of jobs, long hours, you know?"

"You were alone a lot," he said, reading between the lines.

She nodded. "But it was okay. I was always a bit of a weird kid, a loner. I stayed out of the cliques. I wasn't a cheerleader or voted most likely to succeed… I just… got by, like my mom."

"Boyfriends?"

Max had a preoccupation with her love life. "Not really," she said. "My mom always said I was too smart for the losers in our neighborhood. Truth was, I wouldn't know what to do with a guy if he stripped naked and promised to have amnesia the next day."

Laughing, he swayed in to kiss her shoulder before swaying back. "When did that change?"

"I don't think it ever did," she said.

Beneath the covers, he took her hand and guided it to his dick that was thick and proud when he coiled her fingers around it. "Yeah, baby, it did."

She was no expert, but if he was happy with her performances, so was she. "Like a lot of people, I lost it in college," she said, turning on to her back as she thought about her first boyfriend. "Dunc was a senior, he worked in the library." Smiling, she curled her tongue in her mouth. "Boy, did he give me an education."

"Okay," Max said. Taking her hand off his dick, he yanked her across the bed, sweeping her arm up over his shoulder around his neck. "We're done with that conversation… What did you never learn?"

Another thing Rob had asked her. Max took in details even when he wasn't outwardly paying attention, she'd have to remember that.

"To drive," she said. "I never learned to drive. We never had the money and I never cared. I could walk to school and to the library, those were the only places I needed to go, and I wasn't afraid of the bus."

"The library? Again? You liked the library."

"One of my mom's earliest jobs was in a library. I was about six or seven maybe, I had to hide under the desk while she worked because I wasn't supposed to be there. But she'd sneak me in after school and hide me under there with a juice box and a pile of books… I guess it's no surprise I grew up socially awkward. I got used to my mom taking me to her different jobs and hiding me in closets or in dark corners when I was tiny because she couldn't afford childcare and my dad was useless."

"Or not around."

"Yeah," she said. "After that library job, I didn't want to do anything else but read. I didn't want coloring books or games. I wanted books, non-fiction mostly. At first it was the pictures that really fascinated me. My dad taught me how to draw; I was never as good as he was, but it was the one thing he gave me. Anyway, I read about art, and classical musicians… I always tried to talk to my dad about it. Maybe I was trying to get him to notice me… who knows. I was never good at being creative, but I could learn about those who were." His expression didn't change. He was listening, but she began to shrink. "Sorry, you don't want to—"

"If I don't want to, I'll tell you I don't," he said, anticipating what she was going to say. "And books are cool… we never had none in my house… but I guess they're better than drugs or getting yourself fucked up like other losers."

Drugs and teenage pregnancies were rife in her neighborhood, but she'd stayed indoors or kept her nose in books. Her mother struggled to make ends meet and her father usually spent whatever spare cash they had on his art supplies or on weed.

Seeing the stress her mother lived under was enough to make Tally wary of getting herself involved in any kind of relationship. Her parents fought all the time, or drifted around each other, living separate lives like they were ghosts who couldn't see each other. When things were especially tough, Tally often felt like a ghost herself because her mother was just too busy to interact with her.

"What about you?" she asked. "What was it like for you growing up?"

"You don't know already?" he asked, peering down his nose at her.

Tally couldn't tell if he was pissed or teasing her.

So much for them not talking about his father. "Teddy did hire a PI to find you, that's how I ended up here… but he was more interested in locating you than learning what you were like. Getting to you was important; you're sort of his last hope. He would never let a woman take over the business, it just wouldn't happen. When Laura, his wife, was killed, he was really messed up. He tried to hold it together, but I've never seen him like that."

"Sounds like you care about him."

Did she? Maybe. "Your father's given me a lot," she

said. "But he's a tough guy to warm to, he's quite… severe."

"Yeah, I had a bunch of stepdads like that," he said, skimming a hand down over her hip. "I guess my mom has a type… Sick fucks who treat her like crap. They beat the shit out of her, take her for everything she's got, which is never much, and then they toss her ass on the street."

There was so much anger in his words that Tally reached up to stroke his face. Her heart broke for him. Seeing his mother be hurt by every man she ever had in her life must have been tough.

"Baby," she murmured and pushed up to kiss him. "I'm so sorry."

"No problem," he said, pulling away from her hand and her kiss, though he didn't leave her embrace. "Her choice, not mine… I got tired of fighting the fuckers when I was fourteen and bailed. Didn't matter how many I kicked out, she always found a new dirt bag… not my problem."

"But you still see her? Your mom, is she still in your life?"

"Sometimes," he said. "I didn't see her for like five years. She moved into the neighborhood for a while then took off with a new deadbeat. If she asks me for something, she'll get it, she's my mom, you know? I'll always do whatever I can to keep her on her feet."

It was nice that he still cared about his mother. Though he must have seen some horrific things as a child if the men she'd brought into his life were all violent. Maybe that was why Max wasn't like that; he didn't throw his weight around, not with her, even though he had the physical strength to take most people apart.

He'd probably figured out the value of his fists when he was young. If his mom's boyfriends were violent with her, some were probably violent with him. Learning to take care of himself involved staying in peak fitness, and the kit in his room was a testament to how hard he worked on his ripped form.

But she could understand how frustrated he had to be as a youngster, standing in front of his mom, taking the hits, or beating the guys who hurt his mom, only to have her take them back or bring new guys in who were just as bad or worse.

"Is she still choosing the wrong men?"

Max shrugged, putting an arm around her, he moved onto his back. "She wouldn't say that, she says they're passionate." He scoffed the word like it was ridiculous and it was.

Kissing his shoulder, she couldn't stop stroking his body, or pressing herself into him. "You're passionate," she murmured, and his eyes dropped to watch her tasting his torso. "But you'd never hit a woman."

"How do you know? Maybe I just never got caught."

She had seen his rap sheet, mostly it contained petty theft charges from when he was younger. There was one incident involving a bar fight, but the details on that were sketchy. But he was right, a person's criminal record just showed what they'd been caught for, not what they'd actually done. She'd already found out from his friend that he had stolen cars and sold them for parts, that wasn't on his record.

"If I thought you were capable of hurting me, I wouldn't be here," she said. "And after spending tonight with you… You're a decent guy, Max… You're more than decent. You care about people."

His snigger was meant to be dismissive, but she'd guess that he wasn't used to taking a compliment. "I care about what I care about," he muttered.

"Like your business," she said. "That's something to be proud of."

"It's all homers, word of mouth, for buddies. We do maintenance jobs, whatever needs done. We don't take it too serious."

Still, he and his friends had accomplished something. "It pays the bills."

The slow close of his eyes as he averted them in a kind of shrug told her he didn't want to talk about it. "How'd your mom hook up with the wine guy?"

The wine guy. She smiled. Okay, so he only half listened. "He's an art professor, or he was, he's older than her, retired now. After college I took her to a charity auction thing, it was one of the first Stretton events I attended. They met there and, I guess, hit it off. She went to France with him a couple of months after they met."

"Spontaneous woman."

Yeah, it had surprised her too. "She deserved it. Yeah, it was a risk, but I was educated, starting my life, she did her bit with me. It was her time."

Bobbing his head, he nuzzled her face. "So your dad dying worked out for you, huh?"

"The life insurance, sure," she said. "We didn't even know he had it until after he was gone. Turned out he did care about us after all. But, yeah, my mom told me to get a trade. I just needed a vocation… I wasn't good at the creative stuff, so it was teaching or accountancy, and I figured I'd be better in a job I could do myself instead of standing in front of a group. I'd hate that."

"Numbers, huh?" he asked. "I thought you were an assistant."

Taking a deep breath, she laid her face against him to breathe in that scent she loved. "There was a recruitment thing at college, senior year, and I met your father by accident, he was there looking for talent for the company. I guess he liked me because he offered me a position… the rest is history."

Her life hadn't turned out the way she'd thought it would. But she'd never really been good at knowing what she wanted; only what she didn't want. Max had made it clear he didn't want to share much more about himself and she wanted to take advantage of being close to this man, and his scent, while she still had him.

Biting into his chest, she startled him enough to make him look at her again and she grinned. "Oh, it's like that?" he asked. Grabbing her, he flipped her onto her back, locking his fingers between hers to pin them above her head. "You like it rough, Boss?"

It was a sign of trust.

Yes, Max's possession made her aware of every hair on her body, every cell of her being, but it was the intangible that heightened her connection to this man; the feeling that he'd defend her with everything he was. Just like he had tonight on a superficial level when men tried to move in on her.

But he had honor too, he'd taken her to that club, and even when other, much more beautiful women were throwing themselves at him, he hadn't wavered, not for a single heartbeat. That was integrity, proving what she said about him caring for people.

"I'd never had sex in public," she said. Her heart lost its steady rhythm. She wrapped both arms around the back of his head, stroking her fingers through his hair and letting it tickle her forearms as she rubbed them through his locks. "I'd never dragged a guy into an alley and demanded that he have sex with me… I'd never had an orgasm on a dancefloor or given head in a bathroom… until you."

He kissed her. "Next time you'll receive."

Smiling, she tried to remember their agreement while simultaneously knowing that there would never be a next time. "What is it about you, Max Flynn, that makes me crazy?" She exhaled, her eyes rolling back in her head when his lips slid down to her neck. "Are you some smooth operator taking me for a ride and I'm just too dumb to see it? Is this what you do with all the girls? Drive them crazy with your intense "challenge me" glare and the ownership of your hands?"

His hands curled around her waist, gripping her tight and shifting her body under his, proving her point. "Oh, I own you, baby… you want me to own you?"

He breathed in her nipple, suckling her hard and rubbing his fingertips through her cleavage. "Yes," she whispered, gripping his shoulders and whimpering. "Oh, God, Max, I do."

"Open those legs for me, Boss, I'm hungry for your pussy. The sweet girl needs worshiped, and I've got the tongue to do it."

Where was her confidence? Where was her sense? Tally couldn't let her soon-to-be-boss worship any part of her. But as he descended further down her body, she parted her legs, freeing him and opening herself for his mouth.

Yes, this was crazy. But tonight, he'd asked her to be nothing more than a girl enjoying her guy. It wouldn't last, but while it did, she was going to enjoy it.

SIX

LYING IN HIS BED, the morning after, Tally could feel him stroking her face with the back of his fingers. She didn't want to open her eyes, so smiled instead.

"I'm going out for coffee, okay, baby?" Max murmured. "How do you like it?"

Her smile got wider. "Fast, hard, and dirty," she whispered, taking her hands out of the blankets to slide them down his body, but instead of grabbing his dick, she got a handful of denim that made her huff.

Max laughed and touched his lips to hers. "When I get back, okay? I gotta see a guy real quick. Just stay right here."

It seemed she'd have no choice except to wake up, but Tally resisted and kept her eyes closed. "What time is it?" she murmured.

"Nearly noon."

It had been a long night, but a fun one, and she wasn't ready to wake up from the dream yet. "Hmm," she responded and tried to curl into his body, then she realized what he'd said. Oh no! She sat bolt upright. "What? Oh my God!"

"Got somewhere to be, Boss?"

Tally scrambled off the bed to try to locate her clothes. "Damnit," she whispered. "I am so fired."

"Cool," he said, and she stopped panicking to notice him stretching, fully-clothed, on top of the sheets they'd slept in. She didn't appreciate him being happy that she might have lost her job, but he shrugged. "If he fires you, I don't have to go to this dinner."

"You do remember that I said I live in his house, right? Jobless, homeless…"

But Max wasn't stressed. "Come crash here," he said. " 'Til you get on your feet."

He didn't even get it. "You do know Mr. Stretton's going to ask you to move into the mansion. You won't have an apartment anymore, you'll be living there."

Max sat up; his nonchalance became a frown. "What else will he be asking me?"

"To work at the company," she said. "You'll have an office on the top floor, an assistant, a lawyer—"

"Whoa, wait, what? I don't want to work at his damn company."

She rolled her eyes. So much for him paying attention, he hadn't heard anything she'd tried to explain about his father or what was expected of him.

"You don't have to do anything there; you'll be a figurehead. Maybe sit in on some meetings and walk away with a few million in the first year." His brows rose. "I know it will be a culture shock and you'll want to push back. He's a confident guy who will expect your respect, he won't try to earn it."

"This gets better and better," he muttered.

It might not be the best of news, but she had to be honest. Giving Max the hard sell was more difficult now that they'd been intimate. Knowing him like she did, it felt right to be honest and that meant not circumventing any inconvenient truths.

"On the plus side, I don't think there will be any big emotional father-son reunion. So don't worry about tears or heartfelt conversations."

His attention dropped to the bed. "Goodie," he

grumbled.

Maybe she'd said the wrong thing. Going to him, she crawled onto the bed to kneel in front of him. "Unless that's what you want. Do you want an explanation?"

He shook his head. "I don't want fuck all from him."

That didn't make sense. "Then why are you going to the dinner?"

Max leaned in to kiss her. "Because you're the boss, baby," he said and vaulted off the bed. "The shower has attitude, you need to give it a minute to warm up."

After he disappeared into the bathroom, Tally heard the shower going on. A second later, Max returned to the bedroom and went to a corner closet to retrieve a towel. She waited until he had it in hand before she spoke again.

"Lover," she said, picking at the sheet.

In her peripheral vision, Tally saw him spin toward her. "Uh-oh," he said. "I can tell that tone isn't good."

She hadn't meant to put him on edge, but when she looked up, it was impossible to keep the apology out of her eyes. "You remember I asked you about that favor in the kitchen yesterday?"

"Oh," he said. Exhaling a laugh, his hand went to his chest. He tossed the towel to her. "Shit, yeah." Coming over, he sat on the end of the bed. "Before we get into that, I've gotta ask something."

"Okay," she said, and as he became more serious, her suspicion grew. Those wary feelings intensified when he picked up her hand to kiss her knuckles. "Max?"

"Did he tell you to fuck me?"

Wow, he knew how to slap a woman in the face. "No!" she said, pulling her hand away. "Jesus, Max!"

Shoving out of the bed, Tally took the towel with her and wrapped it around her nude body because she didn't feel like being vulnerable, or exposed, right now.

"What?" he asked. "You said he tells you who to date."

How could he think this? How could he believe that what they'd had was orchestrated and fake? She'd opened herself up to him last night, talked to him, trusted him, and here he was asking if she was a hooker!

"What we've been doing goes way beyond dating," she said, her heart pounding and her cheeks burning. "I have never sold sex! I think you'd have got that I wasn't a pro just from…" She gestured at the sheets.

Bounding to the corner of the bed, he prompted her. "From what?"

"How much I suck at it," she snapped, resenting him for making her say it. "God, Max, thanks for…"

Why was she so angry about this? It was irrational, and his question was reasonable. Except she was more than offended, she was hurt.

"You don't suck at it," he said, leaping up to snatch her hands again and he took both to his mouth this time. "Geez, baby, you don't even see how you've got me by the balls and we've only known each other for like a week. I said you were my favorite and I meant it. I want this. I want you."

Oh no!

Warning bells made her step back, but Max wouldn't release her hand. "You want to know how you can be sure I wasn't sent here to seduce you?" she asked, though didn't let him answer. "I don't even feature. If your father wanted you pussy-whipped, he'd have sent someone far more adept than me. He wants you single, you know how I know that? There are at least three women lined up for you already."

"Three—what?"

This was truth beyond what she'd meant to share. "Women, for you, dates. He won't know for sure who he wants you with until he finds out what you want. Do you want the trophy wife who'll spend your money, and charm other wives, or the supermodel who'll make other men drool, but be high maintenance? Or it could be that a business alliance will be more beneficial to everyone. Trouble with the last one is you'll have to get a good balance. You don't have boardroom experience, so if you get the wrong woman she'll take over and make you look ineffectual. Teddy will hate that. But if you get the right one, she'll guide you and let you lead."

Shock opened his mouth and widened his eyes. "What the fuck is this?" he asked and as he retreated he dropped her hands to let his go into his hair. "Wife? I don't want to get married."

"That's okay," she said and smiled to reassure him because the last thing she wanted to do was deter him from going to the meeting. "You're a guy, you'll have plenty of time to play the field. You can wait ten years, hell, you can wait twenty, as long as you produce a boy eventually."

"Produce a…" She'd never seen him so pale or stunned. "What the fuck? You said there was a sister, does she work at his company?"

"Kimmy? No," Tally said. "She shows up at the company sometimes, she likes to float around and chat it up, but she doesn't have an official role. She does a lot of charity stuff, and… She helped her mother with the Stretton social functions. That's kind of… on the backburner now. Though there's a gala at the end of the month and that's… Well, you don't care about that."

He shook his head slowly. "I don't know if I can…"

The shock was understandable, but she'd never had so much faith in a person in her life. "Sure you can," she said, going to him on impulse. "It's one day at a time, that's all, and everything will be done for you…" Tally looked at his jeans. "Do you want me to get you a suit?"

"A… what the fuck? Babe!"

Now that Max was beginning to panic, she could see him sliding into anger like it was his defense. "No? Okay, that's fine," she said, doing her unthreatening thing. "I just… if you wanted me to help I could, that's all I was saying. No one expects you to be anything you're not."

"No one except the fucker who dumped my mother," he said. "He wants me in a fucking office, in a goddamn suit, screwing models and corporate sluts."

Okay, yeah, that was kind of what she'd said. "Look, I'm an assistant," she said, trying to backtrack. "I don't know anything about anything. I'm a nobody. All I was told was to come here and get you to the mansion, that's it. If you want to know more about what your future's going to be, get close to Heath or Blair."

"They're like his boys?"

"Blair is a woman," she said and smiled. "And she has slept with Teddy, but she's slept with everyone. She'll get to you eventually."

"I don't fucking think so," he said. "Hos ain't my thing."

Had she put her foot in it again? Time to backtrack some more. "Oh no, she's the classiest thing you'll ever lay eyes on. She's beautiful, and smart and—"

"You want me to sleep with her?" he asked and tilted his head. "Are threesomes your thing?"

"What? No! I've never… I mean I haven't…" Tally cleared her throat and scratched the back of her neck. "Taking me to bed with Blair would be an insult… to Blair. And I'd just get in the way, if you had a figure like hers to play with—"

"You mean, if I had your figure to play with," he said, moseying closer to grasp her waist. "She'd be left getting coffee."

Well, that was sweet, but she took it at face value, given that she was naked in his bedroom, and he'd never laid eyes on Blair. His tune would change after he did.

"Heath is Teddy's number two," Tally said, picking up his hand to kiss his palm. "Don't be surprised if he's hostile, I think he wanted to take over the company. What he doesn't know is that Teddy doesn't really like him. He trusts him, and Heath is good. Very good. He's the best. But he's also…"

"He's what?"

Describing Heath to someone who'd never met him was tough. "He thinks a lot of himself," she said. "Sometimes Teddy feels disrespected."

"Poor Teddy," he mocked without any sympathy.

"Your father would never say it," she said. "But, yeah, Heath can be quite snooty, and he is obsessed with boobs."

That was shocking enough to make Max's head duck forward. But it was meant to be a light-hearted fact about the man who'd hate Max on sight. "He has a… what?"

"Yes, I doubt he knows what any of the assistants' faces look like, but he'd recognize us by cleavage." His half-smile was understanding, and she nodded. "He hates Blair with a burning passion. They've slept together, course they have, but she doesn't give him the time of day, and the guys at the corporation chase their tails for her. I guess Heath resents how good she is at using sex to get what she wants… he has a little less… finesse."

"He doesn't get dates?"

"Not willing ones," she said and then thought she was being too harsh. "That's unfair, I guess… I mean, he's rich, and he works a lot, he'd probably be a good guy to marry. But wouldn't be a guy who'd burn up your sheets. Once a year, we assistants draw straws to, you know…"

She shrugged and lowered her eyes, which made him grab her arm. "Sleep with him?"

"No! Flirt with him, make him feel good around Blair's birthday when she's inundated with attention… She sends out a memo to make sure everyone remembers to buy her a gift. One of the assistants, Gemma, she did sleep with him, and she said—" Coming to her senses, Tally blinked and shook her head. "God, I'm sorry. What am I doing?"

"Giving me a lay of the land," he said. "I like it."

She shook her head again. "No, I'm influencing you unfairly. These people are your peers. I shouldn't be…" Backing away, she took a deep breath. Heath and Blair were his peers and her superiors, just like he was. It was time to get real. "I'm going to leave you my number, okay? If you need to know anything, give me a call and I'll answer your questions."

"Wait a minute," he said.

But that had been the problem, her procrastinating. Tally shouldn't be here. She shouldn't have spent the night. The fantasy was over, and it was time to face reality.

Deciding to shower at home, she dropped her towel while picking up her bra and skirt from beside the door. She couldn't stay here anymore. This was getting too hard.

"When can I see you again?" Max asked.

"I don't know," she said. "I'll be buzzing around at the house, and I'm at the office some days… I run a lot of errands between the two… you'll see me around."

Max was shaking his head as he approached. She

dipped to pick up her shirt. "Not good enough," he said. Grabbing her arms as soon as she was upright, he pinned her to the door with a thud and pressed himself close. "I'm going to this damn dinner because of you, *for* you, and now you're telling me we're through?"

If there could be another way, she'd love to embrace it. If he was any other guy, she'd be crawling back into his bed. But he wasn't, and she'd always known this was going to have to end.

"Not through," she said. "I just… I think you should wait to see what he can offer you before you make me any promises."

His eyes got heavy. Already she'd learned that as his eyes grew drowsy, his dick woke up. "Is that what you want?" he asked, tracing a line back and forth over the swell of her breast to her cleavage. "Promises?"

Yes, and she wanted to make them too. Being impulsive was so unlike her, somehow this man brought it out in her. It was so unfair that he was the worst man in her life that she could fall for. Tally had to be the level-headed one and that meant saying it plain.

"No," she said, catching his finger. "I want you to go there and give this a chance. Think about your friends. I know it will be uncomfortable and you'll want to walk away from the trouble, but think about all those guys out there who would kill for a chance like this. You're having money, family, and security, thrust upon you and yeah, sometimes it will be a nightmare, but people who grew up dirt poor, with nothing, they'd kill for this. Walking away from it is an insult to all your buddies, all those guys who would love even half a chance to make a go of this."

"Hmm," he muttered. "Guilt. That's a low tactic."

"No, not guilt, inspiration," she said. "Push through the difficult part and you'll come out the other side in a dream. Enduring the pain will be worth it."

As tough as it would be for her to lose him, he was about to wake up in a full color, 3D fantasy. He'd see that she was right, she knew he would.

"And you?" he asked. "If I decide you're what I

want?"

The woman in her was screaming with joy, but the employee was screaming in terror. The truth was, it would never happen. He'd be seduced by the glamour of the life; she'd seen it happen and could understand the allure… to a point.

"Then we'll cross that bridge," she said and winced because she had to move on to another difficult subject. "But that favor I wanted to ask…"

"You don't want me to tell them about us."

It was a relief that he'd figured it out, so she didn't have to say it aloud. "And the guys, if you take them to meet anyone, can you make sure they don't say anything to anyone either? I doubt they'll think to mention it, but just in case I'm around…."

Another scowl made her nervous. "You don't want them to talk to you?"

But there was no reason for him to be offended, she liked his friends. "Oh no, they can talk to me," she said. "Everyone knows I came here to proposition you, so it's reasonable to assume that I'd have met your friends. But the us… together part…"

He wasn't happy, but more resigned than angry. "I don't get it, you say I'll live in this dream world where I can have anything I want, then I say I want you and you… say I can't have you."

Touching his face, Tally wanted to kiss him. "You'll get it soon," she said. "I'm not saying you can't have me, I'm saying your options are about to increase and I'm…"

"You're what?" he asked because he never let her get away with anything. "What are you, Boss?"

There was no way to be subtle about it, so she lifted a shoulder. "I'm the girl who blows you at your desk over lunch… not the girl you bring home to your bed."

This was the morning for surprising him. "Wow," he said, and his grip loosened. "Just… wow."

"Yeah," she said. "Like I said, all kinds of options for you now." Linking her fingers at the back of his neck, she pulled him down for a quick kiss. "I'll leave my number, call me if you change your mind about the suit."

His nod of acknowledgement was absent, so she took the opportunity presented by his distraction and eased him back to open the door. He probably had too much on his mind to realize this was the first and last time they'd ever wake up together, but she was aware of it, and it was making her heart break.

But Tally had known all along that this would be harder on her than on him. The relationship part, not the adjustment to Stretton-life part; she didn't envy him that.

His life was going to be turned upside down, but she believed what she'd said, if he pushed through the early difficulties, his life would get so much better.

SEVEN

A SUIT.

A fucking suit.

Why the fuck would she think he wanted to wear a fucking suit?

Just the suggestion of it made Max make less of an effort. He didn't even bother changing his clothes after work; he left the garage and went back to his place to have a beer without even thinking about cleaning himself up. A fucking suit. Propping himself against the kitchen counter, he gulped down half the bottle.

This was important to his girl, but he couldn't figure out why. Maybe she just cared about this Stretton guy more than she was telling him.

Max didn't know what it was about her that got him going. But from the first minute he'd seen her standing outside his apartment, he'd been intrigued. What kind of woman stood outside a stranger's apartment all night in a neighborhood like this? She could've been there for hours for all he knew… He'd have to ask her how long she waited and make it up to her.

Memories of their night in his bed made him scrub

his hand over his eyes and down more beer. When he'd met her in Fitzpatrick's he'd meant to mess with her head, thought it might be fun to ruffle that sweet little demure personality, figuring she could stand to be wrinkled a bit.

Boy, had that backfired on him.

He'd told her to make the world believe that they belonged to each other and she'd ended up convincing him that they did. His casual interest in her neat body had become an inferno of need.

If it wasn't for her impressive performance, he'd have kept his hands to himself, maybe not his lips, but his hands for sure, if she hadn't made it so clear that she wanted him bad. Not in a million years had he expected her to pull him into the alley. Max would've put serious amounts of money on her being more modest than that.

But, if what she'd told him later was true, he hadn't been wrong. It was just that he brought it out in her, and he wasn't sorry that he did.

Something about their connection made her crazy and he liked that. He wasn't immune either. Seeing how she got a boost of confidence around him, and the way her eyes started to sparkle any time he touched her, drove him nuts.

Except, he was hyperaware of her vulnerability. She was so small, petite, and clueless.

It was tough to believe that she grew up in crappy neighborhoods because she didn't have a lot of street smarts. But he'd known kids like that, the socially awkward ones who didn't make friends and just locked themselves up inside. The guys ended up as forty-year-old virgins and the women usually found themselves trapped in the first bad relationship that found them, or as crazy cat ladies.

His girl shirked that stereotype. Her dad kicking it had given her an out. One she deserved.

She'd done good.

And now he was trying to drag her back down to his level.

A car horn blared outside. He took his time about finishing his beer before he bothered going to the window. Using the neck of the empty beer bottle to push the curtain aside, he looked down to the street.

What the fuck?

This was crazy.

He couldn't go down there and get in to that dumbass fucking limo; he wasn't a limo guy, never had been.

Taking a step backwards, he glanced over the breakfast bar at the coffee table in the living room. Tally's card was there. If he bailed on dinner, he could call her instead. It wouldn't take much to convince her to come over and once she was here he'd make it up to her, she'd forgive him… He knew how to work his girl.

Stretton might not be so understanding. Max didn't care about that bastard, but in the same breath, he didn't want to be responsible for her losing her job. If she did, he'd take care of her. Damn right he would. He thought it might be fun to have her around more, but Tally wouldn't go for that and she shouldn't, her career meant something to her… as did the family she worked for.

Her education gave her opportunities, but for some reason, she'd decided Stretton was the only one she wanted to work for. Max couldn't fuck that up for her just because he didn't want to sit in a limo or eat a fucking plate of food.

Knowing that this was one of those situations where a guy just had to hold his breath and get it done, he growled and turned around to toss the beer bottle across the room into the trash. Right. He had to just fucking do it. It was a dinner. A fucking dinner. No worries.

Doing this would be way easier if he had his girl at his side. Except he wouldn't. Without her to get him through it, he'd need to take a few buddies to keep him company. Retrieving his bottle of Cuervo from the back of the cupboard, he took a few long slugs then grabbed a couple of beers from the fridge and slid them into his jacket pockets.

If he got drunk enough, he wouldn't remember this clusterfuck tomorrow, and if he offended this Stretton guy, he might lay off. Bonus.

After secreting the Cuervo in his sleeve, Max opened a third beer bottle, tossed the lid, and started for the door figuring he might as well get this over with.

Still looking for any excuse to delay, he hoped to see someone on the way out of his building. He knew most people that lived around here and there was always a chance of a party going on somewhere.

Whenever Max needed to be somewhere, he couldn't walk ten feet in his building or his neighborhood without seeing someone he knew. So why the fuck was it that the whole fucking street was deserted now when he needed some bastard to distract him? A better offer would give him an excuse not to show up for dinner.

Sure, he didn't want to explain this stupid car, but he was in no rush to get to this fucker's house.

No, fuck, he had to do this. Didn't he just get through telling himself that?

In any other circumstance, he'd tell the guy to go fuck himself. Not because he had any anger towards this Stretton guy, fuck that, he had no daddy issues, and no resentment. Max was indifferent about it and had never craved a relationship with his father. He'd barely spared the guy a thought through the years. Yeah, maybe his life would've been different if his mom and Stretton had stayed together, but seriously, he was no idiot, and knew how the relationship would've gone down.

Max's mom, Cindy, gave Stretton what he wanted; the dude was happy to take it and split. Plenty of guys would've done the same thing… plenty of them did with his mom. It was just Max's luck that he'd been conceived. There was no Cinderella story. He knew guys like Stretton who used women they saw as trashy for their perverted fantasies. They got to do the dirty and then fuck off back to their own cushy lives without a thought for the consequences.

That's all he was. A consequence. An ignored one. But that was just fine by him.

Loitering on the sidewalk, he drank some more beer, keeping his distance from the car. But the front door opened. A guy got out and started toward him.

"Mr. Flynn?" the guy asked as he adjusted his hat.

Max smiled. It was fucking hilarious how out of place the Stretton folk were around here.

"Max," he said, putting the opening of his bottle to his lips as he swiped the guy's cap from his head and thrust it against his chest. "No hats, no Mr., and I really don't give a fuck about the rules." Taking a beer from his pocket, he offered it to the guy. "Beer?"

"Uh…" The driver glanced at the bottle and shook his head. "My employer doesn't allow—"

"Yeah, I don't give a fuck about that," Max said and strode past the guy to head for the front of the car.

"Sir, if you'd just—"

Turning to lock eyes with him, Max glared. "If you think about trying to tell me how things are done your way, you know, like opening a door for me or sticking me in the back of any rolling showboat like this, I'll have to show you how things are done my way and you'll end up eating asphalt."

The driver wasn't used to guys like him, Max could tell from the way he made fish faces for a minute before saying anything. "Yes, sir."

"That goes for calling me sir, too," Max said. "Now let's get this show on the road. Faster I get there, faster I can split."

Jumping in the front of the car, Max was tempted to do the driving, but he wouldn't be able to drink his beers as easily if he did. So he settled back, stretched out his legs as best he could and waited for the driver to follow him in to get them moving.

The fuck off fancy house was surrounded by a massive fucking wall that had some fancy iron gate. Max was ready for a nap by the time they got there, and almost drifted off in the time it took to get from the gate to the house.

He'd chatted with the driver a bit, but the guy was off his game, least that's what Max figured. Either that or the guy was just boring as hell.

Soon as the car stopped, Max got out, even though the driver called after him. He didn't need any gaunt-looking fucker in a costume opening his door or escorting him anywhere. If he was here for dinner, he was going up those stairs and into that house.

Despite knowing it was good manners to knock and

be invited in to a stranger's house, Max walked straight through the front door. He didn't want any ceremony, none of that *"Please wait here, sir,"* shit. Sir, he fucking hated that.

But when he got inside, he stopped short and lifted his eyes to the domed ceiling towering thirty feet above. He wasn't impressed. Shit like this didn't impress him, and he certainly wasn't awe-struck by its beauty. Show him a decent pair of tits or rev a perfectly tuned engine and he'd acknowledge beauty; this was bricks and mortar, no different from his place or any other place as far as he was concerned.

"Can I help you?"

Spinning around, Max saw a beanpole in a costume approaching from a side arch. "Pizza guy," Max said, tipping the last of his beer into his throat.

"Very good," the costume guy said. "You're Mr. Flynn, I assume. Your father will receive you in the dining room, please follow me."

The folks around here had good manners, even if they were dry. If he'd come here without meeting his girl, he'd probably have judged them a lot more harshly, and mocked their snooty attitudes.

But his girl could be snooty, and it wasn't because she was superior, far from it. It was because that was what this Stretton guy demanded of his people. Though God only knew why, because it made it difficult to relax around here.

Strolling along behind the guy who was walking like he had a pole in his asshole, Max looked left and right at the fancy paintings on the wall and the shiny gold statues. He didn't get it, didn't get why this was interesting or why it should make him fall over himself.

The beanpole stopped at the end of the corridor in front of two massive double doors and took his time about opening them, like Max might need time to compose himself before he saw what was on the other side. He didn't.

Striding on, he gave the beanpole his empty beer bottle then swept him aside with one outstretched arm, so he could throw the doors open himself. He swaggered on in while sliding one hand into the opposite sleeve of his jacket.

There was a man at the head of the long table that

probably had twenty places on each side of it. It was fucking laughable that this guy needed something so big for such a small party, and Max immediately wondered how fast he could fill the joint with his buddies from Fitzpatrick's and how Stretton would cope when the guys got rowdy and the couples started copping off.

His girl feared this guy that was standing there now, staring at him like he didn't know what to say, but Max wasn't intimidated. The first thing he wanted to say was that Stretton should be grateful for the fuckable assistant he'd sent to retrieve him because if it wasn't for that girl, Max wouldn't have come within ten miles of this place.

Instead, he sauntered a few more steps into the room and pulled the bottle of Cuervo from inside his sleeve. "Wanna hit a few shots?" he asked, holding up the liquor.

The guy at the table stepped back, like maybe he'd been slapped, but Max knew he wasn't that fucking lucky. "I'm Theodore Stretton," he said. Max had figured that out for himself, not that he'd say there was any family resemblance. "I'm your father."

He ignored that declaration. "I thought you uptight fucks were all about minding your manners," he said, twisting the cap from his bottle. "Don't matter, I'd only have been faking it if you gave me a glass. I prefer it this way."

Putting the bottle to his mouth, Max tipped his head back to down a few mouthfuls of the liquid that reminded him of the first time he'd laid lips on his girl.

"This is unorthodox, I expected—"

"Manners," Max said, inhaling and smacking his lips when he lowered the bottle. Tossing the lid to the floor, he sauntered deeper into the room. "Take a good look, this is what happens when daddy spunks and splits." Opening his arms for a second, he was just buzzed enough to laugh before grabbing a chair and dropping into it. "Ah, I'm fucking with you Teddy… I don't give a shit, Cindy used to scrub up nice; I get it." He slapped a hand on his stomach. "Let's eat! I'm starved. What have we got? Quail or some shit?"

"Steak, the finest," Stretton said, seating himself. "But we're waiting for the other two members of our party before we begin."

"Right, don't worry, this will keep me going," Max said, swigging more liquid.

Stretton was still blinking at him. Max figured he was supposed to be the curious one, the one in awe, but he just didn't give a fuck about this guy or his flashy house and his fancy company.

"A gentleman should have composure," Teddy said.

He could see the sneer forming on the old man's face. Usually seeing anyone turn their nose up would make Max want to beat their brains in. This guy was no better than him; no amount of money could make that happen.

But just when he was about to say that, he thought about his girl. She valued her place here and that was the only reason he'd shown up; he couldn't fuck up her life.

Gritting his teeth, he put the bottle on the table and pushed it away. "He should," Max said, though it pained him to agree with this bastard who kept his employees on such tight leashes. "But I'm not like you..." He gestured to the room. "This isn't life for me. In my world a guy has to be tough or other guys take from him, you get me?"

Stretton nodded once, seating himself and folding his hands on the table. "You're bold, and aggressive, neither are bad qualities. This will be your life, I promise you that. No matter what it takes, we'll make sure it happens. You don't need theatrics to prove yourself to me. You were born for this, born to learn from me. I see you have pride, and you know how to be a dominant force. You have everything you need, Max, all the basics. It's in your blood; there's no denying it."

Breathing in, Max suppressed a belch and squinted at the guy sitting at the head of the table. "If you're coming onto me, I gotta tell you, you're not my type."

With a smile, Stretton rose and started toward him. "I can see Cindy in you." It surprised Max that the sound of his mother's name on Stretton's lips made his fingers curl. "She didn't suffer fools." When Stretton got to him, he slapped a hand on his shoulder. "You are just what Stretton Chemicals needs. You're strong and unapologetic... the rest, that will come, I'll teach you how to conduct yourself. In time, you'll be the man you should've been from the start. I'll free your potential."

Sounded like some New Age shit to him, but Max tipped his chin to look at the guy whose expression was creeping him out. Maybe the booze was dulling his senses, but there was a real happiness, and an optimism shimmering around this guy, even if he was king of the pole-up-the-ass gang.

Stretton slapped his shoulder again, proving he didn't know much about touching other guys without their permission. If Stretton tried this in Fitzpatrick's, he'd be wearing his drink and swallowing his teeth within sixty seconds.

A door opened, and two more people came in. Their conversation died the moment they saw him. The woman was the first to smile, and it didn't take much for Max to realize she was a woman in heat. But fuck her, if that was the ho his girl had told him about, he wasn't going near her. Not that he'd be going near her anyway, he had the only woman he needed in his life.

The guy with her was a weaselly-looking sort. The disgust and annoyance on his face made Max want to smile; that fucker thought he was competition and he wasn't going to disabuse him of that idea. It would be fun to play with the guy some.

"Heath and Blair," Stretton said. "Let me introduce my son, Max Flynn… my heir."

Max caught a glimpse of the Cuervo bottle from the corner of his eye just as Stretton began to cajole him up to shake the hands of these two new people. The woman, skinny bitch with a triangle head and no tits, held on longer than he liked, but even when he tried to pull his hand away, she clung tighter, pressing her shiny talons into the back of his hand.

"Mr. Flynn, it is a pleasure," she said, batting her lashes. "I didn't expect you to be so tall."

And he didn't expect her to be so obvious. Those words were about to slip from his mouth when the reminder of his girl slipped in. He couldn't be rude, he didn't care about fucking this up for himself, but he couldn't fuck it up for Tally.

Biting his tongue, he told himself to say the opposite of what he wanted to say for the rest of the night and say nothing if he couldn't think of anything that didn't include a curse word.

"I didn't expect to meet Stretton's friends." There, he figured his girl couldn't be mad at him for that.

"Please, let's everyone sit," Stretton said. "We have much to discuss and plans to make."

Maybe this could work out for him, if Heath and Blair were here, Max figured he'd be expected to say very little. He'd eat what they gave him, nod, and sit quietly until he could get the hell out of here.

Then first chance he got to get his hands on his girl, he was going to make sure she showed him just how damn grateful she was for putting him through this dog and pony show.

Damn woman had him pussy-whipped already, but keeping her happy did something to him, and it wasn't something he wanted to lose. Not yet. Maybe not ever. He was doing this for her and if he would go this far, he doubted there was anything she wouldn't be able to make him do.

EIGHT

IT WAS AFTER TEN-THIRTY at night when Tally got the page. Dinner had to be over and maybe this was her being called in for a debrief. Had Max said something about them or did Teddy have another task for her? Hopefully it wasn't another illegitimate child.

She wiped her face with her towel and hooked it around her neck as she ran up the stairs. Tugging her headphones from her ears, she caught the wire and picked up the pace. Teddy didn't like to wait, especially at this time of night when he might be thinking about retiring to bed.

Tally knocked on the drawing room door and stepped inside. Instantly, she slowed. Teddy was here, as were Kimmy, Blair, Heath, and a glaring Max. So dinner was over, but the party was still going on... kind of.

"Sir?" she asked, drawing her eyes off Max, who hadn't looked at her yet, to look at Teddy.

"You were in the gym?" Teddy asked.

She glanced down at her shorts and racer-back top. "Yes, sir."

He scowled at her. "I do wish you'd do that in your

own time."

This was embarrassing, but she should've known better than to make assumptions. If Teddy had been alone, he probably wouldn't have noticed what she was wearing. But showing up dressed like this, in front of company, even if it was just Max, was an affront as far as her employer was concerned.

"Of course, sir," she said. "I apologize."

"When is her time?" Max asked, fixated on the dark bourbon in his heavy-base glass.

Everyone else was surprised by the abrupt question. "Three AM to five," she muttered then spoke up to Teddy. "Sir, I got a page, is there something—"

"I need the Abacus files," he said. "You'll need to go into the office."

A request like this wasn't unusual. It was less typical at this time of night, but she'd gone into the office at all hours. Except if this was a social function, she didn't quite understand why they were addressing business. If Teddy was trying to seduce Max by giving him the impression that he was being let in on family affairs, he was going the wrong way about it.

"Yes, sir, but…" She paused and inhaled, gathering her courage before being presumptuous. "The Abacus files are in the third-floor archive."

Telling him he was wrong might not be well received, but Tally knew she was right

But Teddy sort of glossed over her comment. "Yes, Pierre will—"

"No, sir," she said, asserting herself. "The third-floor archive here at the house."

He was surprised and glanced at Heath who shrugged. "They were moved in the flush?" Heath asked her.

Everyone seemed twitchy, but Tally guessed that made sense. Max was out of his element, which would make him tense and probably angry. Heath didn't want Max here at all. Blair probably wanted to make a move on the newest associate but wouldn't be able to in this room full of people.

No doubt Teddy had figured out by now that Max

wasn't as malleable as he might have liked his heir to be, so his mood was probably fraught.

Still, she was here to do a job, not speculate or interfere. "Yes, sir, Mr. Cable."

"Did you make the Whittaker call today?" Kimmy snapped.

Always ready to make herself known, Kimmy liked to interject as often as she could. Tally was sure it made the woman feel important.

"Yes, Miss Stretton, I'm awaiting confirmation on the discount negotiations."

Kimmy huffed. "If you hadn't been missing for half the day, we'd have an answer."

Reminding Tally of where she'd woken up and why she'd spent half the day AWOL wasn't wise given the company they were in. But still, Max didn't even look at her.

"Yes, miss," Tally said and backed away toward the door. "I'll retrieve the files. Unless there's anything else, sir?"

Teddy shook his head, but Heath spoke. "Are you swimming later?" he asked, smiling as he looked her over.

Oh great, now she had to endure Heath's leering. He wasn't a horrible-looking guy. He wasn't stunning by any stretch, but his appearance wasn't offensive. Shame that the same couldn't be said about his attitude or personality.

"I wasn't planning to, no, Mr. Cable."

"You should, the upgrades make quite a difference."

This was as close as Heath got to flirting. Tally wondered if it had ever worked on any woman or if it was just his money that made them respond. "Yes, sir," she said.

"You prefer to swim in the morning, don't you?"

It was so creepy that he knew that, but it was true, and there would be security logs to prove it because she had to type her code in to the pool door before she could enter the health suite. She swam as many mornings a week as she could be bothered. She had to do it early and she was always aware that Teddy could need her any minute, but Tally enjoyed the water and hadn't been caught out yet.

"Yes, sir," she said, feeling a bit odd having this conversation about her routine in front of an audience.

"I'm here for an early breakfast in the morning. Call me when you're in there, I'll come down to see how you like it."

Oh yeah, she'd so be forgetting to do that. Thank God she didn't answer to Heath directly. "Yes, sir," she said, trying her best to return his smile.

Kimmy and Blair were whispering to each other on the couch. It was odd that she should be more self-conscious about her figure being on show for the women rather than the men. But women like Kimmy and Blair made sport out of finding other women's flaws.

Teddy went to the desk, Max was still staring into his glass, and Heath was smiling. Tally backed away, out of the room and closed the door.

The Abacus files, how odd. Guessing it wasn't her place to question his logic, she set about doing as she was told. A door opened behind her and she turned to look down the corridor only to see Max coming out of the drawing room she'd just left.

Tally gasped and dashed back to him. "What are you doing?" she whispered. "Go back in there."

"Told them I wanted to see around this pile of bricks," he said, curving a hand around the back of her head and she was so shocked when he pushed his mouth down to hers that she froze, much like she had the first time he'd kissed her.

But she got it together and pushed on his chest, forcing some space between them. "You can't do that here," she hissed. "Are you crazy?"

"Oh, baby, you owe me," he said, coming for her as she started backwards down the corridor. "This has been the worst night of my life."

She smiled, still walking backwards. "Slept with Blair yet?"

Stalking her, he let some space grow between them, but kept her in his sights. "You can put a ho in a pretty dress, she's still a ho."

"Oh, you would do her, don't deny it," she teased.

Her back hit the double doors at the end of the

corridor. Before Max could reach her, Tally turned the handle and dashed through the door. After bolting up one flight of stairs, she crashed into Sean.

"Whoa, slow down, girlie," Sean said. "That was a quick workout."

"Yeah, I got called in," she said.

"To the dinner?" he asked and sniggered, scanning her workout gear. "Heath hit a boner when he saw that much skin?"

She shivered. "I kept my eyes up," she said and moved to pass him then stopped to turn. "Hey, do you know if the Abacus files were brought over in the flush?"

"The Abacus?" he asked, leaning back on the top banister. "No, they weren't moved in the flush. They've been in the archive for… months."

"That's what I thought," she said, wondering why Teddy would make such an error.

"You know sometimes I'm amazed these people accomplish anything," Sean said. "They wouldn't if it wasn't for us, you know that, right? Especially you, you know everything about this damn family and their company."

Brushing off the compliment, Tally moved closer to Sean and lowered her voice. "Is there a file at the office labelled Abacus?"

"You think he wants something that's not what it says it is?" Sean asked, and she shrugged. "Depends whose office… Teddy doesn't do his own filing, he wouldn't…" He trailed off when Max came strolling up the stairs at their side. "Uh, are you lost?"

She laughed and nudged Sean. "This is Max Flynn," she said. "Teddy's son."

Wearing grubby jeans and sporting grime under his fingernails, Max didn't exactly scream billionaire heir. She thought he looked yummy, even despite what was probably engine grease smeared on his tee-shirt, but she was a little biased. From the shock that spread on Sean's face, Max obviously wasn't what he was expecting.

"No way," he said and regained his senses enough to stand up straight and clear his throat. "I apologize, sir. Sean

Morgan."

He introduced himself but didn't offer his hand.

The clear line between what was right and wrong was stark for Sean, Tally had kind of smudged it… well, more than kind of.

"It's okay," she said. "You can shake his hand. Max…"

Max was peering at Sean. Employees weren't usually supposed to be forward in touching superiors, but her colleague lifted his hand. Her persuasive drawl of his name made Max do the same and the men shook, but that just shocked Sean more.

Tally leaned in between them, clasping her hands at the small of her back. "Sean's the guy who arranges poker in the upstairs kitchen at the end of every month and strips us all of our wages."

"Hey!" Sean chastised her because that wasn't the kind of thing they shared with superiors.

She squeezed his forearm. "Trust me, Mr. Flynn will keep the secret. Besides, if you invite him, you might clean up at heads up."

He scowled at her, but she knew Sean too well to take his wrath seriously. "Want me to check out that thing for you?"

"Sure," she said. "But tomorrow, or whenever, there's no hurry."

"Cool," he said. "We're upstairs when you're done." She nodded, and he turned to Max. "Nice to meet you, Mr. Flynn."

Sean disappeared up the stairs and she started to move again, but when she glanced back, Max hadn't moved, he was glaring at the stairs, and she hoped he wasn't thinking about going after Sean.

She went back to grab his forearm to pull him along with her. "Everyone is chilling, it's late," she said. "If you go up there now you'll just freak them all out. This is down time. Our superiors never go up there. I'm not sure Teddy even knows where the employees' rec room is."

"That's what's up there?"

"Yeah," she said. "That and our bedrooms. Some of the household staff have rooms in the basement too. But that part of the house is only accessible by that stairwell and the rooms are small, so it's useless to the family. So up there is where me and a couple of others stay."

Max hadn't relaxed. "Guys?" he asked, pulling her to a stop.

"I'm the only female living up there, yeah," she said. "But Sean, Johnny, and Pierre are like my brothers, they're protective. They would never think to…"

"Fuck you?"

Slapping a hand over his mouth, Tally looked left and right. "Will you please watch what you're saying around here?"

"Doesn't matter, baby," he said, cupping her face. "I'm not coming back here, no chance."

"What?" she asked, panicking about what might have gone on at dinner. "What happened?"

"That's a long conversation."

And one they didn't have time for now. Except the pressure was on for Tally to convince him to give his father a chance.

"Come here," she said and pulled him back the way they'd come to the stairs Sean had used. She took him up past the rec room and the guys' bedrooms to carry on to the top floor where her room was. Pushing through her door, she flicked on a light and dragged Max inside. "Will you wait here, just for a minute?"

"Wait? Why?" he asked. "Where are you going?"

"I have to get the file to your father, he needs it for a reason and doesn't like to wait." She backed to the door, leaving him to examine her bookcase. "I'll tell him you went outside for some air. That should buy us some time." He tipped his attention to her and she smiled, reading his mind. "Not enough time for that. Just wait here and don't make a sound."

Maybe that was a ridiculous thing to say because the guys in the rec room downstairs would assume any noise up here was just her getting ready for bed. Though that did mean she'd have to get to the archives, and back to the drawing room without running in to anyone who could tell the others that she wasn't the one upstairs in her bedroom.

Getting to the archives and back downstairs was easy enough. She handed over the file, made excuses for Max and then tried to back out as the men huddled around the file.

"Oh, Tallulah," Teddy said.

Ahh! Didn't the man know that she was trying to be speedy? "Yes, sir?"

"We're going to need you to work with Max some more," he said. "He's joining us at the Walker Benefit next Friday and he said he'd feel most comfortable with someone he knew on his arm. It may work out for the best, coach him, you know, what to wear, what to say…"

"What not to say," Heath said, and the men exchanged a look.

Just like she thought, Max had been his wonderful self and it had shocked the shit out of these civilized men.

"Of course, sir," she said, though she was silently seething. "I'll take care of it."

Before Heath could say anything sleazy, she departed the room and wasted no time in bolting back to her room. Ignoring the noise in the rec room, she went straight to her bedroom and locked the door from the inside.

Max was sitting in the middle of the bed, barefoot with his legs stretched out, his fists propping him up as he bounced. "You ever had sex in this bed?"

His lie pissed her off enough that being facetious came naturally. "Yes, hundreds of sex, millions of it. I'm on my back with a different dick in me every night."

He stopped bouncing to peer at her. "Something wrong, baby?"

Marching to the bed, she pulled off the iPhone she had strapped to her arm and tossed it onto the ottoman at the end of her bed along with her headphones. "You're never coming back here ever in your life, but we're going to the Walker Benefit together next Friday? How does that work?"

She bent down to take off her sneakers and socks. "I'm not coming back here," he said and glanced at the bed. "Well, I'll come back here to this bed, but down there, to them." He shook his head. "Not doing it. No way… But sure, I'll go to their fancy party with you before I dump them."

"Oh, so that's the plan?" she asked, climbing over the ottoman to get onto the bed with him. She straddled his shins, resting her ass on his feet. "You use them to get a ticket to the most coveted party of the year, then dump them after one date with me?"

Relaxed, and amused, Max didn't have any shame. "I don't give a fuck about the coveted party bit, you know that," he said, "the date with you part, yeah, that's my bag." Growling out her frustration, Tally sagged forward, putting her hands over his knees, and resting her face on his thighs. "North a bit, babe."

Oh, so he wanted to tease, was that it? He thought this was all some big joke? If he wanted to play, she'd play. Pushing up, Tally slithered north and parted her lips over his as she squeezed her hand between them and began to rub his dick through his jeans until it was nice and thick and hard.

"That what you want, baby?" she whispered on his mouth, easing away when he tried to kiss her.

"Oh, yeah," he growled.

"Do you like it when I do this?" Opening the buttons of his jeans, she tucked her hand into his underwear and began to work his shaft. "Mm," she purred. "You're so hard." Tally had never talked dirty in her life, but his eyelids got heavy and he tried to kiss her again, but she ducked back. "Can I kiss it? Can I, lover? Will you let me suck you off?"

"Baby," he grumbled.

"That what you want?" she murmured, still tugging him in her tight fist. "You want my mouth? You want me to run my tongue all over your thick, hard cock? Want to push your dick into my throat? To fuck my skull until your hot, delicious spunk explodes in my mouth?"

She squeezed him tighter and rolled her thumb over his head. "Yeah, baby," he hissed.

Adding in a few breathy whimpers, Tally inhaled his exhale. "Yeah?" she asked, almost kissing him but not quite. "You want that?"

"Yeah," he murmured.

She smiled then shoved away. "Well, tough," she said, and gave him a push. "God, Max, you came here to make friends with your family and instead you're up here thinking about having sex with me!"

"More than thinking about it," he said and lunged forward to snatch her back onto the bed. She whooped when he pinned her face down with the weight of his whole body. "You got me going, baby, you're gonna give it up."

Wedging his hand down the back of her shorts, he squeezed her ass and kept on going, using his own legs to force hers apart so he could slip a finger into her.

Her inhale cracked, his finger felt so big in her with her legs this close together. Trying to hold on to her anger was impossible as his digit stimulated her.

But damn it, she wanted to be mad, not turned on. How did he always do this to her? He always got her hot and made her focus on him so completely that everything else in her life became insignificant.

"Stop it, Max," she hissed.

She couldn't shout, not with the other guys' downstairs. The call of surprise she'd released when he pulled her back might have been masked by the TV. But if it wasn't, and they'd heard it, they might be on alert listening now trying to figure out if she was okay.

But Tally wanted to call out, like she could at Max's apartment. If she could scream and kick, and put up a fight, she could fulfil another of her fantasies with him. Getting physical with him, more physical than normal, was something she'd daydreamed about. Max was possessive but let her take the lead. More than anything, Tally wanted to know what it would be like to be overtaken by his want.

"You don't want it?" he breathed into her ear, sliding another finger into her. They came out to circle her clit and then slid back down inside her. "Come on, where's my hungry little boss who knows what she wants?"

Oh, she was right there, but it felt good not to give in, to make him think he was working for it. She could be his, was his, in any way he wanted to take her. But playing it reluctant was a new and thrilling game.

"Stop it," she said, trying to struggle beneath him, but he was too heavy, too strong. "I mean it, Max. Get your hands off me or I'll scream."

Another whoop came out of her when he reared up and flipped her onto her back. Concern framed his scowl. "Are you really saying no? Baby, I would never take—"

"Hush, Max," she said, pushing his arm aside to clamber out from under the cage of his body that had been braced on all fours over hers.

Dashing to the stereo, she turned it on to the maximum allowed, which wasn't much, but it was a better disguise than nothing. Max still looked worried when she came back toward the bed, but Tally pulled her top off over her head and then shimmied out of her shorts and shoved his shoulder to put him on his back, so she could climb on top of him.

She brushed her lips on his. "In future, remind me I shouldn't start games I don't intend to finish, I'll always lose."

"If this is losing, sign me up," he said, grabbing her ass to pull her pelvis down onto his. "You had me worried for a second, I thought I was being a jerk, forcing myself on you."

Stroking his face, she kissed him and gazed down into his eyes. "Not possible," she whispered. "I was about as pissed as I could be tonight, and here I am. Damn me for it, Mr. Flynn, but I crave you."

"Crave," he said, playing it dumb. "That's better than want, right?"

Her smile lowered until she was kissing his jaw. "Means I'm obsessed with you," she murmured, dragging her teeth over the angle of his jaw. "Addicted."

Grabbing her into his arms, Max rolled her onto her back. "I can live with that," he said and pulled one of her legs up over his hip. "Remind me how this goes again."

Letting her eyes grow heavy, Tally used her most sultry voice to say, "Fast, hard, and dirty."

"Gotcha," he said and grabbed her arms to stretch them high over her head. "If dinner ends this way every time, I might have to rethink eating here."

Tally didn't want to be his reason for coming to his

father's home. Being his reason was flattering, but it put pressure on her and one day, Max was going to come face to face with what he had signed up for.

As much as she wanted to mean something to him, she feared that their intimacy was distracting him from reality and that wouldn't work out for any of the parties involved.

NINE

KICKING MAX OUT of her bed had been a novelty. It had been fun to watch him leave in a grump, but even if Tally had wanted to, she couldn't let him stay. It was against Stretton rules for employees to invite anyone onto the premises let alone have them stay over. But the joke ended up being on her because after he'd gone, Tally had struggled to sleep in her sheets that smelled of them. Every time she almost drifted off, she'd reach for him, and then remember she was alone.

Before leaving, she'd told Max to avoid the employees in the room beneath hers, and given him directions back to the drawing room where the others were. He must have followed her instructions because she wasn't told otherwise by her roommates or employer, and he never came back to her bedroom.

That Saturday, Tally got the oddest call from Max's friend, Robbie, asking her to come to Fitzpatrick's. Max hadn't been in touch since the night of his dinner, so the call from his friend was perplexing. Robbie hadn't said much other than it was urgent, which only made her worry about Max.

So after asking one of the other girls to cover for her,

Tally went straight over there without taking the time to change out of her floor-length chiffon cocktail dress. The crystal detailing around her waist stopped glittering as soon as she stepped into the dark atmosphere of Fitzpatrick's.

It wasn't busy, but all the patrons who were there had chosen to gather at the furthest, darkest end of the room. Trey was behind the bar, and she immediately saw what was making the other customers nervous.

There at the bar were two plainclothes cops. It wasn't only their stern expression that betrayed their profession, she knew these particular guys personally. She'd liaised with them after the car accident that killed Laura, Teddy's wife, when it was discovered that jewelry and personal effects had been stolen from the scene.

Detectives Sanford and Calder had been more than thorough in their investigation and had interviewed all the Stretton staff from the estate, which was how they'd become part of the employee poker games too.

The last place she'd expected to see them was here at Fitzpatrick's. Three people rushed from the back of the room, and she barely made them out as Robbie, Ryan, and Mark. But she didn't wait for them to reach her, she headed straight for the bar.

"Sanford?" she asked.

The cop closest to her turned around. "Tallulah."

She accepted his kiss on her cheek, and Calder's too. "Calder."

Ryan, Robbie, and Mark skidded to a halt. Trey was definitely examining her, but she was focused on the cops. "We pulled you away from something," Sanford said, looking at her dress.

"Yes, and I can't thank you enough for it," she said, smiling. "You saved me from the Yates engagement. Is something wrong? What's going on?"

He took a small plastic baggie from his pocket and put it on the bar; inside was her diamond earring.

Oh no.

"Got a report of this. Someone sighted it, said it might be stolen," he said. "When we came to check it out, we recognized the stamp on the gold, it's a Stretton."

"Yes," she said.

All valuable jewelry that was custom made for the Stretton family was etched with a specific identifying mark.

"We called in and the guys checked out the insurance docket… this is one of a pair of earrings Laura gifted you three years ago."

"Yes," she said again, looking at the stone on the bar.

"We were going to arrest him, but these guys said it was legit," Sanford said, nodding backwards at the trio. "Said they knew you… is that true?"

Glancing at Trey, it was clear he didn't expect her to vouch for him. Robbie, Ryan, and Mark looked similarly concerned. "Couldn't anyone get in touch with Max?" she asked Robbie, who shook his head.

Calder, the other cop spoke up, nodding at Trey. "All he told us was it belonged to Max's girl."

Sanford looked at the trio on their side of the bar. "These stooges said they knew who Max's girl was… Are you Max's girl, Tally?"

Well that was a complicated question for so many reasons. She didn't want to answer because these cops might have contact with the Strettons. If Sanford and Calder had been at Fitzpatrick's for a while, they might have learned just how intimate she'd been with Max on her first night here, when she'd dragged him from the bar and screwed him in the back alley.

Calder's hand began to move as though he was going for his cuffs. "Tally?"

"Yes," she said on a long blink. "Yes, I am… and Trey did nothing wrong, the earring was given to him as a gift. That's all."

A gift or payment, she didn't really want to commit. Sanford and Calder sneered at the environment. "You can do better than a scumbag from this joint."

These cops were her friends, but offense scalded her, and she had to remind herself that they didn't really know what they were talking about because they'd never met Max.

"Maybe," she shrugged and smiled. "But he's *my*

scumbag."

"Okay," Sanford said, and straightened up. "You call us if you think of anything else." Or change your mind, that's what he was saying. It seemed that he was leaving it open for her to change her story when there weren't so many witnesses around. "Do you want us to take you home?"

As cops, they were supposed to look out for citizens. Choosing not to look deeper than that, she accepted their question at face value and ignored its undertones.

"No," she said, holding her clutch in two hands in front of her. "I'm good here for a while."

The Yates' engagement party was still going on, and she could go back, or go home. But she felt it was important to show a sense of solidarity by standing here. Tally wanted to prove, not only to the cops, but to the patrons, that she wasn't afraid to be here, and that she didn't share Sanford and Calder's disdain.

"You sure?" Calder asked, sneering at the guys around them and the customers who were beginning to spread out again. "It's not safe around here... especially for a woman dressed like you are..."

So he was going for direct? But that was okay, he could warn her as much as he liked, Tally wasn't scared anymore. "I'm Max's girl," she said and as soon as she uttered the words, an odd, unexpected heat spread through her. "And now everyone here knows it." Even if it hadn't been her plan to out them. "That makes this room the safest place in the world for me."

They didn't seem to understand. The cops exchanged a confused look, but Sanford tipped his invisible cap at her and glared at the trio behind them before heading for the door.

When they were gone, the whole bar let out a collective breath that they'd been holding all this time.

"Someone get this girl a drink!" Mark called out, but Trey was already pouring tequila.

He held it up for her and she went over to retrieve it. But when she took the glass, he didn't let go. "Your drinks are free in here, forever," Trey said, and she was touched by how relieved he looked. "That would've been my third strike."

He took her hand and kissed the back of it. "Okay, okay," Robbie said, coming over to pull her hand away from Trey. "Didn't you hear her say she's taken?"

She sipped her tequila and Robbie turned to demand that the music be turned up. Now there was a real party spirit and it seemed like she was the guest of honor. Tally was standing next to the stool she'd been sitting on when Max taught her about fitting in around here. His lessons gave her an idea.

"Do you have scissors?" she asked Trey, who frowned but ducked down to retrieve some from beneath the bar.

After taking another drink, she put her glass on the bar and bent to cut into her dress. Max's lessons got her approval because when others saw her hacking the length from her skirt, they cheered along, and she laughed as Ryan and Robbie bent to help her rip it free.

Sliding the scissors across the bar to Trey, he caught them and the skirt that Ryan tossed at him next. Now she fitted in much better. Taking a deep breath, she relaxed. Despite the circumstance, Tally felt so much happier, and so much freer here. In fact, she was so glad that she wasn't at the stuffy Yates engagement that all the tension slipped from her shoulders; she just couldn't stop smiling.

"Come and dance," Robbie said and pulled her toward the jukebox at the back of the room. "There's a card game going and pool, do you know how to play pool?"

"Pool?" she asked, calling over the music. "No, but cards… what cards?"

Robbie stopped to turn back to her. "Texas Hold'em," he said, suspicious as he examined her innocent expression.

"I… might give that a go."

His smile was slow to spread, but when it did, she laughed. Yes, she knew how to play, but she wasn't going to tell anyone that. Sean had taught her how to hustle, though she'd never believed she'd have the chance to use those skills.

"You got it, MG."

That wasn't a name she'd heard before. "MG?" she asked.

"Max's Girl."

"Ah."

It fitted, at least tonight it did, and it was sort of insurance that if the cops ever came around again, everyone would know who to call. But this wasn't a night for worrying about tomorrow. Tally let Robbie pull her over to the jukebox and didn't hesitate when he demanded that she choose the next song.

She had never known Fitzpatrick's existed before she heard the name on Max's lips, now, the place was starting to feel sort of like home.

TALLY HAD BEEN BANNED from the card table. In the nicest way possible, that was how Ryan had explained it to her when he drew her away from her seat. What he really meant was that no one wanted to play with her anymore because they'd figured out that she knew what she was doing.

But she was alright with giving up poker; it gave her a chance to watch the pool game. Standing with her back to the card game she'd been banned from, Tally observed others playing pool and tried to work out if she wanted to give it a go.

Something hit the back of her leg and she looked down to see there was a poker chip on the floor. Doing a good deed, she crouched to pick it up, but she wobbled when she surged back to her feet, probably as a result of the alcohol streaming through her system. Someone put their arm around her and she pushed back against the embrace until she looked up and met the eye of a surprised Max.

Identifying that he was the one steadying her, Tally relaxed. "Hey, handsome," she said, and smiled before turning out of his arms to face the table. "Who does this belong to?" Tally held up the chip, but the last two players, Doug and Andy, weren't looking at her, they were growling at each other. Edging the chip toward her cleavage, she waited for one of them to claim it, and hoped she'd distract them before they could make something of their obvious tension. "Going, going, gone…"

"Mine, MG," Andy growled.

She flicked it over to his stack. "Please, boys, play nice. Winner gets a dance," she said and they both perked up. "As long as there's no more fighting."

They had the decency to appear contrite. "Sorry, MG," both men muttered.

An arm came around her and this time she assumed it was Max's, so she didn't resist when it pulled her away from the table.

"Hey," she said again when she looked up and saw he was scowling.

"What the hell are you doing here?" Max asked her.

"MG!" someone hollered, and she turned to see Ryan holding up a glass.

"Oh," Tally said, pushing away from Max. "Excuse me."

Hurrying to the other end of the pool table, she accepted the drink and was swallowed into the circle of men she'd been hanging with.

"So are you going to do it?" Bobby asked her.

But Max loomed large behind them. "What the fuck is going on here?"

"Where the fuck were you earlier?" Robbie asked, noticing his friend for the first time.

"Cops were in here asking questions," Ryan said, and a somber kind of mood spread through the group that made her smile.

"Ms. Taylor saved the day," Mark said, leaning over to kiss her cheek.

All the men did the same, making her laugh. It had become a joke at the poker table. Whenever she'd won a hand, they'd all kissed her cheek in congratulations. They probably assumed she'd be lousy, except, she'd started to clean up, and the frequency of kisses became so ridiculous it was laughable.

"Who?" Max asked.

Her smile fell, and she rolled her eyes as she held up an open hand at shoulder level. "Me."

"Huh," Max said, taking a second to look at her.

"Trey kissed me too," she said, touching her liquor and licking it from her finger. "Everyone around here is damn friendly."

The guys sniggered. All except Max. "Yeah, until you took them all for a bunch of losers at poker," Robbie said. "She's a hustler, Max, man."

"They banned her," Ryan said. "After Dib was tossed out on his ass for squaring up to her."

Max's brow rose and his shoulders went back. It was like he seemed to grow, and as he tensed up, she sensed danger, so quickly worked to calm him. "It's okay, I was taken care of and Trey barred him…" Leaning to the side, she tried to seek out the bartender behind the bar. "I think he likes me."

"I think he loves you," Mark said. "I think we all do. If Trey's gone then this place shuts down and then where would we hang out?"

He hugged her and then Robbie did, and she laughed as they each showed their appreciation.

"You fuckers are all drunk," Max snapped. "What did I tell you about three feet?"

"Hey, you're supervising, aren't you?" Ryan said, sliding an arm around her waist.

"Oh," Tally said, tugging at her skirt. "Not too tight, honey. My skirt rides up over my ass if anyone holds me too tight."

The guys jeered and laughed. It hadn't been deliberate, but her skirt had ended up shorter at the back than at the front when it was ripped off.

"I need a fucking drink," Max said and spun around to storm away.

Oops, maybe it wasn't fun to be the sober one around a bunch of drunkards. The others saw her wince, but she kept her eyes on Max as the guys called after him, mocking him for being grumpy.

After gulping down her drink, Tally began to follow Max, but the guys kept shouting. Walking backward, she tried to tell them to cool it with a gesture, then she hurried over to the bar where Max was braced on two outstretched arms.

In a brief crouching move, she ducked under his arm, putting her back to the bar. Linking her fingers at the back of his neck, she tried to get his attention. "I'm sorry, lover," she said. "If I'd known you'd be pissed at me hanging out, I'd have left as soon as I got here. I didn't like the way the cops were sneering at the place and trying to take me home like I was unsafe here."

He glanced down at her. Trey came up behind her and slid a drink onto the bar. Max tried to offer him a bill, but Trey refused it and ruffled her hair before going to another customer.

"What the fuck happened in here?" Max asked, holding the bill in mid-air.

"You can put it in my bra if you like," she said, eyeing her chest, but he scowled at her joke. "My winnings are in there. You didn't notice I'd gone up a cup size?"

Maybe he was just resigned, but he folded it and tucked it into her cleavage. "That's the rest of your dress up there, right?"

She glanced back to see Trey had draped her ripped skirt behind the optics like a flag of victory.

Scrunching her nose, she nodded. "It's a long story."

"How you came to be here alone on a Saturday night to bail my buddies out of trouble with the cops? How you got to be best friends with the hardest guys around here? How you cleaned up at poker? Lost half your dress? And got us an open bar? Yeah, I guess it would have to be a long story."

That was a lot, but really, it was simple. "I was worried about you," she said. "I only came because I thought something might have happened to you… I can leave if you're angry with me."

He sealed his lips as his eyes met hers, subtle anger burning in them. "I wasn't around when my friends needed me, then I find out some cunt thought about putting his hands on you? I'm angry, Boss, but not with you."

She grinned. "That's why you're angry? Because you weren't here for us?" He nodded. "Oh, you're so sweet… Do you want to tell me where you were?"

"Tracking down my mom," he said. "Figured I

should tell her about this Stretton shit."

"Did you find her?"

"Yeah, but I don't know if you'll like what she said."

Too intrigued, Tally had to ask. "What did she say?"

"That I should take him for every cent I could, that he owed me," Max said, his conversation with his mother probably didn't put him in the best of moods. "It's weird, I never really see her, but when she was saying goodbye to me…"

"What?"

He shrugged. "I don't know. It was like she thought it would be for the last time. And I guess she thinks if Stretton gets his hooks in…"

That there wouldn't be a chance for his mother to compete or that his mother wouldn't be interested in having a relationship with her son? It saddened her that there might ever be a scenario when his mother wouldn't be interested in him.

Tally couldn't even picture feeling that way herself. "I'm here if you need any help."

But he seemed to have forgotten about his mom already. "Baby," he said, hooking her loose hair over his fingers to push it over her shoulders, letting it flow down behind her. "I'm sorry I wasn't here."

She shook her head because no harm had been done. But this wasn't the place for them to get heavy or mushy, so she decided to help him take his mind from his troubles.

"It's okay," Tally said. "I'll forgive you if you kiss me."

Stooping to merge their mouths, Max's tongue glided between her lips making everything in both their worlds brighter. Their kiss didn't get much further than that; it was interrupted by cheers and wolf whistles coming from the other end of the room. They were the focus of everyone in the place.

Tally laughed and he swept an arm around her waist to boost her onto a stool so he could slide himself between her thighs.

"Do you think they're expecting a repeat of the first

night we were in here?" he asked, kissing her cheekbone and her jaw.

"If you keep doing that, they'll get one," she said, running her hands over his ass before sliding them up and inside his tee-shirt to feel the flesh of his back under her nails.

He kissed her neck, and dipped her back against the bar to kiss her throat. With her head all the way back like this, he could kiss her upper chest, but he kept on going south until he was sucking the supple mound of her breast that was plumped over her neckline.

"MG," he said, lifting his head like it was a question he'd meant to ask before. Dazed by want and endorphins, Tally couldn't form words to answer. "Why does everyone keep calling you MG?"

"Max's Girl," Trey said from behind her as he came over to top off Max's glass. "I won't stop you going at it right there, but that girl deserves a bed and some privacy, buddy. She's a queen."

Trey disappeared again, and Tally reached for Max's belt, but he intercepted her hand. "He's right. Let's say goodnight, baby." It was crazy how disappointed she was, and Max must have read the sulk on her face because he smiled and kissed her. "You want me to fuck you?" Her features lit. "Here? In front of everyone?" Biting her lip, she reconsidered. This wasn't a random audience, these were his friends… and she was with it enough to know that she was too drunk to make smart choices. "Come on."

He linked their fingers and eased her body in front of his. Bringing their clasped hands up to her abdomen, she held his protective forearm against her as they moved back toward their friends. Max finished his drink just as they got to the group.

"We're leaving," she said and there was a collective groan of disappointment.

"You just got here, Max," Mark said. "You haven't seen how cool this girl is yet."

These guys really were drunk if they thought she was cool. The comment made Tally laugh. "Max knows how cool I am, he was sleeping with me before any of you knew I existed," she said. "Hell, we were having sex out the back of this place a half hour into our first date—" Her mind caught up with her mouth and she twisted to look over her shoulder at the man she was leaning on, heat flooded her cheeks. "I just said too much out loud."

"It's okay, sweetheart," he said, bowing to kiss her. "We weren't discreet about it. I don't think it's a secret around here."

Did that make her feel better? Maybe. Yes, because she hadn't embarrassed him, and she'd hate herself if she ever did. Downside was, every person in the place knew she was a hussy.

Turning all the way around, she buried her face in Max's chest, and he didn't grope, just draped his arms around her.

"That's good," Mark said. "Take her out back for a service if she needs one, and then bring her back in to play with us."

"You watch your mouth," Max said. "I really don't want to put my fist through my buddy's face… but I will if he disrespects my girl."

Oh, this was all going wrong, now there was anger between the friends. Mark was drunk, he didn't mean any disrespect. But Max was being kind in making sure no one treated her like a slut.

"Excuse me," Tally said.

Pushing away from Max, she headed to the restroom, and after going through the motions, she looked at her reflection.

Since meeting Max she'd become a different person. She was wild and confident with him in a way she never had been before. Yeah, she'd always been able to talk to people if she had to, but she wasn't taught to assert herself in the Stretton house. She was taught to blend in, not to talk unless she was addressed. She was taught to apologize, that everything was her fault if that's what she was told.

Max was different. He taught her to hold her head up. Made her feel desired for who she was, not who he told her she had to be. He wanted her. Let her be free to act as insane as she wanted to. Being with him made her feel good about who she was, and she trusted him. She couldn't be too much or take things too far with him. He accepted her no matter what.

She was so lucky to be with a man like Max. Except she *wasn't* with him.

It was like there were two Maxs; the Max who lived in his apartment, hung out here, and drank tequila with his friends. And the Max who was Teddy's son and heir, the one she'd been supposed to track down and persuade to have dinner with his long-lost father.

Except that job was done and she was still here. Why was she still here?

Why had she been so scared earlier when Robbie summoned her to Fitzpatrick's? Why had she been so terrified by the thought that something might have happened to Max? Why had she hung around with his friends all night drinking tequila and laughing at their jokes when she should've rushed back to her boss at his party?

Teddy might have needed her, yet she'd chosen to stay here and risked him finding out that she'd not only abandoned her post, but she'd gotten drunk as well?

It was Max.

Max was the reason she was here. He was the one she wanted to be close to. The one she wanted to be with. The one she loved.

Her thoughts skidded to a halt. She watched her eyes in the mirror widen in horror. She loved him. She loved Max Flynn. Oh God, what a disaster! Tally loved the man she'd said she couldn't get attached to. The man she'd told not to make her promises.

She had to get out of here.

Pushing away from the sink, Tally stared at herself for another half beat before rushing to the door and into the hallway. To the right was the fire exit that she knew from experience would take her to the alleyway and into the street. To the left was the bar, Max, and his friends.

So what should she do? Go back to the party like nothing was different, or to freedom where she could have

some time to come to terms with her major fuck up?
Right.

TEN

THE MONEY IN HER BRA had been a godsend, because she'd left her clutch behind the Fitzpatrick's bar for safe keeping. Her winnings got her a cab home and as soon as she was back, Tally sent a text to her own phone to say she was safe knowing that Trey was likely to give her purse to Max when she didn't come back from the restroom.

Tally ordered a new company phone and called to get her number transferred onto it, rendering the old one effectively useless. Even in spite of her hasty departure, Max didn't try to call, but then he thought he had her phone, so that wasn't much of a surprise.

Unfortunately, she couldn't avoid him forever and on Friday night, the Stretton house was in full-on grooming mode. As Teddy and Kimmy prepared for the Walker Benefit, Tally was sent on ahead in a limo to swing by to pick up Max.

She'd had a tux couriered to him and had received notification that it had arrived, but that was it. Max would probably be livid about the outfit, but she hoped that he put it on because it would win him points with Teddy.

It wouldn't win him points with her, in fact, Tally found herself uncomfortable with this whole process. Still, the point was to get Max comfortable in society not to keep her happy. Tally had to effectively groom him into what his father wanted him to be. Her own needs and wants were irrelevant and remembering that was going to be crucial to Max's success.

Her problem was that she loved the current Max exactly the way he was now and didn't want him to change, not even a little bit. The idea of seeing her Max in a tux, trussed up like one of Teddy's fancy friends, made her squirm. She wanted him in his faded jeans, wearing a grubby tee-shirt, with his hair finger-combed at best. That's how she wanted him. That was her Max.

But that wasn't who got into the back of the limo.

The Max who got in with her wore the tux and more than that, he'd shaved and styled his hair. She immediately felt sick. As soon as the door closed, the car started to move.

He slid toward her. "Mm, white," he said of her dress. "You playing the virgin tonight?"

Her sheath dress was backless and elegant, but it was long, and he had to bend to find the hem. If he got his hands on her flesh, he would break her resolve. So she intercepted him before he could touch her.

"Don't," she whispered.

Tally had made sure the limo's privacy screen was up before Max got in the car, which was weird for her given that she'd usually speak to the driver when she was in the car alone with him. But she'd sold it that she'd have to brief Max about the night ahead and didn't want Pierre to hear her gossiping.

"You still feel bad?" Max asked, stroking her hand. "It's okay, baby, no one cared."

She was confused. "I don't... what?"

"For telling everyone we fucked in the alley? I figured that's why you ditched me, you were embarrassed... right?"

If that was what he thought then that worked for her and as he got more concerned she worried he was reconsidering his assumption, so she smiled. "Yes, uh huh, sorry. Yes, I was embarrassed."

The corner of his mouth curled. "Don't worry about it. You didn't have to stay away from me all week."

Putting his arm over her waist, he pulled her to him. But she resisted. "Don't, you'll crease the dress."

He relaxed and scrutinized her dress, then frowned at her. "You don't give a fuck about your clothes when I'm touching you. Do you want to try that again?"

The smile she'd tried to sell didn't cut it, and although she'd done her best to keep her voice neutral, it had come out strained. So even if he'd bought it for a minute, Tally hadn't put him off the scent of the truth. In fact, pushing him away just pissed him off and the last thing she needed was the confined atmosphere to be charged with any kind of emotion.

"I'm just not in the mood," she mumbled and straightened so she was facing the front of the car, hoping he'd let it go. But it was a fool's hope.

Still irritated, Max didn't hide his feelings about her attitude. "We've gone without all week and now we're alone, you don't want to fool around?" he asked. "Or are you telling me you've been getting yours somewhere else this week?"

She'd thought he might consider her fickle or that he might assume she was playing hard to get to force him into chasing her. The last thing she'd considered was he'd guess she'd been screwing around.

"What?" Tally panicked and flipped back around to face him. "No!"

"Then what the fuck?" he asked, his volume rising.

She touched his lips, trying to keep him quiet. "Please, don't get angry," she whispered. "We just… can't."

His anger was highlighted by his scowl; he didn't make any attempt to subdue his impatience. "Can't? Why not? You're coming back to my place tonight, right?"

She hadn't even considered that he might think that they'd be spending the night together. Tally played that scenario out in an instant and knew there was no way it would work. But going back to his apartment would only make things worse anyway, so it had never been an option, much as she might have wanted it to be.

"No, I… I couldn't," she said. "The driver will take you home, if I went upstairs with you…"

"What?" he snapped. "Everyone would know we're

hot for each other and you can't live with the shame of screwing a lowlife like me?"

Horror hit her hard. "No!" she exclaimed, how could this conversation be going so wrong? Why was he being so defensive? "You're not a lowlife, you're heir to billions, you're—"

"There are plenty of rich scumbags," he said and opened his arms, his face tense, set by the same anger that dominated his voice. "Look at the fucking state of me! I'm wearing this damn monkey suit 'cause it's what you wanted." But it wasn't what she wanted and as she shook her head, moisture gathered in her eyes. "I'm doing this shit to make you happy, Tal. This is what you want, right? You want a guy all trussed up like a fucking punk and—"

Tears slipped from her lashes. "I hate it," she wailed and covered her mouth as though she could stuff the words back in.

"What?" he asked, his anger loosening to shock.

"I'm sorry," she whispered, her tears in freefall. "I know you did it for me. I know you're here because of me. I know you're trying to be everything the heir apparent should be but…"

"You hate it," he muttered.

"Baby, I'm sorry," she said and wriggled closer. "I don't want you to touch me because… because like this you're not… my Max. I don't know what you are, I don't know who I think you are, but… I hate it. You look like a stranger."

More tears flowed. She grabbed for the champagne bottle to pour some into a glass, so she could gulp it down, and try to dampen some of her overwhelming grief.

"Tal," he said and touched her bare back.

But she pushed his hand away and slid as far down the seat as she could to get away from him. "You need to do this," she said to him, but it sounded more like she was giving a pep talk to the ether. "It's what's best for you. I tried to tell you… to tell you that it would be like this. I tried to warn you that it would take some getting used to. But, ultimately, Teddy is going to give you a good life, one with security that you can be proud of."

His anger was all gone, he sounded as resigned as she felt. "But to have that life, I have to be this guy."

"We'll both get used to it," she said, letting her gaze fall to her drink. But she was so disgusted with it, and herself, that she put the flute aside. "It's good. This is good. We needed distance. This will let you be who you need to be without our… flirtation getting in your way. I should've tried harder, I should've been stronger. I was the stupid one who went and fell in love. It's complete insanity. I was careless and ignorant. But this is good. This will help me remember, I'm not MG, not really. I never was. Never could be. You belong to them. You need to belong to them. It's what needs to happen—"

Max grabbed her wrist and yanked her along the length of the seat to his side. Thrusting her arm up, he forced it around the back of his neck, clamping it in place, so she couldn't go anywhere. When she was helpless and pressed to him, his face ducked to within an inch of hers.

"You fell in love with me?"

She nodded, making more tears fall from her lashes. "I'm sorry… That's why I ran out of Fitzpatrick's," she whispered her confession. "I wasn't embarrassed about what I said. I was looking at myself in the mirror and I realized… I love you." He dipped to kiss her, but she turned her mouth down to prevent them making contact. "We can't."

"Fuck that," he said, some of his irritation returning. "You need me to wear dirty jeans and my leather jacket, we'll turn this tank around and I'll change. The fuckers at your party will wait."

"You won't get in dressed like that," she said, and just the idea of him in his jeans and jacket made her insides flip.

"Then we'll make our own fun," he said and pressed his mouth into her hair. "We've always been good at that." If she closed her eyes, she could vaguely smell her Max, but she resented the mist of cologne that covered the scent she truly loved. "Come on, baby, let's go home."

Shaking her head, it took a couple of tries of her tugging her arm to get her hand back from him, but he eventually let her go and she slid away. "No, this is your future,

Max, and I won't take that away from you."

But he was on the defensive and wasn't letting himself see that she was right. "My… I never gave a fuck about this prick and his money. It's not worth it if it doesn't make you happy."

Nothing about this situation was simple. "But it does," she said. From everything she'd just said, she understood why he thought the opposite; she wasn't being clear, so she tried to explain. "It makes me happy that you're connecting with your father. That you're going to get what's owed to you, what's rightfully yours. You've struggled all your life and it's only right that you get what should've been yours all along. You're smart. I know you'll figure out all the business stuff fast and the rest of it… that's nothing. You'll figure out a way to fit in. And when this all comes together for you, Max, it will be spectacular. You'll be living a life full of opportunity where you have everything your heart desires."

Something had faded from him, and he was no longer vehement. There was a dejection in him that he tried to mask, but Tally saw it and it broke her heart. "Everything but you."

He was handsome, there was no way anyone could deny that with his square jaw and keen eyes that he was one of the most stunning men available and the money would only make him more eligible.

"Max, I… I've been around rich, influential men most of my adult life. I work with them. I live with them. I've dated them and slept with them. But not one of them came even close to making me feel how you did that first night in Fitzpatrick's. Hell, I was attracted to you the minute I saw you in your hallway… But this is about more than just sex. The way I feel, it's about the way you make me feel, and the man you are. Except, this week I've had to come to terms with the truth that this will change you." Lifting her eyes to his, she could read his concentration. He was trying to follow, to understand. "They will change you… And that will be good for you."

"But bad for you," he said. "You don't want a rich, influential man."

There was more to it than that. "It's not the money,

or the power, it's… the way you carry yourself. Take tonight for example, you won't be able to hold me or kiss me, even if our relationship was public, the most you could do is hold my hand or kiss my cheek. And it's not about getting physical, it's… you won't be able to be proud of me, I won't be able to show how proud I am of you. No one will be happy for us, accepting. We'll be just the same as every other detached, demure couple there. We won't be laughing and playing, and I guess, I need to be able to relax in the way only my Max can make me relax." She smiled at his blank expression. "You don't get it, do you?"

"No, I do," he said. "I just… I don't get why we have to go if it's going to be such bullshit."

"Because it's where you make connections," she said, taking his hand. "It's where you'll meet people and tell them about your accomplishments. It's where people come to bow down to you. You'll meet people tonight that you'll see next week in the board room, on the opposite side of negotiations, and events like this help you learn about them, and ingratiate yourself."

"But I don't give a fuck about that."

"You will," she said, it was almost like coaching a belligerent child. "This is baby steps. Everyone starts somewhere, you're just starting later than most. Think of it like going to prison, you find a friend, someone to watch your back and introduce you to the right people. They'll tell you who to avoid, what to do, how to act, what not to do… then before you realize it, you've found your comfort zone."

"I find my comfort zone. And what do you do?"

She shrugged and sat back to check her make up in a mirror that folded out from a panel. Taking a tissue from the box on the side, Tally dried her tears and mopped up the smudges in her makeup. "I'll wake up and go to work on Monday," she said. "It might be a first for me, but other women the world over are their boss' dirty little secret. I'm not unique."

"Hey," he said, reaching over to take her hand, drawing the tissue away from her face. She turned to look at him. "You were never my dirty anything."

She pushed out her lower lip in a mock petulant pout. "I liked being dirty with you."

It was too soon for teasing; the light of interest in his eyes flared fast. But the car stopped and the door on his side opened. They were there.

She scooted over next to him. "Get out first, then take my hand and hook it inside your elbow." He looked at her and she didn't know if he was nervous or appreciative. "Just think of it as role play."

Something they hadn't done, but it might make him feel more comfortable. Tally had been nervous at her first society event and she was a woman, so she could at least trust that she'd be led by a man. Max didn't have that safety net.

Here, for his first time, someone had to show him how to lead and Tally was honored to be the one, even if her heart was breaking.

ELEVEN

MAX DID EXACTLY as she'd instructed and held her close after they got out of the car. "This is fucked up," he mumbled from the corner of his mouth.

She pointed at the door. "Usually people would stay out here to greet each other and fawn," Tally said. "And if there are photographers, the ones who are fame-hungry linger for as long as they can."

"We're not fame hungry?" he asked her. She smiled up at him and shook her head. "Okay, got it."

"Tonight, you're lucky to be basically anonymous and I'm completely insignificant. Once people start to learn your face and know who you are, they'll start trying to talk to you more. You'll have people intercepting you, they'll compliment you, and don't be surprised if they use your date to get to you. They'll compliment her, engage her in conversation about how amazing she is, and depending on how shallow and ignorant she is, that can be frightfully effective."

"You're not shallow or ignorant."

Tally had to hold her skirt up with her clutch hand to ascend the portico stairs. "Well no one's going to try to talk to me because I'm poor, so that makes me invisible... I've actually met almost everyone who will be in the room tonight. You know who'll remember my name? The staff; security guards and the drivers, that's it. The rich partygoers will think they're meeting me for the first time even though I've been around for years… Though they'll recognize me fast enough if they want a space in the schedule."

"You'll never be invisible to me."

It was sweet that he thought so, but she wasn't so naïve. "Give it six months," she muttered, then nodded ahead. "You have to open the door for me."

"Can I smack your ass as you walk past?"

Tally had just broken up with him three minutes ago and already he was making her laugh. Instead of saying no, she twisted to face him as she went by, nodding in thanks and preventing him from getting near her ass.

Waiting for Max on the inside, Tally took the invite from her clutch and handed it over to him. "You have to give that to the attendant at the top of the stairs," she said and took his arm again. "Everything here is old-fashioned. It's a male-dominated world, I'm nothing but the breasts accompanying you for the evening."

Moving through the lobby, Tally saw a couple of security guys from another family's detail. They bowed and tipped their invisible caps when they noticed her, and she nodded in regal acknowledgement then grinned.

"Know those guys?" he asked as they crossed the wide space.

"The three in front gave me self-defense lessons after I was mugged."

"You were mugged?"

She nodded. "Wasn't a fun night for me. They're good guys," she said, then got back on point. "But, okay, so you're the man. You have to take charge of everything, but you're good at that."

"You never complained," he murmured, sending a chill down her spine.

It was difficult not to make everything he said intimate, but she'd have to get out of the habit. "I meant like getting drinks for the ladies and making sure your date is happy. You're attentive anyway, I don't have to teach you that."

"You don't have to teach me anything," he grumbled. "These fuckers can take me or leave me, I don't care."

His mood was petulant, but she probably hadn't helped it given their conversation in the car. She just had to remain calm and try to make him see past their relationship. "Yes, but your father does. If you do anything to embarrass him, he'll be angry."

"I'll sleep fine."

Tally smiled. "Yeah, but I won't, because I'll be on the street," she said. "Remember the point of me being here is to keep you in line."

"Good luck with that," Max said and started up the stairs, but she slowed him when she had to lift the front of her dress again.

When they eventually got to the top of the stairs, they went to the podium and handed over the invitation.

"Tallulah!" the guy at the podium exclaimed. "You look good enough to eat."

Max tensed, so she pulled him closer to her. He didn't really move, but her increase in grip told him to calm down. There was nothing to be jealous about here.

"Hey, David, why are you out here?"

"Covering for Jamie, he's out back having a smoke, fighting with Alicia."

"Oh," she said. "They haven't fixed things yet?"

He shrugged. "Dunno, they're fighting or fucking, I can't keep track. You coming to the wedding?"

"Next month? Absolutely," she said. "Sean and I got the day off… he's promising to bring his Harley… I can't wait."

David laughed. "Don't show up the bride, we don't want any more hitches. It's about bloody time they just did it, right?" David said, scanning Max. "Anyway, I best let you get in there. Your table's in the usual place."

"Thanks, honey."

Turning to the grand double door, the doorman opened it for them and Tally offered him a polite smile as they went through.

"Honey?" Max asked. "You screw him?"

"David is gay," she said. "So, no. And next time you see him, don't repeat any of that. He spoke to me as a friend because he didn't recognize you, so he assumed you were one of us. As soon as he knows who you are, he'll be embarrassed, and he'll treat you with nothing but deference."

Max's offence level was rising. "Maybe I don't want deference," he said. "And what the fuck is one of you? I'm not one of you?"

"No," she said, nodding at the glitterati, the rich and beautiful people they were moving towards. "You're one of them."

The marble floor was shining, the chandeliers gleamed, and the room was filled with the country's richest. "They don't look like nice people."

She couldn't say that all of them were but smiled instead of saying that. "Just smile and try to look friendly."

He stopped walking to glare at her. "I don't smile for no reason and I don't want any fucker to think I'm friendly."

"Hmm," she said and thought about it for a second. "You do pull off the brooding thing well, maybe just do your best to look bored and mean. The superrich can afford to be aloof to the point of rude. So bored and mean. Go with that."

"You got it, baby," he said, and that made her laugh though he meant it.

"Your father always likes a table close to the action and on the dancefloor. He gets annoyed if people get too close to the table, but he likes a good view. Most of the hotels and venues hold the same events every year. You'll get used to where he likes to be in each room."

"And no one else gets a say?"

They wound through the tables, giving her a chance to think about it. "Not now, but I guess over time, you might. It depends how your relationship with him progresses."

"I'll get my own damn table. I like dark corners."

And she liked to be in dark corners with him. "I know you do, but in time you'll probably come around to your father's way of thinking. If you can see who's talking to who,

who's dating, it helps the business. And people have tells; sometimes you can pick up blackmail material just by watching how people respond to each other."

"So if I grab your ass now—"

"Don't even think about it," she said and smiled, widening her joy when the Stretton table came into view. "Okay, when we get there, you have to move around the table, shake every man's hand and kiss every woman's cheek. If Teddy doesn't introduce you, introduce yourself. Whenever a woman stands, any woman, for anything, you have to stand too. You can sit down when she leaves. Stand up again when she comes back, before she sits. When she sits, you sit. And if you're beside her, pull her chair out for her."

"Yeah," Max mumbled, sounding again like that stroppy child. "We should've just gone home."

Just as she said, when they approached, everyone at the table stood up. "Ah, we thought you'd never arrive," Teddy said, reaching for Max's hand. "Everyone, this is Max, my son."

She eyed the people at the table, encouraging Max to go around and shake all the male hands as he kissed all the female cheeks. His was the last vacant seat at the table, opposite his father and next to her. Tally wasn't at all surprised to see Blair positioned on his other side.

When Max sat down, a server rushed up behind him to provide them both with champagne. Max sipped it and scowled. "What's this shit?" he murmured at her.

"Cristal, I think," Tally said, moving her glass to his position because she wasn't allowed to drink it.

Sliding his hand along the back of her chair, he leaned closer to her while putting his back to Blair. "Why don't you have to kiss everyone?"

"Because I'm insignificant," she said. "It would be an insult for me to greet people as their equal when I'm subordinate to everyone at the table." She pushed his thigh. "Sit straight in your chair and don't slouch. And don't turn your back to a lady, it's rude."

Leaning even closer, Max's proximity was verging on being inappropriate. "I wanna give you a hickey so bad right now," he mumbled.

God, he was awful, and her look of horror probably conveyed that to him. Though he was quite proud of himself as he turned back to the table and guzzled more of his champagne.

"Max, how was your trip?" Kimmy's date, Brian, asked.

"What trip?" Max asked. "Where'd I go?"

"No, I meant your journey here," Brian said, glancing at the others at the table. "Some of us were stuck in the construction tailbacks uptown. You know, where they're resurfacing."

"Oh, I live on the south side," he said. "No resurfacing there, the city don't give a fuck about our roads. There are more holes waiting to be filled in our streets than there are in whores at a fucking brothel."

Okay, this was… not going so great if the looks of shock going around the table were any indication. But Max didn't care, he was busy poking at the central plate of canapés, picking out pieces he wanted to eat… which seemed to be the pieces on top because he was ignoring the bases beneath.

"And uh…" Heath said, glancing at Teddy. "How do you feel about joining us at the office next week, Max?"

Max stopped poking to scan the table. "I don't give a flying fuck about your business and I ain't interested in clocking in for a nine to five when I can make as much dough as I need knocking over liquor stores." Something startled him because he jerked back. Max landed narrow eyes on Blair, then reached under the table to pick her hand off his leg to drop it onto the table. "No cock for you to ride in these pants, sweetheart. Plenty of rich fucks around here with dodgy tickers for your pussy to play on."

"Okay," Tally said and stood up. "Excuse us."

Grabbing for Max's arm, he didn't even have the decency to look contrite when she pulled him up and dragged him over to the dancefloor. Lifting his arms into place, she wasn't surprised to feel his hand slide around to her lower back, but as long as it stayed off her ass, it was progress.

"Are you trying to kill me?" she asked. "You're not

content to get me fired, clearly, you want me to die of sheer mortification."

Again, like a bored child, he shuffled and looked around, but his heart wasn't in it. "What?"

"Okay, maybe it was my fault. I didn't spend time prepping you. You have to dial back the swearing, and yes, words like cock and pussy are classed as swear words in this room." They got a few side glances. Tally had to temper her mood to lower her voice. "We don't talk about whores or brothels. When in doubt, a simple yes or no will suffice. Now, don't get me wrong, when you're with just the men at the country club or smoking cigars out back, I'm sure there is plenty of demeaning talk about women. But at the table, at the start of the evening, when everyone is sober and there are women present, you have to think polite, think demure, think…"

"Boring."

"Yes," she said, a grin splitting her face. "Yes, don't go for shock value. Just imagine your mom is sitting beside you."

"Hmm," he said and considered that. "My mom curses worse than me."

"Then act the complete opposite."

"Good advice."

"Good," she said, glad she'd found a way to get through to him and help him understand. "And with Blair, you have to be subtler. The dirty talk will only turn her on. Remember what you said about the classier the girl, the dirtier she likes it? Well, just think of Blair as the classiest woman on the planet."

"So the dirtiest?"

"Yes," she said, but her pride in herself was short-lived. "Wait… that makes you want her, doesn't it?"

"Do you care? Didn't you just try to dump me?"

Deflated, Tally didn't need the reminder of their conversation in the car. That had to be the root of his sulk, but there was nothing she could do to change the facts of their predicament to make it better.

"Yes," she murmured, trying to ignore the stinging

that strained her shoulders. "Sorry, you're free to sleep with anyone you want to."

But Max didn't play games with her. "Doesn't matter, I already figured that about her, if she'll screw a guy and then go after his son, she's got no boundaries… I like a woman with boundaries."

He was trying to reassure her or make her feel better. Her eyes drifted to his and she saw the light of interest, something that shouldn't be there, that she should ignore, but that light drew her in. He hadn't lost his power over her and she doubted that he ever would.

"You get this certain look in your eye when you're thinking about sex," she murmured.

"I'm surprised you've ever seen me without it."

Seeing past the outfit and the grooming, she could fixate on the man and recognize her lover in those eyes. "I'm just letting you know, you have a tell, so you might want to work on that for future… women. If you want to be brooding and mysterious, you'll have to disguise it."

His eyes narrowed. "Can I get something straight?" She nodded. "If we met on the street, or in a bar, just a guy and a girl, without this Stretton connection, you would be with me, wouldn't you?"

What a question. At least she had her answer about his mood. Clearly, he was still thinking about what she'd said in the car. It probably hadn't been fair to end their relationship and then bring him here, but in her defense, she hadn't planned to lose control like she had.

His question put so much in perspective and she wouldn't lie. "Yes."

"But because I'm related to that schmuck over there and he wants to turn me into this corporate flunkey and load me up with dough, you don't want to be with me, do you?"

Inhaling, she hated that it made her sound like such a bitch to put up arbitrary boundaries. "No."

"Well, fuck," he said and shook his head. "That takes the fucking biscuit. Every bitch who's ever ridden my cock has wanted more or dumped me for some dude with more money or a better car or whatever shallow shit they care about.

I find me a woman who doesn't want to change a damn thing about me, and she dumps me 'cause it turns out I've got a rich daddy."

"Max—"

"No," he said and stepped away from their dance. "I love your honesty, you don't screw around. You give me the truth upfront… It's one of the things that made me fall in love with you." He loved her? He hadn't said that in the car and now that they were surrounded by people, she didn't even know how to respond. He ran the back of his finger along her jaw. "I'll play nice, Boss. I'll do whatever makes you happy. Whether we're fucking or not, it doesn't change the truth."

"The… truth?"

He came to her, right up close, to murmur. "That we're crazy for each other. Love, huh? Pretty damn cool." He turned but didn't get far before he came back. "Oh, and you'll always be MG. I don't give up. This…" He lifted his head to scan the room before looking at her again. "This I don't give a fuck about. You make me the richest man in the world. Only you."

TWELVE

THE WALKER BENEFIT was winding down.

Tally was at the Stretton table typing into her phone, Kimmy and Brian were a couple of places away from her, and everyone else was away schmoozing or drinking. Ready to go home, Tally stifled a yawn with the back of her hand. But she didn't get to decide when they left, it was her responsibility to be here until the bitter end.

Just as she was about to put her phone into her clutch, it began to ring. "Hello?" she answered.

"MG!" Robbie called down the line. She smiled when she heard the cheering in the background. "Max said you were coming out tonight, where you guys at? Drag his ass out of bed and get down here, Trey's got this cocktail book, he's so fucked up, it's hilarious. We're having a lock-in later, you up for it?"

Hiding her smile by bowing her head, Tally leaned back in her seat. "How drunk are you, Rob?"

"Want me to put you on speakerphone?" he asked and didn't wait for a response. "She's on speaker!"

A rabble cheered so loud that Tally had to hold the phone away from her ear. Kimmy and Brian must have heard the noise because they looked over at her. Tally averted her gaze and quickly turned down the volume of her handset.

Concealing the conversation, she put the phone back to her ear, and this time shielded her mouth by cupping a hand around it to direct her voice to the microphone. "Hey, guys," she said.

"Sounds like she's whispering," Ryan said.

"Is Max sleeping?" Mark asked, probably assuming she'd tired him out with sex. "Wake him up. Max! Max!"

Everyone started to chant his name, their enthusiastic rhythm made her laugh. They were having so much more fun over there than she was having here. Like he'd promised her on the dancefloor, Max was playing the dutiful son, doing everything he should do, and he was watching what he said and his manners too. While being at this fancy event was a novelty for him, she was bored out of her wits.

Tally turned to stop a server as he passed. "Can you bring me three shots of tequila, please?"

The server frowned. "Tequila?"

She nodded. "Yeah, the cheapest stuff you've got."

Though perplexed, he left with a nod. Another cheer echoed down the phone. "Did he wake up yet?" Robbie asked. "Or we can bring the party back to your place?"

Her place. They were classifying her place as Max's place, which it wasn't, and never would be.

"Guys," she said, trying to calm them down. "Guys, we're at a party."

"A party? A fucking party?" Robbie exclaimed.

"Oh, and we weren't fucking invited!" Mark shouted and everyone on the end of the line started booing.

They were just hilarious, Tally was laughing again when Blair came to sit down at the Stretton table. But Tally twisted away to block the superior beauty out when she drew her scornful eyes away.

"It's not like that," she said. "You know I love you."

They kept on booing. "We're having a party tomorrow night, right here, want an invite? 'Cause maybe you and your boyfriend won't get one now."

Tally should be staying away from that part of town,

especially after last time when she'd bolted, but maybe that was why she was tempted to go back, to redeem herself.

"I want an invite," Tally said, playing along. "What do I have to do?"

"Play pool," Robbie said, and everyone laughed.

"Yeah, for money," another voice said, and it took her a minute to recognize Doug had been the speaker. "Give me a chance to get even."

Tally raised her eyes as someone passed her and sank into the seat beside hers. Max identified himself by sliding a hand along the back of her chair, but she leaned forward away from it.

"Who's on the phone?" he asked, but might not have been talking to her, because Blair answered.

"Her boyfriend," Blair said. That wasn't true, and she had no idea how Blair had reached that conclusion. Surprise made her twist, and Tally found herself being met by glares from everyone at the table, the most intense being Max's. "She said she loves him."

Had she said that? "What the—" Before he could swear, Tally took the phone from her ear and held it out to Max. His scowl deepened, but he took the handset from her and put it to his ear. "Yo?" His expression loosened as clarity came to him and a second later he smiled. "Yeah, I'm awake now, what's up? Jesus, fuck, Rob, you're wasted."

He rose from the table and wandered away, touching her cheekbone with an absent fingertip as he left.

"Rob?" Blair asked.

"One of Mr. Flynn's friends," Tally said, straightening up everything in her reach on the table.

"You know his friends?" Kimmy asked, moving down to Blair's date's chair to get closer.

"Uh, some of them, yeah," Tally said. "I met them when I went to his apartment."

"What's it like? His apartment?" Kimmy asked.

Tally couldn't blame her for being curious about her brother. Blair's interest was more unsettling.

"It's an apartment," she said. "One bed, shower room, open plan living area."

"And it's on the south side?" Kimmy said and rested a hand on Blair's forearm as she shivered. "Weren't you just terrified to go over there?"

Tally shook her head. "No, I didn't really think about it being dangerous when I went the first time and after I met Max, he always made sure I was safe."

That statement raised some brows. "Max?" Blair drawled.

Oh, oops, her cheeks heated. "Mr. Flynn, I apologize."

The server came over with the three shots on a fancy silver tray. It looked crazy, but he placed them in a row and she smiled.

"Thank you," she said, and pulled a bill from her clutch to hand it over.

The alcohol was free at these events, but finding cheap liquor like this probably took some time, so tipping felt right.

"You visited him a few times, didn't you?" Blair said. "Do you think he trusts you?"

Tally didn't get a chance to answer because Max came back, handing over the phone as he sat down. "They're having a ball over there," he said and examined the shot glasses. "What's this?"

"A reward," she said, lifting two over to him while she took one.

He raised his glass to her and they tossed back the first shot together then he quickly threw the other down his throat too. "Oh, I love that shit," he murmured and again stretched an arm along the back of her chair, but this time he leaned over to whisper in her ear. "Let's get a room and fuck, right now. I'll do you fast and dirty, baby, any way you want it."

Oh no, maybe the tequila had been a bad idea. The taste was an instant reminder of their encounters in Fitzpatrick's, which were always steamy. Tally could already see Max's other hand sliding off the table and it would be a short journey for him to reach her leg. With Blair so close there was no way the act would go unnoticed.

But Tally was saved from having to stop him when Teddy marched over to the table with fury spread on his face. "Miss Taylor, are you consuming alcohol?"

Ah, fuck, oops. She shouldn't have drunk that tequila! For some reason with Robbie on the phone and Max nearby, she'd forgotten all about the no-alcohol rule.

"Sir," she said, the center of the table's attention. There was no way to miss Blair's smug enjoyment of her embarrassment. "I apologize, I—"

"Your services for the evening are terminated," he said. "I am heartily disappointed that you would flout our long-held rules."

"Yes, sir," she said and rose. "Again, I apologize."

"Wait a minute," Max said and stood up beside her. "She was drinking with me. And she's worked hard keeping me in line tonight. She deserves a reward."

"You don't understand our procedures yet," Teddy said.

Max inhaled, but Tally rested the back of her hand against his chest, remaining side-by-side with him. "Don't," she murmured.

"She used his first name a minute ago too," Kimmy said, and Teddy's jaw literally fell.

Damn, the meddling little minx never passed up an opportunity to get someone in trouble. Tally's face was burning, she was usually classed as the good, responsible one. It seemed those days were gone.

"That was an accident," Tally said, "I apologized and—"

"Whoa," Max said. "I told her to use my first name, I don't like all this Mr. Flynn shit."

"You have to get used to it," Kimmy said. "It's a mark of respect. A subordinate using your first name is insolent."

Kimmy had been taught by her father so of course she felt that way. "Well I guess I like that," Max said.

"Stop it," Tally said and tipped her chin up to look at him.

It was clear that Max was angry, and she was touched that he was standing up for her. But he didn't understand that all he was doing was damaging them both.

"Do not speak to him that way," Teddy said. "I don't know what's come over you, Miss Taylor, but this is unacceptable behavior."

Oh God, was she about to lose her job? "I'm sorry, sir," Tally said. "Truly, I am."

"If this is what alcohol does to you, I would say abstaining is appropriate for you. Now, if you wish to keep your job, you will retire and take the weekend to consider how important your position is to you."

Ooh, ouch, a suspension, that was as unveiled as it could get. Blair folded her arms as she sat back, sneering down her nose. Kimmy was wide-eyed and interested. Brian wouldn't lift his eyes from the table. Teddy was furious, and she couldn't even bear to look at Max.

Grabbing her clutch, Tally spun around to head for the door. Getting out of here seemed like an excellent idea. It was funny how they'd worried about Max being the one to get them in trouble, yet it ended up being her who crossed the line.

She had just gotten to the top of the stairs outside the ballroom when Max caught up with her. "Baby," he said, louder than she was comfortable with given where they were.

But he didn't seem to see anyone except her as he rushed over wearing a scowl.

"Max—"

"Good, well at least they haven't got in your head enough to make you question using my name," he said, clasping her elbows to urge her close, but she took a backward step. "Babe—"

"No," she whispered. Paranoia webbed through her when she scanned the people standing nearby, who were side-eying them, and probably taking notes for future reporting to their gossip buddies. "Please, I can't afford to lose this job, sir."

His worry became instant rage. "Don't you fucking dare. Don't you fucking think about using that 'sir' shit on me. Try it and I'll go back in there and tell that bastard to go fuck himself."

But this wasn't as simple as what they felt for each other. It frustrated her that he held the power to ruin her life, and he didn't seem to understand how these little details could cause her world to implode. Tally understood that he was trying to stand beside her, but what she really needed was for him to calm down.

"I'll lose my job," she begged, pained that he didn't understand how vital this family was to her existence.

None of his determination ebbed. "Sorry, baby, I don't give a fuck," he said. "I'll stay as long as it doesn't affect us. You don't want me to touch you out here, fine." He held up his hands and backed off a step. "But you call me sir one more time and I'm taking both of us out of here... I don't give a fuck if it pisses you off, we'll start again from my place. Dirt poor is better than hearing that word come from your lips."

The most terrifying part of his vehemence was that he meant every word. His resolve was absolute. "Don't talk like that," she whispered. "Max, I have to leave, and you have to go back in there."

But he didn't seem ready to accept the way it was. "Why?" he asked. "Why do I have to go back in there?"

"Because I've screwed up enough," she said and pressed the back of her hand to her forehead. "What was I thinking of drinking tequila? How could I have—"

"You were safe," he said, misinterpreting her dismay. "I was around. Doesn't matter how drunk you get, I'll always look after you."

He tried to take her hand, but she moved toward the stairs. "No, that's not it. I broke the rules, I deserve to be benched."

"One drink doesn't break any rules," he said. "It's insane. And using my name? What the fuck is the sister all about? She's a fucking bitch trying to drop you in it."

Tally stepped down one stair. "She's your sister. Your family. And you have to connect with them. I have to go before I do any more damage."

He was calming enough to start thinking. "Okay," he said, moving forward to put his hand over hers on the banister. "If we can't talk here, meet me at Fitzpatrick's."

Having expected to go home alone, she didn't know what to do with that invite. "What?" she asked. "I can't."

"The guys will look after you," he said and must have seen her reluctance because he ducked. "Baby, you go to Fitzpatrick's or I'm gonna kiss you right here, right now. I'll pick you up, put you against that wall and what we are won't be a secret anymore."

And the sinister glint in his eye betrayed his veracity. That wasn't an idle threat, he meant it. "Okay, I'll meet you. But you have to go in there and be charming for another half hour. Don't say anything in defense of me. Don't even bring it up, and if anyone else brings it up, you say nothing, understand?" He growled, showing her his clenched teeth. His need to protect her made her smile. "I know you'll want to. But it will only make things worse…" Lowering her voice to a whisper, she straightened his tie. "Teddy wants to talk to you about moving into the mansion. You have to do it. You have to say yes. You know you have to."

Swagger flavored his smile. "You asking me to move in with you?"

Exhaling a laugh of sorrow and appreciation, she smiled at him. Just looking into his eyes, some of her troubles drained. "God, I love you," she whispered, without really thinking to make the admission aloud.

"Good answer," he said and picked up her hand to tuck it into his elbow.

"What are you doing?" she asked when he began to lead her down the stairs.

"Putting you in a cab, I'm not sending you out there alone. I'll get you a ride, then go back inside and make nice. I'll meet you at Fitzpatrick's in an hour."

The valet was waiting outside and hailed a cab for them. Max put her inside and spoke to the driver, giving him money and the address before patting the roof and watching her go.

Tally closed her eyes and rested her head back to watch the city drift by. This night had been full of downs and shocks, but she'd been impressed by how well Max adjusted to minding his manners. He didn't like spending time with Teddy, but she'd noticed him being polite to others who spoke to him and he was honest in answering questions without being crass.

She hadn't expected to be dismissed tonight because of her actions, but she was proud of Max for making it through.

Going to Fitzpatrick's dressed like this would be a nightmare, white would get dirty in a hurry and she didn't feel like customizing another of her dresses. So Tally slid to the front of the seat and redirected the driver to Stretton Estate. If she was quick, she could change and still make it back to Fitzpatrick's before Max got there.

THIRTEEN

OKAY, SO SHE'D BEEN WRONG.

Tally paid the cab driver and dashed into Fitzpatrick's to see Max there already at the bar, leaning over to talk to Trey as the other guys jeered him for his apparel. But when someone noticed her, they all called out and Max spun around to pin her under his disapproval.

She went to him, pouting her apology. The guys parted to let her move up close to him.

"Thought you stood me up," Max said when she pulled the strap of her hobo bag over her head to dump it on the bar behind him.

"I went home to change," she said, holding her hands out to present her ruched-bodice, strapless black dress with its micro-mini layered skirt.

"I like it," he said.

Before he could touch her, Tally reached up to loosen his tie. He watched her with keen eyes as she opened the top few buttons of his shirt. "How's that?"

He rubbed his throat like it had been constricted for days. "I can breathe again."

Pushing his jacket from his shoulders, she laid it on

the bar and whipped his tie from his collar to tie it around her bare neck as a choker. Just then Trey held up a drink.

Tally nodded and smiled. "Thanks, honey," she called out.

Instead of reaching for the drink Trey had put on the bar, she took out Max's cufflinks and shoved them into her bag before opening his shirt in one confident tug.

Everyone whooped and cheered, while Max grinned down at her. "What's this?" he asked but let her take his shirt off to toss it over the bar.

She drew a fingernail down the center of his chest to his navel, but when he bowed to kiss her, she leaned away and grappled for her bag.

"You don't fit in around here, honey," she said, running her hands into his hair to mess it up again. "Let me give you a few tips."

"Oh!"

Everyone else jeered, but they didn't get the joke like Max did. The corner of his lips curled and the light in his eyes glowed brighter.

Yanking the plastic wrapped tee-shirt from her bag, she ripped the packaging open with her teeth and spat the wrapper away to pull the brand-new tee-shirt over his head.

"I grabbed it from the stock in the gym," she said, feeding his arms through the sleeves and pulling it down over his torso. "I figured you'd be more comfortable with this."

"And you would," he said, wrapping her in his arms now that he looked more like her Max than he had all night.

"There you are," she whispered, and he squeezed her ass in both hands. "There's my man. Where you been, handsome?"

"Hey, baby, miss me?"

The guys crowded in behind them and Robbie came close enough to speak in her ear. "Come play pool, MG," he said.

The others pulled at her. She smiled at Max and shrugged as she retreated from him. Tally had told him they couldn't be together, so they shouldn't be canoodling anyway. This was a good distraction, one they needed.

A flare of hope made her wonder if maybe she could keep this even after they were no longer sleeping together. She'd come to enjoy Fitzpatrick's and the guys in Max's life. Beyond the Strettons, where even the staff was all dedicated to the family and their rules, she had no life. This felt like freedom, it was fun, and she didn't want to give it up.

One of the guys brought her drink over. She finished it and got another while the current game of pool was going on. "You've never played before?" Andy asked.

The guys were all mulling around the table watching the game. Tally was in the corner where the waist-high tables, that were fixed to the wall, met. Andy was at her side, propped against them too.

"Nope," she said, sipping her drink.

"Don't worry," he said, leaning in to whisper in her ear. "We'll go easy on you. Doug sucks anyway."

It felt weird when she realized his arm was behind her. While he wasn't holding her, his limb was stretched across her back, his hand spread flat on the table top. Shrugging off her weird feeling, Tally kept watching the game. It was a good minute later that she felt his fingers brushing up and down her opposite arm. Yeah, his arm was around her now.

Luckily, she didn't have to ask him what he was doing, because Robbie grabbed a cue off the guy who'd just lost and thrust it at her. "You're up, MG," he said and grabbed another cue. So her first opponent was a friend? That was good. "You want to break?"

One of the other guys was setting up the balls, and she shrugged. "Sure."

"Just whack it hard," Robbie said.

Everyone cheered her on. Their encouragement was inspiring, so she bent over the table and tried to figure out how to rest the cue on her fingers. Mark came over and helped her out, earning her a few jeers. Tally rolled her eyes in good humor and pulled back the cue, then… missed.

Everyone laughed. She stood up feeling like an idiot, but curtseyed, appreciating that everyone was having a good time, even if it was clear that this wasn't going to be her game.

"Go again, MG. You're doing good," Mark said, and

everyone cheered to encourage her.

"I'll help you," Andy said, coming up behind her. Tally felt uneasy about him standing so close but figured this was all in good fun. They were all friends and she wasn't going to make a scene. Andy put a hand on her waist and another on her shoulder. "Bend over, darlin'."

Okay, that weirded her out enough that she shuddered, but no one else seemed to be bothered by him helping her. Tally bent over, and he bent with her. She hated this; she felt pinned down, restricted, violated. He took a long time to show her how to line it up and then used his own hand at the back of the cue to follow through hard. When the shot was done, his other fingertips brushed the back of her thigh.

No, she couldn't do this.

While everyone else was cheering the break, she stood up and went to her drink, noticing how close Andy stayed to her side. While still grinning, she leaned in to Ryan who was watching Robbie take his shot. No one seemed to notice that she'd gained a shadow who was currently trying to take her hand.

Finding Ryan's ear, she whispered, "Get Max." Ryan glanced at her, his smile faltering for half a beat when he read how serious she was and then he glanced past her to Andy who was smiling at the table, she leaned up to whisper again. "Discreetly."

Ryan didn't hesitate to put his drink down and disappear into the crowd. She didn't want a confrontation, didn't want to start a fight. Everyone was in a good mood and Tally wanted it to stay that way. Andy had just drunk too much and forgotten for a second that he was moseying into another guy's territory. He wasn't making a serious play or trying to be an asshole, he was just tipsy and caught up in the atmosphere.

Too soon it was time for her next shot. Everyone spouted their suggestions about which ball she should try to hit, but she was too aware of Andy who was staying glued to her to listen or make sense of them.

"That one," Andy said and put a hand on her hip to line her up. He pushed her toward the table. "Bend over, darlin'."

And then like the proverbial knight in shining armor, a second hand touched her hip and she looked over her shoulder to see Max edging Andy aside. "I've been in training for this position, buddy," Max said, making everyone laugh.

She appreciated that he'd chosen to make a joke rather than to punch Andy in the face.

Yanking her hips, Max lined her ass up with his pelvis and gave her a reassuring squeeze. Tally rocked into him, pushing back and squirming against his groin in appreciation for him coming to her call. Already she felt better, more relaxed, and could focus on the cue ball.

They bowed over the table and his breath warmed her cheek. "How am I doing?" she asked, turning her face toward his.

"You're looking the wrong way," he said and though the music probably hid their words, everyone was laughing at the couple's exchange.

"Oopsy."

Opening her mouth, Tally dragged her teeth over his cheekbone and he turned his face to kiss her ear. He ran his tongue around the shell, making her shiver. "Can I knock him out?" Max murmured.

Maybe he wasn't as relaxed as she thought, but she arched her back, forcing her ass deeper against the prominent ridge nestled against it.

"Oh, man, now they're on the foreplay," Robbie called out.

"This is gonna be a long game," Mark said.

Max whispered a couple of tips into her ear, but she was too aware of him to really listen. He stayed wrapped around her to take the shot for her and sank three balls in a row this same way. They were both holding the cue when they stood up straight.

Tally kept herself against him, not only to conceal his boner, but because she didn't want any other guy to have an excuse to sneak into his place.

They backed away until Max was seated on a stool by the waist-high table with her between his legs. She twisted to look at him over her shoulder while Robbie considered his shot.

"I'm messing with your head," she said, roiling in guilt. "I'm sending out mixed signals, telling you we can't be together then asking you to rescue me."

But he just blinked cool amusement at her and looked back at the pool table. "Obviously you didn't hear what I said when we were dancing at that shindig," he said. "I'll do whatever it takes to make you happy and you'll always be my girl."

"What happened after I left?" she asked. "Was there a fight?"

"No, I didn't say much."

And he still wasn't saying much. "Did Teddy ask you to move to the house?" she asked. He didn't respond, he just rubbed his hands up and down her belly then up over her breasts. But Tally needed an answer. Curling her hand around his face, she drew it around to make him look at her. "Max, what did you say?"

"You told me to, didn't you?"

When his eyes fell she felt his sorrow like he really didn't want to be giving up his independence and she understood his grief. Leaving his old life behind would be difficult, and it would be hard for him to see the positives until he took the leap.

Turning in his arms, she coiled hers around his neck and pulled herself as close as she could, holding him to reassure him that he would be okay, that he'd done the right thing, that she appreciated him. He squeezed her so tight that her heart broke. He was using her for comfort, as an anchor, and she wished she could take his anxiety away.

His head moved down to urge hers aside until he could look her in the eye. "Give me this weekend," he said, begging her with his intense gaze. "No talk of whether we'll make it or not. I told him I'd move on Monday. So give me this weekend, baby… please."

He'd be her Max all weekend, and it would be his last weekend in the life he knew; the only life he'd always known.

Nodding once, Tally was honored to be a part of his farewell.

His lips curled before he leaned forward to take her mouth. It had been a week since they'd kissed like this, more than a week, and she'd missed it so much. As she coiled her tongue around his and felt his hands drift down her back, she wondered how she'd go the whole rest of her life without feeling this.

After this weekend, he'd belong to Teddy Stretton and she'd be consigned to memory. Truth was, Tally needed this farewell as much as Max did.

FOURTEEN

TALLY WAS ON MAX'S COUCH, wearing his tee-shirt, when the guys showed up at the door the next day. Since her lover had left to get breakfast quite a while ago, she'd thought it was possible that he was carrying so many things that he didn't have a free hand to open the door, hence the knock.

But it wasn't her lover, it was his friends.

The guys wasted no time making themselves at home, taking over the TV, and raiding the kitchen. She was just grateful that they didn't evict her from the couch. Robbie sat at the end of the couch beyond her feet. Mark and Ryan were in the armchairs, while Tomas and Bobby sat at the bistro table behind.

She was in the middle of a satisfying stretch when the front door opened. Max came in carrying two coffees in a cardboard tray and a brown paper bag. But he stopped short when he saw his apartment was full of people.

"Look, honey, we have guests," she said and then yawned.

"That's like the tenth time she's yawned like that," Ryan said, pointing at her. "Did you let her get any sleep?"

"Not much," Max said, dropping his weight against

the door to close it. "What are you bastards doing here?"

"You told us to drop by," Mark said.

"Yeah, I meant whenever, not first thing," Max said.

The guys laughed. "It's like three in the afternoon."

She and Max had discussed in great detail how he would have to tell the guys what lay ahead for him. It had been daylight by the time they got home from Fitzpatrick's and sex had been the only thing on either of their minds.

They'd done little else but nap and screw all day, but they had come to the conclusion that it was time for him to tell his friends the truth. Tally had only got out of bed after Max said he was going to get coffee. She'd have been happy to stay wrapped in his sheets all evening and all night.

Robbie patted her ankle. "Your lady has been looking after us," he said. Max zoned in on the sight of his friend's hand on her leg. Either Robbie didn't notice, or he wanted to rile his friend because he slid his palm up her shin. "She has really amazing legs, the guys and I were talking about them before you got back."

She raised her head slightly to look at Robbie's hand on her leg. "Max came there this morning... and I haven't showered."

Robbie lifted his hand straight up, his face contorting in disgust as the guys laughed. Max smiled at her and winked.

"Bit far south of the mark, man," Ryan said.

"He came there too," she said and let her smile turn saucy. "And a few other places."

"Okay, I feel like I should move now," Robbie said, pulling himself onto the arm of the couch.

Max came to the back of the couch and bent to kiss her then pulled a coffee from the tray. "Skinny mocha triple shot," he said, ensuring she had proper hold of it before letting it go.

She breathed in the intoxicating scent of coffee and sighed. "Oh, I love you."

"Is she talking to the coffee or the guy?" Ryan asked.

Max bowed to kiss her again. "I bought bagels—"

She pushed up higher, hope increasing her heart rate. "Did you get the—"

"Cinnamon raisin," he said. "Yes, I only had to go to three different stores."

"Aww," she said. Putting her coffee on the end table, she climbed to her knees and leaned on the back of the couch to grab his jacket to pull him down for a long, tongue kiss. "Thank you, baby."

"You feel like we came at the wrong time?" one of the guys muttered as she nuzzled her mouth on Max's and hummed out her adoration for this man who went above and beyond for her.

"I don't think there's a right time to hang with this pair. They seem to be on all the time," Mark said.

Max put his coffee and the bagels by hers, then shed his jacket and leaped over the back of the couch to take her previous place, managing to scoop her into his lap at the same time. Keeping his lower legs hanging off the edge of the couch, he bent a knee to give her a kind of nest to settle in. Then he returned her coffee to her and handed over the bagels.

"Can you turn off the TV, please, Ryan?" she asked, opening the bag of bagels as Max took a drink from his own coffee.

He drew it down from his lips and squinted at her. "You want to do it now?" Max murmured. "Let them chill a while."

"Oh, I just thought... I figured it was best to get it out of the way," she said, the scent of the bagels drifting up to her. "We can wait."

But as they looked around, it was impossible to miss how intrigued the guys were. Ryan grabbed the remote and turned off the TV.

"Okay," Max sighed. "I guess now works... I have to tell you something."

"MG's pregnant," Robbie said.

All the guys straightened up.

"No!" Max said then looked at her. "Are you?"

She huffed and scowled at him. "You don't think I'd tell you that before I told him?" she asked, pointing at Robbie.

"I don't know," Max said, and his attention fell to her

stomach. "Maybe we should do a test, just in case."

Curious, she left the bagel bag on her lap to twist toward him. "What part of this situation makes you think a baby would be a good idea?" she asked. "I don't even know how we would make that work. I'd have to…" She thought about it a second and a strange parallel struck her. "Wow, that would be history repeating all over again."

"Okay, so she's not pregnant, what is it?" Ryan asked. "We hitting Vegas next weekend?"

"For a wedding?" Mark asked.

Tally was excited by how excited they seemed. "No, we're not getting married either," she said, not looking at Max or giving him a chance to get any other crazy ideas. "It's not us news, it's just Max news… Something amazing has happened and… it means him and me won't be seeing each other anymore."

"What?" The shocked horror brought them all to the fronts of their seats. Tomas and Bobby came around to stand in front of the TV and all eyes were on them.

"You're incredible together," Robbie said.

"Yeah, we're jealous as hell," Ryan said. "You seem into each other."

"Our buddy has never been happier," Mark said.

"It's okay," she said, smiling at them all to show she wasn't upset. "We're good until Monday morning."

The guys all looked at each other. "You put an expiration date on your relationship?" Robbie said like it was the weirdest thing ever because it *was* the weirdest thing ever.

She sagged back and looked at Max. "I'm not explaining this very well. Do you want to start at the beginning?"

He caught a length of her hair on his index finger and swept it back. "You're sexy as hell, you know that?"

Pulling his hand from her hair, she tore off a piece of bagel and stuffed it into his mouth. "No dirty talk," she said. "Tell the guys what's going on?"

"Okay," he said and exhaled. "Tal works for a guy."

"Theodore Stretton," she said, eating her bagel and drinking her coffee.

"Right, and it turns out…" He looked at her, he wasn't happy about admitting this, but eventually accepted that he had to. "He's my father."

"What the fuck?" Robbie said, which was similar to everyone else's shocked reaction.

"That's not the most surprising part," she said, slipping more of the bagel between Max's lips; he caught her hand to suck her fingers clean. "Tell them the most surprising part, baby."

"He's worth a shit ton of money," Max said, tilting his head to run his tongue down the length of her finger.

His mouth was mesmerizing. Each touch, each kiss and lick, sapped some of her energy and some of her sanity. The guys were talking, but all she could see was Max's mouth nibbling on her as his hooded eyes stayed trained on hers.

"You're rich?" Ryan asked. "How rich?"

"He has a company," Max said, sliding his fingers from her wrist to link them between hers. "It's worth a few billion."

The guys were out of their chairs, gasping and swearing, cheering and rejoicing over this news. Max got a few smacks on the shoulder and she tore her eyes from his to join in with the celebration. It was nice to feel vindicated, Tally had said that these guys would leap on the chance Max had been given and they were proving that she was right by their reaction; this was like winning the lottery.

Robbie bowed to hug her, and she got kisses and hugs from all the guys who were still babbling, exchanging ideas and praise. "This is fucking amazing," Ryan said. The men began to settle again. "Guess we won't be seeing you at the garage anymore."

All the guys were part owners of the garage, Max included. "Yeah, man, we'll do what we can to buy you out as soon as possible," Robbie said, glancing at her. "You still going to look at the books for us, MG? You remember promising us you would last night?"

She nodded. Accountancy had been her major, but she'd let that fall by the wayside when she picked up with the Strettons. When she'd talked to Robbie about how much she'd like to return to it, he offered her a position keeping their books as it was a messy job that none of them really understood.

"I remember, and I'd be honored. I can figure out what you can afford," she said. "Maybe come up with a payment plan."

"Naw, nah," Max said, waving a disapproving hand. He reached over his shoulder to discard his coffee on the end table, and hers too when she handed it to him. "I don't want money. I'm not giving up the apartment either. I told him I'd go stay in his stinking house and give this a shot. But I'm not gonna fuck up my life in case this doesn't work out."

The guys exchanged looks with each other. Tally wondered if their thoughts were anything like hers. "You have to, man," Robbie said. "If you don't throw yourself into this all the way, your old life will always hold you back."

"I'm guessing that's why you're ditching Tal," Ryan said and the next expression they all bestowed on her was pity. "You want to check out your options."

She widened her smile to convince them she wasn't going to fall apart. "Guys, don't look at me like that. Really, I'm fine."

"And I'm not ditching her, she's dumping me," Max said.

Okay, this was going a weird way. "You guys don't know what it's like," she said and sighed. "The temptation that's out there…"

"Temptation," Max said, and she was shifted a little when he rose from his slouch. "You think I'm gonna fuck around on you? You didn't say that before. Babe, you were sure I'd bang that Blair bitch and she did fuck all for me."

Tally exhaled. "I don't mean that. You just… you're going to have options, like Ryan said. There will be a lot of sexy, classy women throwing themselves at you and I guess… I want you to have the full experience."

"And you don't want to lose your job."

"Is that so awful?" she asked. "Right now, keeping this job is the only way I can still be involved in your life."

He got snarky. "Or you could keep fucking me, that's

pretty deep in my life."

There was so much about his new life that he didn't understand yet. "Being a Stretton mistress comes with all sorts of rules," she said. "I don't think it would work for either of us."

"A mistress," Mark scoffed. "Our buddy can have a fucking mistress."

"Yeah, we just call them fuck buddies," Ryan said, earning himself a laugh. "Guess when a guy has money, even his one-night stands get a title."

"But hey, MG," Robbie said, leaning over to poke her shoulder. "You'll still come by Fitzpatrick's, right? You're part of the gang there now."

He was sweet, they all were, and she hoped that he meant that and wasn't just being polite. "You have my number," she said. "And someone mentioned a party tonight, am I invited to that?"

"Sure thing," Robbie said. "We can grab food first if you want."

"Definitely," she said. "I brought a change of clothes last night, so I'll have an actual planned outfit to wear." For maybe the first time.

Max drove his fingers into her hair, turning her toward him. "You knew you were coming home with me before you came to the bar last night?"

Busted. She hadn't known for sure, but given how things usually went between them, she didn't think it hurt to prepare with some extra panties, being that he did like to steal or rip them from her.

"Maybe," she said. "We know what happens when you get me drunk in that bar. I thought it was best to be prepared."

"Yeah, and I guess we're all going to be on Tally duty from here on out," Ryan said. "When Max is out of the picture, you'll be fair game, girl. The guys are going to be lining up."

"Out of the picture?" Max asked, offended and confused. "I'll still be at the bar."

That earned the biggest laugh of the day so far. Tally

patted Max's chest as Mark spoke. "Yeah, buddy, I doubt that. You'll be off in your fucking mansion, drinking champagne, lining up sluts to fuck—sorry, Tal—" She dipped her head in a nod of acceptance and smiled. "You're not coming back here."

"Now that he's rich, we should bet him on that. Squeeze out a few cents for the old neighborhood," Robbie said. "One billion or two?"

They laughed. Max looked pissed, but they were right and that was how sure they were that he wouldn't be coming back to this apartment or Fitzpatrick's. Max was going up in the world and the rest of them would be left behind. It was nice that his friends were embracing this and weren't expecting to be rewarded or being resentful.

"I'm not leaving the planet, just the neighborhood," Max said, his snit getting hotter.

"Yeah, for a goddamn mansion," Ryan said.

"Tal lives there now," Max said.

She laughed and pulled another lump of bagel from the bag on her lap. "Yeah, in staff quarters," she said. "It's not quite the same thing."

Robbie held up a hand. "Oh hey, if Max is keeping this place, we'll have a permanent crash pad for you, Tally. You've got a key, right? One of us has a spare somewhere, we'll get you it."

How would she feel about sleeping in Max's apartment without any prospect of sharing it with him? "Need to make sure Andy and his crew don't know she's up here alone though," Ryan said. "He was muscling in last night. He'll be the first to make a play."

"But she'll be single," Robbie said. "She can fuck who she wants."

Though that was true, she still had her tastes. "Not Andy," she said, screwing up her face. "It felt really weird having him on top of me last night."

" 'Cause you're not used to it," Ryan said. "Rob's right. We'll get used to seeing you with whoever… We'll come up with a signal for if you need help."

"Trey's cute," she said.

"And a business owner," Robbie said, nodding like he approved.

"And a felon," Ryan said.

"Ha, what the liquor board don't know…"

"He hasn't been in prison for years," Mark said. "Yeah, he's a good guy, and if they hook up, we might see Tally working the bar."

"Ha, turnover would explode, Fitzpatrick's would be standing room only."

Glancing around as they laughed, she fixed on Max who was scowling at her. Tossing the bagel bag to the table, she turned to press her chest to his torso and touched her mouth to his.

"Our time isn't done yet," she whispered on his lips.

Max tipped his head back. "Okay, guys," he called out. "We'll see you at the bar later. Me and my girl need some alone time."

"You can't kick them out," she said and sat up straight.

But the friends were already shaking hands and bumping fists with Max, each man kissed her cheek and then a minute later, she and Max were alone.

"I don't want you sleeping with anyone else," he said as soon as the door was closed.

Tally should've known the eviction of his friends was about more than them being alone. "Max," she whined and pushed off him to get to her feet.

"I know, it's hypocritical, you're telling me to screw my way through all the daughters and nieces of society's elite and I'm telling you to stay faithful, but—"

"It's okay," she said, crouching beside him. "It's weird now, but believe me, once you get into the swing of the parties and get to know the women, it won't be a big deal. You'll forget about me, and the guys, and Fitzpatrick's."

Shaking his head, he shifted to open his thighs around her crouched form and doubled to cup her face. "I won't forget. I don't want to forget."

"You heard how happy they were for you," she said. "I told you they would be, didn't I? That's what I was talking about in the bedroom that time you accused me of using guilt as a motivator. I wasn't. I just knew that your friends would want this for you. Just like you'd want it for them if it arrived on their doorstep."

He exhaled, and she could feel his frustration. "I feel like... there's this choice, either I go and work hard to really make this work for every person like me, the guys who have worked their whole lives and just never got a break. Or I stay..."

"And?"

"Marry the woman I love."

Her heart slowed but only because it was overwhelmed. She didn't know what to say. The man she loved was offering to fulfil her dream. A selfish part of her wanted to leap into his arms and say yes. But the practical part, the part she'd always been taught to embrace, took a deep breath.

Shifting onto her knees, Tally pushed her hands to his thighs to rise and kiss him. Stroking his face, she tried desperately to keep her tears at bay. "I'm not enough, Max," she whispered. "If you give this up for me now, you'll resent me in the long run. We'll be fine and in love for a few months, maybe a few years, then we'll start to struggle financially, and we'll argue. We'll forget about how we used to play in Fitzpatrick's, or it won't be as important anymore, and we'll grow to hate the sight of each other."

"Because if I give up this opportunity, you have to quit your job to be with me?"

"Blair already asked me if I thought you trusted me. I don't want to be used against you. I don't want us to be played off each other. If I'm still there and you're not... they'll blame me, and my life would be hell."

"And you don't trust me to look after you?"

"I don't want you putting that pressure on yourself," she said. "You go out to work all day and I'm left home alone and bored."

"You can work, you'll find another job."

"Without a reference? If I don't declare my history with Teddy, I'll have to explain a huge career break. It will make employers suspicious," she said. "I can't even say I was raising kids."

"Then we'll have a kid," he said, skimming his hands up and down her arms. "Anything you want, baby."

She couldn't believe they were really talking about this. It made no sense to give up all relationships with his family and all chances of inheriting a fortune just because they were infatuated with each other.

"You're scared. That's all this is. You said your mom wanted you to take him for everything you could. You're doing this for her and for the guys."

"So why can't I get you out of my mind?" he asked. "If this is such a great idea, why am I so focused on losing you? I don't even think about the money, babe. I know, it's weird, but I... you're what I think about."

But it made sense to her. "It's abstract, that's why," she said. "Once you get there and see what this money does for you, then you'll begin to understand and everything else will fade away. Put it this way, you'll never know unless you try, right? What's the worst that can happen? You have your apartment to come back to, and the guys will give you a job."

"But you," he said. "How long will you wait? How long before some other guy steals you from me?"

Going by her track record, she only had a boyfriend once or twice a decade, so the odds were good that she wouldn't be hooking up for a while, not for a long while. Certainly, Max would be rolling in the hay with other women before she even looked at another guy.

Smiling, she kissed him again. "Didn't we say we weren't going to talk about this? This is our time to enjoy each other."

Leaning forward, he hooked her thighs and stood up, wrapping her legs around him. "You're right, Boss, sorry," he said and carried her to the bedroom to fall on the bed, cradling her beneath him. "I'm taking advantage of you as often as I can... while I still can."

And that was what she needed him to do because there were no promises to be made. Neither of them could predict what would come next for them. This was their time.

The last time they had left.

THE ALARM BEGAN TO BUZZ on Monday morning and then it stopped. When Tally blinked open her eyes, she saw Max's face on the pillow beside hers, just an inch away.

"You didn't hear that," he whispered, picking hair from her cheek to tuck it away with her other locks. "It's just a dream, go back to sleep, baby."

Her voice was weak from sleep. "It's Monday."

"Shh," he said, stroking his fingertip on her cheek. "No, just close your eyes."

But they were already watering. "I'll never wake up with you again."

"Shh, baby."

When he pulled her close into his body, she sobbed and breathed him in. They had to do this. They knew it would be impossible to be together when they were employer and employee, and she wouldn't fit in as an equal of the Strettons; she didn't want to.

But as she closed her eyes again and let her tears flow free, Tally promised herself that she would never settle for a love less than this one.

Max had given her so much, more than she could express to him, and the least she could do was bow out of his life quietly.

FIFTEEN

BLAIR HAD BEEN A PILLAR for Max. In addition to Teddy's only female confidante, Max was dating two other women. Tally made a real effort not to keep tabs on his love life. Being without him was hard enough without having to listen to every salacious rumor whispered around the Estate about him. But it was difficult to be ignorant when everyone was fascinated by this new, secret Stretton family member.

It had been six weeks since he'd moved into the mansion and other than a few minor hiccups, she heard through the grapevine that he was doing well fitting in. Max had his own assistant, Mandy, who hated her, and he was driven to the office every day. There was always someone with him to guide him… and keep tabs on him.

The fact that the Stretton social calendar was full made it impossible for them to have any contact, which was probably for the best. Teddy wanted to show off his new heir. Keeping busy distracted the Stretton's from dealing with actual issues like their familial relationship or Teddy and Kimmy's grief.

Tonight, there was a function at the Stretton Estate. Kimmy had planned two for the month ahead. This one was a memorial for her mother; the family had started another charity in Laura's name. Tally didn't need to be at the party itself but was on the side-lines just in case someone needed something, so she had to make herself presentable.

In a black square-neck dress, she had a loose chain belt around her waist and her cell phone in her hand. Given that she was on call, she remained in the hallway at the top of the stairs, watching the rich and beautiful arriving at the house. Standing just at the edge of the upstairs banister was her favorite spot. Hidden by the hallway wall, she could peek around and watch Max greet guests.

He, Teddy, and Kimmy stood with their backs to the stairs, shaking hands and speaking to guests as they arrived. Their dates stood with them. Max was with a blonde tonight, Anika. He seemed to have developed a thing for blondes in the last six weeks.

This woman was the daughter of a Stretton family friend. The couple had been out a few times; it was a good match. Tally said that in her head to remind herself this was what she'd expected to happen, but it still made her sick to think about his hands on Anika in the way they'd once been on her.

People always lingered with Max, he was the draw of society at the moment. Some judged this illegitimate child and his elevated position in the family. Some even spoke about him being favored over Kimmy and Heath, who was not enjoying the competition at all.

Her cell vibrated in her hand. Confused, she glanced down at the device. Given that she was on call for Teddy, and she was looking at him, it was impossible for him to be the one on the other end of the line, though he could have instructed someone else to call her.

"Hello?" she asked, answering the number that didn't come attached to a name. The line was open, but no one said anything. "Hello? Who is this?"

"I know this is probably a bad time, but I need a favor."

Surprise struck her. "Robbie?" she asked.

Tally had seen the guys, but Max hadn't. He called a

few times in the first week, but his calendar filled so fast that he'd had no time to breathe. His friends were disappointed, but not surprised, and she talked him up every chance she got. The last thing she wanted was him losing friends.

"Yes, I… Tally, I need your help."

Okay, so she had a new priority for the night. Whatever Robbie needed, she was going to make sure he got. "Tell me what you need."

Another pause. "We need something from Max."

Her mouth opened as she whipped around to look at Max, who was still at the bottom of the stairs with his back to her. "He's with… people," she whispered.

"Yeah, I figured. Look, it's not him we need. It's something he has… something he had. I don't know if he's still got it. But if he doesn't, Bobby's fucked."

"Okay, slow down, what's going on?" she asked, wondering how she'd pull Max away discreetly while he was the center of attention. "Where are you? I can tell Max—"

"No, he can't know. This is… it's not his concern anymore, you know? If he finds out about this, he'll go postal. We don't want to fuck up this good thing he's got going, you know?"

Narrowing her eyes, she stepped back into the shadow. "What kind of trouble are we talking, Robbie? Are you in danger? Where are you?"

"We're here, at the place, this fancy fucking house," he said, and her mouth dropped open. They were on Estate grounds! "By the fountain thing with the weird wing thing on it."

That was in the courtyard and far from where the guests would be arriving. "How the hell did you—"

"We were going to break-in. We called Cindy, she gave us directions, but… fuck, there's this party and there's fucking security everywhere."

Tally knew little about Cindy's affair with Teddy, but it stood to reason if it was more than a one-night stand, Cindy had been here and might remember her way around the place.

But that wasn't what was sending Tally into a daze. "You were going to break in?" she hissed. "Are you nuts? If

Teddy found you, he'd have called the cops. Hell, you could've been shot! Why didn't you call me?"

"Because it's not your fucking mess either, Tal," he snapped. "If Max knew I was involving you in this shit, he'd—"

"What is it you need?" she asked, thinking there would be time for explanations later.

"Max has something. It's probably in his room. I don't think he'll carry it on him… I tried his apartment, it's not there, so he must have brought it to this fancy fucking castle."

Max had brought most of his things with him, not because he wanted to erase his connection to his old place, but because the crime rate in his old neighborhood was high. "Okay, what is it?"

"A key, he used to keep it in his wallet," he said. "Do you think you can get it for us?"

His wallet, oh yeah, no problem. Damnit. Tally covered her eyes. "I can try, what's it for?" Robbie didn't answer. "I'm not prying, I just… I have to know that whatever it's for… that it won't hurt him." More silence. "Shit, Rob, you're asking me to steal from him."

There was a long, lingering pause that didn't fill her with confidence. "Max knew you were going to rock his world even before your first kiss in Fitzpatrick's," Robbie said. "He told me after, just touching you was like a sucker punch to the gut."

Maybe she'd asked for it. Robbie was trying to put her at ease and to let her know that Max probably wouldn't consider it stealing because he trusted her. They'd once been so close that he'd have let her have anything of his without question.

She didn't know how far they'd come from there, but Robbie was trying to remind her that the secret of her relationship with Max brought them all closer and reinforced their trust. But his words had a secondary effect he probably didn't expect… They gave her a flash of that first night… her first date with Max.

Stepping into the hallway light, Tally looked down at

the man greeting the glitterati in the gleaming foyer of this sumptuous home that he'd one day inherit. She couldn't connect the man at the bottom of those stairs with the one who'd pulled her dress down and told her she needed to kiss him to fit in.

The memory made her ache. "I don't want to think about that night," she murmured, wishing for the numbness that had gotten her through her heartbreak.

But he didn't listen. "You didn't kiss him back," Robbie said. "He said the look of shock on your face grabbed him by the balls and he knew he had to have you… don't think he expected it to happen that night in the alley—"

"Okay, I get it," she said, understanding that his friends would never ask her to hurt him and they'd certainly never con her into it. "Go toward the north courtyard entrance and follow the path behind the rose bushes, there's a basement entrance hidden behind a big stone pillar with a thing that looks like a frog carved into it."

"Okay."

She glanced back at the guests and was happy to see a large group had just arrived. They'd give her cover to get away for a while. "Give me five minutes. Meet me there."

Concern came down the phone line. "You know if we're seen in that house we'll embarrass Max," Robbie said. "I don't want a confrontation. Are we going to fuck this up for him?"

The Max she knew wouldn't be embarrassed by anyone he cared about. But it had been six weeks since they'd been intimate, she couldn't say how much his attitudes or opinions had changed in that time. Teddy's influence could be overpowering. Max might not realize just how big an impact his new role and position had had on his nature.

Once or twice she'd been called into a room where Max was present, but he never looked at her. The first few times, it hurt, but after that, she came to understand why he did it. She was the past he had to forget.

"No."

"Cindy said Stretton would put Max's rooms in the heart of the house, somewhere close to the action and I—"

"I'm not leaving you outside in the cold. I don't know how long it will take me to find it," Tally said. "You can wait in my room, no one ever goes in there."

She said nothing for a minute. There was sheer gratitude in Robbie's voice when he spoke again. "Thank you. You're an angel."

They hung up. She clutched her phone tight and ran along the hallway. She didn't need it to ring again, she needed a window of time to help the guys. Taking a detour by the frantic kitchen, she grabbed a plate of food and a bottle of champagne. Everyone was so busy trying to keep the wheels greased that they didn't pay any attention to her.

Hurrying along the basement corridor, Tally went up the three stairs to the sunken entrance and peeked out. Huddled at the top of the stairs were three figures and she gestured them down.

"Seriously?" she asked, recognizing Robbie, Ryan, and Bobby. "There are three of you?" Robbie opened his mouth to speak, but she held up a hand. "Just come this way, I'll yell at you later."

It was too dark to pick out their features, so she couldn't read all their moods. But there was no time for conversation. With the champagne under her arm, she took Robbie's hand and led him down. They continued along the basement corridor until she got to the stairs that led up to the drawing room level, and then she kept on going up until she got to her bedroom. When they were safe inside, she locked the door.

The men bundled forward, breathing into their hands and rubbing them together. "God, you look freezing," Tally said. "Sit."

Bobby sat in the wingback chair she had in the corner, Ryan on the bed, and Robbie on the ottoman. Tally left the food and champagne on the dresser and went to the heater in the corner to turn it on full. The guys weren't even wearing jackets, so she grabbed blankets from a drawer and tossed one to each of them.

"Is someone going to tell me what's going on?" she asked. The guys looked at each other. "Do you want my help or not?"

"We owe some guys some money, that's all," Ryan muttered.

"That's all?" she asked and shook her head. "How much money?" None of them spoke. "Guys, I can't believe you wouldn't trust me."

"We trust you," Robbie said, putting his blanket on the ottoman as he stood up. "We just don't want you mixed up in this. That's all."

But she knew there was more going on; Robbie tried his best to look innocent and Ryan stayed so still, he didn't even blink. Setting her sights on Bobby, she noted that he wouldn't look at her. Something drew her closer to him and that was when she noticed the bruising around his eye and the blood on his temple.

"Oh my God, what happened?" Tally asked and dashed into the bathroom to dampen a washcloth. "Hell, guys, please!"

She began to wipe the blood from Bobby's face and though he resisted, she crouched and pulled him to her.

"They caught up with me," Bobby said. "That's all."

"Why would you owe people money?" she asked. "The garage is doing okay. I—"

"We borrowed it a long time ago," Ryan said. "It's a long story. Are you going to help us or not?"

"With this key," she said, standing again and scrutinizing them all. Whatever was going on, it was no joke if people were getting hurt. "Okay, stay here, eat something and get some rest."

"Tal—"

"I'm not sending you back out there if there are people who want to hurt you," she said.

"You're not gonna tell Max, are you?" Ryan asked. "We talked about it and we don't want him to know about any of this shit."

"I won't—"

"You've got to promise us, Tally," Bobby said. "Please, you won't tell him. Promise."

"I promise," she said, nodding.

This was the strangest thing, but it was important to support these guys who were clearly in need. Maybe it was a pride thing; Max's life was going well and they didn't want to tell him that theirs weren't working out so well. But from the certainty radiating from these guys, she knew their desire to protect Max came from a place of love. He was doing great and they didn't want to cause him any trouble that might jeopardize what he had… Tally could identify with that feeling.

"We just need the key," Robbie said. "We have a safe, but we need all three keys… Max doesn't need what's in it now. Cindy made us promise we wouldn't take Stretton's money. We don't want it anyway, that's what Max is owed."

"Okay, I'll get it. Just stay here, eat, and then get some rest. I'll be as quick as I can."

Surging to her feet, she took her phone from her bra and left it on the dresser. What she was doing now was more against the rules than not answering her phone, but it was a risk worth taking.

SIXTEEN

TALLY LEFT THE RELIEVED MEN in her bedroom and ran to the household office to look for the spare key to Max's suite. Most doors in the house weren't locked, but Max would lock his, out of habit if nothing else. She'd never been in his suite before to know for sure, but his mentality couldn't have changed that much.

Running her hands over the various keys, she found his and snatched it from its hook. She covered her tracks by moving another key over and hoped that no one would notice his keys were missing. It didn't matter that she'd get them back as soon as she could or that no one should be in the office because the household staff was all hands-on deck for a party like this, she was still nervous.

Tally had never lived a life of crime and this experience was proving to her that she wasn't cut out for it.

She thanked her workout routine for keeping her going as she hurried the full length of the house again to run up another set of stairs from the first floor to the third. Usually, Tally avoided this part of the building. She never really had any reason to be here, so it wasn't hard to stay away.

But with her pumping heart and dry mouth, she slowed her pace and focused on his door. She'd always promised that she wouldn't come here, that she wouldn't enter his bedroom. But she didn't have a choice right now. When she got to it, she rested a hand and her forehead against the wood. This was it, the line she didn't want to cross.

Tally liked to picture him in his apartment, in Fitzpatrick's, in bed, she didn't want an image of where he lived now because it would be confirmation that their previous life had been erased. Sliding her hand down the door, she tried it and it wouldn't give. She smiled and put the key in the lock. At least one thing about him was the same.

Taking a deep breath, she knew she couldn't linger in the hallway because that would give someone a chance to see her. So she slipped inside and closed the door. Resting against it, she looked at the large square room with its central living area and wall-mounted TV above the fireplace, just like at his apartment. Except, in contrast, the furniture here was pristine and there wasn't a speck of dust in sight.

Knowing the layout from how other suites on the Estate were setup, Tally was aware of the position of each space. The office was on the left. The terrace was through the double-doors on the far wall and the bedroom was in the far right corner. She couldn't hang around, she needed to find his wallet. If the key wasn't in there, this could take quite some time; there were a lot of places to check.

Tiptoeing across the room, she didn't like feeling as if she was in enemy territory. She couldn't even turn on a light or someone outside might notice that his room was lit up while he was downstairs at the party.

Going inside the bedroom, Tally was all set to do her hunting and didn't expect to be hit by the scent of Max. Not just any Max, but her Max. Swinging around, she closed her eyes and pressed her face to the inside of the doorframe as the door clicked shut.

"Damnit," she whispered, hating the moisture that stung the corner of her eyes.

She could do this, she didn't have to look at the bed, didn't have to touch his sheets, or smell his clothes. Yet, after another half dozen breaths, she still couldn't open her eyes. She hadn't expected to freeze, and she couldn't stay here like this all night. What should she do?

Forcing her head to roll against the wood, Tally peeked through one eye at the four-poster bed minus its canopy in the middle of the wall. There were nightstands on both sides, and a door to his walk-in closet beyond. There was a family bathroom off the main living room. But if this was like the other suites there would be a shower room off the walk-in too.

That bed. It was huge. Magnificent. She got a flash of herself and Max in his sheets at his place. But it was superimposed here. She imagined standing by that foot-post and him coming up behind her, scooping her hair aside and kissing her neck.

Closing her eyes, Tally lost a breath. How could she still want him like this? He was her boss now, heir to the family fortune, businessman. But it wasn't the man at the foot of the stairs she saw in her fantasies. It was the man who'd sat at the bar in Fitzpatrick's with her. The man who'd laid her on his bed and told her to close her eyes. The man who'd told her Monday would never come as long as he held her in his arms.

"Stop it," she hissed at herself and pushed away from the door.

She was being an idiot. She was here for a reason. If she found the damn key, she could grab it and run, then she could erase this whole experience from her memory.

Pushing down her grief, Tally had a quick look in the nightstand drawers and found nothing. Next, she went into the walk-in. There was no window here, so she flicked on the recess lighting above the mirror and stopped for a minute to examine the rows of suits and shirts. Did he still own jeans? Did he ever wear them?

There were drawers in the furthest corner. She opened the top one to see cufflinks and heavy watches. Slamming it shut, she opened the second. It contained underwear at one-side and socks at the other. Right at the back were older socks. Fumbling around, Tally felt something square wrapped in wool.

Tugging it out, she found his old wallet hidden in a pair of socks. It didn't occur to her, but he probably had some fancy designer wallet now, or maybe he didn't need to carry one, maybe his name was enough to cover bills.

Opening it, she searched around inside and found a heavy silver key with a hexagonal top. Yes, that had to be it. She tucked it into her bra for safe keeping.

Closing up the wallet, she had to put it back as she found it and pray that Max didn't go looking for that key any time soon. She squashed the wallet into its previous place and was rearranging the older socks on top when she glanced up and saw something hanging in the very furthest corner of the closet, behind everything else.

Still holding a random pair of socks, Tally was drawn toward the corner of the closet. Touching the sleeve, she bit her lip. That was her Max's leather jacket. The one he'd been wearing the day they met and one he probably hadn't worn since the Monday he'd left his apartment.

"Lose something?"

Whipping around, Tally gasped at the sight of him in the doorway. He was still in the shadow of the dark bedroom, so she had no idea of his expression, but his tone wasn't impressed. "Uh…"

She hadn't even thought of what she'd say if she was caught here especially by Max himself.

"Your feet cold?"

"My?" she asked with confusion then remembered the socks, which she held up in triumph. "Yes." Tally tried a laugh and stepped forward. "Yes, that's it. Socks. I just needed socks. I put holes in Sean's and he gets upset with me."

"You sneak into my room a lot when I'm not here?"

"No!" Great, now he thought she was some weirdo stalker. "No, actually, this is the first time I've been into your suite. It's beautiful, I love what you've done with the place."

"I haven't done anything."

Really? She frowned. "There's a million five in decorating budget assigned for you," she said. "You didn't use it?"

"Nope."

"Oh well, uh… thanks," she said and held up the socks.

Walking forward, Tally wanted him to let her leave without having to say anything else. Instead, he stepped inside and closed the door behind himself. "Want to try again?"

Shit. No. She didn't want to try again. But her thoughts were harder to control when she saw his stubble was back. Yeah, his hair was still too neat for her liking, but with that scowl, he didn't look polished enough to put her off.

Stopping in the center of the room, Tally couldn't close her mouth, but couldn't think of anything to say either.

"Max!" a female voice called out from beyond the room—from the bedroom, to be exact.

Tally's eyes closed slowly. She whined. "Oh God." This was mortifying; her worst nightmare come true. "You brought Anika upstairs for sex."

And there was no other way out of this closet, so unless Max did her a favor and distracted Anika, she'd have to listen to them going at it. Tally should've known better, she'd been that woman, the one he couldn't keep his hands off. When Max wanted a woman, he did everything in his power to seduce her. Anika was sex on legs; he'd never be able to resist her.

"I came upstairs for a minute alone," he said. "She must have followed me."

A likely excuse, but one he shouldn't have to give because his sex life wasn't her business.

Turning her back to him, Tally faced the drawers. "Please tell me you have an iPod in here or something. Anything, so I don't have to listen to you with her."

"Shh," he said. Tally sealed her lips when she realized his voice was right behind her. Max was right behind her. Trying her best not to move a muscle, she was like a trapped animal when his face descended into her hair. He inhaled her. "Did you come here for me?"

Turning around, she gazed up at him and couldn't remember why she'd come. "Max," she whispered. He began to bend down, but she pressed a hand to his chest to stop him. "Anika is out there."

His jaw ticked. "Shit," he said and backed off. "Wait a minute."

Max strode out of the closet. Tally crept forward trying to hear what was being said.

"I can keep you company," Anika said.

Tally recognized the attempt at seduction in the blonde's sultry voice.

"I just need a few minutes," he replied. "Go back downstairs, I'll join you soon. Enjoy the champagne."

His room key was still in Tally's palm, but she tucked it into her bra with the other key as Max ushered Anika out of the bedroom. After she heard the bedroom door close, Tally shut the drawer she'd been rooting in, and turned off the closet lights before sneaking out.

She crossed the bedroom, ready to dart out as soon as she heard Max getting rid of Anika. If she caught a break, maybe Anika would convince him to go back down the stairs with her, giving Tally a clear route of escape.

Alas, she wasn't that lucky. She had just passed the bed when the bedroom door opened, and Max came striding in.

Keeping herself as loose as she could, Tally tried to sound casual. "I'll just leave you alone too," she said, using his excuse of wanting to be by himself.

Focusing on the door, Tally tried to walk on right past him, but he stepped in her way at the last second.

"Why did you come here, Tal?"

She couldn't answer that, and she didn't want to look at him, so she pointed past him. "Can we have this conversation out there?"

His head tilted. "Why?"

Much as she didn't want to admit it, she did, "I'm hyperaware that there's a huge bed behind me."

The corner of his mouth tilted. "So am I," he growled, and his hands slid onto her waist.

"No," she said, pushing his arms down. "I didn't come here for sex. We can't be doing that anymore."

He didn't let go of her waist, just squeezed and released over and over, his fingers stimulating her memory.

"Why not?"

"You're dating at least two women," she said. "You're on a date right now… Have you slept with Blair yet?" He stopped squeezing and frowned. "Never mind, not my business, excuse me."

That had been enough to cool his jets, so when she moved around him, he didn't try to stop her. He let her go and she could see freedom, she could smell it, she was only ten feet from the suite door when he called out.

"Have you slept with Trey yet?" he asked, and she stopped walking.

How did she answer that? Of course she hadn't, but was that the answer he wanted? Was this easier if he hated her? And she couldn't admit to how hung up she was on him, not when he was moving on. She didn't want him to feel guilty about any intimacies he'd shared with other women.

"That isn't your business either," she said and turned to look at him.

It didn't take him long to stalk toward her. "Like hell it isn't!"

"It's not," she said. "We agreed that we would have a clean break. It's why we agreed no calls, no contact."

He had a new cell number anyway. His friends hadn't even been given it. His mom probably didn't have it either. Tally didn't even have it and she was on the company network. His old number was disconnected. She'd seen him check his new phone when she'd watched him from a distance, that was the only reason she knew he had a new device.

"That was before…"

"Before what?" she asked and didn't like the look in his eye when he turned away. "No." Stepping forward, she grabbed his forearm. "Don't turn away from me. Look at me, Max. What were you going to say?"

Examining her face, he went from angry to longing to pain and back to frustration. "I'm dying, Boss."

"No," she said and widened her smile. "You're doing great. All the reports say you're being civilized and you're learning. You're doing so well. I'm so proud."

"You are?" he asked, probing her with his stare.

"You're proud of me?" She nodded. "And you're happy?"

Well, that was a different question. Her hand drifted from his arm as she reframed it. "I'm super happy with your progress. You did what you said you were going to do. You've thrown yourself into this all the way, no looking back."

When he didn't say anything else, she tightened her smile and began to turn. She could just walk out and she'd be saved from giving him any answers. Except he grabbed her to pull her back and in a swooping move, he scooped her up and rushed her against the wall.

His mouth stole hers before she could inhale. She whimpered in her struggle for breath. But God, he was amazing, and exactly what she needed. This was Max, her Max being powerful and dominant, and that was all she needed to bring back the memories in their vivid glory.

Closing her eyes, Tally opened her mouth and her body to this experience. He was hard against the softness of her center and the feel of him grinding himself against her made her push back.

And that mouth. Clasping his face in both hands, Tally scratched her fingernails through his stubble and a squeal of need accompanied her pulling at his tie to loosen it and rip open the top buttons of his shirt. Without permission, she pushed his head up with a sure hand and closed her mouth around the notch in his throat. Licking her way north, she dug her teeth into him, trying not to suck as hard as she wanted to because she couldn't leave a mark. Except that was all she wanted to do, to claim him, to beg him to be hers again.

Grabbing his hair, Tally pulled his vision into line with hers. "Why aren't you fucking me yet?" she panted.

He growled through grit teeth and pulled back enough to loosen his pants. In a slick move, he pulled the crotch of her panties out of the way and slammed into her. It had been six weeks since he'd been here, and the resistance made her blow out a breath of discomfort, but he pulled back and his next advance took him to the hilt.

He wasn't as coy about not leaving his mark on her, he sucked her neck beneath her ear as he slammed into her. She gasped at the union of pleasure in her pussy with the pain in her neck.

"I've missed you, baby," he said, capturing her mouth again.

She'd promised herself not to be intimate with him again. They were supposed to be apart. This was supposed to be a no-go. So why was her pelvis meeting his thrust for thrust? She didn't care, didn't care about anything except his thick cock fucking into her, sating her need.

Tossing her head back, she gritted her teeth and resisted the urge to scream when she came all over him. It only got harder on the next climax when he grabbed her hips and drove into her, filling her with his seed.

Hot, confused, and at peace for the first time in six weeks, Tally closed her eyes and her head bumped against the wall as they both tried to find their sanity again. He kissed her chin, her jaw, her neck, was he being reassuring or expecting round two?

Pushing his shoulders, she gave him the signal that she wanted her feet again and he complied but kept her hand and kissed her knuckles. Blinking at him, Tally recognized the light in his eyes. She saw the love and then she felt the sorrow.

She'd broken the rules. This was exactly why she'd avoided being alone with him because they just couldn't do this. They couldn't be in the same room without crossing the line.

Taking her hand back, Tally sidestepped, and his satisfaction became concern as she began to move faster toward the door. With an apology in her eyes, she turned and bolted.

SEVENTEEN

PERSUADING THE GUYS to stay until the party was over and everyone was in bed, wasn't that difficult. Tally gave them the key and after that, they seemed to relax, so much so that she had to keep reminding them to keep their volume down. They traded stories about Max and while she got sucked in and laughed along, she was repeatedly stung by memories of how she'd messed up.

To say she was melancholy was an understatement, but she did her best not to let the guys know. She snuck them out while it was still dark out and then went back to bed to grab a couple of hours sleep. Though that was near impossible when all she could think about was Max.

When she couldn't take it anymore, Tally got out of bed and went down to the pool. No one was ever down here at this time in the morning. It was as close as she could get to freedom; she had no place else to go.

Swimming a length and then another, she thought about her own future. Maybe it wasn't here with the Strettons. Since Max had come to join the family, she'd felt stifled. It wasn't his fault. It was just that being with him had made her see how many possibilities existed out there in the world.

She'd become so used to Teddy Stretton's rules that she didn't even stop to figure out if they made sense or were even rational.

At the shallow end, she stopped and stood, but gasped when she noticed a figure in shorts standing on the edge of the pool. "Jesus, Max," she exhaled. "You scared me."

He dropped to sit and dangled his feet into the water. "I've come down here a bunch of mornings hoping to see you."

"You really should get more sleep," she said because he shouldn't be up at this hour of the day while the rest of the house slept.

This was the time for the rich to get beautiful and dream big, maybe he hadn't gotten that memo yet.

The nature of the conversation changed when he braced on one arm and slid down into the water. "You dropped your socks."

So that was his excuse? He'd come down here to give her back the socks that she'd dropped at some point during their session in his suite.

Tally began to back away. "You could've just brought the socks, you didn't have to get in the water."

"To give you back the socks," he said, advancing on her. "No, I didn't." Lunging forward, he caught her arm and stopped her from going any deeper, the water was already over her breasts. When he strode forward, her legs lifted, and he grabbed them to wrap them around his hips. He was hard already and didn't hesitate to push her against the side wall of the pool. "I had to get into the water to do this."

"No," she said, putting her wet fingers to his lips when he moved in for a kiss. "Max, we screwed up. We can't do this here."

"In the pool?" he asked and nuzzled her neck. "I need you, Tal."

Max had always had a voracious sexual appetite, taking on two women wouldn't be beyond him. "Did you leave Anika sleeping upstairs?"

He kissed the corner of her mouth. "Baby, only you, remember? I haven't been with anyone else, I swear."

Okay, that surprised her, but after she got over that and her brows relaxed, she slid her hands up over his shoulders and into his hair. "You didn't sleep with Anika?" she asked. He shook his head. "Probably best, I mean, family politics and such. I'd only sleep with a woman like her if you plan to make a commitment… I can get you a casual girl, I mean, if you want me to send someone to your room I—" What nonsense was she babbling? Tally scowled at herself, was she offering to hire him a hooker? "I… forget I said that, that's just weird, right, I—"

"There's been no one but you, Boss."

"No one?"

"No one," he said.

This time, she let him kiss her. Her hips began to move; she smiled and whispered, "I've never done it in water."

His next smile told her that he knew he had her. He bumped his forehead on hers and brushed his lips over hers. "That's why I'm here, to fulfil your every fantasy."

And running her hands over his defined torso, she could tell he'd been working even harder at it. "You are my fantasy," she whispered and pulled his kiss to hers.

This time was slower, more like making love with the motion of the water enhancing her pleasure as it lapped her breasts and buoyed her body. He moved slowly. The slide of his dick inside her satisfied the desperate need she'd neglected for six weeks.

As soon as he was done, her legs loosened from his hips. Grateful to have the water holding her up, Tally had been left weak and couldn't think of maintaining her balance.

Sliding downward, she reached over her head to grab the pool edge, and she exhaled as her lips touched the surface of the water. "That was amazing."

He bent his knees and came in close to kiss her with their mouths half in the water, half out. "You're amazing."

Losing herself in the hypnosis of his kiss, she almost didn't see the overhead lights go on. But when their glare hit the water, Tally opened her eyes and Max backed off to look at the door. Spinning in the water, she peeked over the edge to see Teddy striding in wearing his satin pajamas.

Max's arm curled around her waist to pull her to him. "Oh no," she murmured.

Teddy's disapproval was written all over his face. "I can't blame you for not understanding how women manipulate rich men, son," Teddy said. "Miss Taylor, please explain yourself."

"I—"

"Hold up," Max said. Putting himself in front of her, he held her with an arm twisted around to her back, pressing her chest into his spine. "I came down here, I seduced her. If you want someone to blame? Point at me."

This was exactly what she didn't want. How could someone have known they were together in the pool? Max's new assistant hated her, Mandy had probably been told to keep an eye on her and report any suspicious behavior.

Tally had been asked more than once about her relationship with Max. People were curious after the stories of their behavior at the Walker Benefit got around.

It had been obvious that while she was avoiding Max, there were efforts to keep her away from him too. Teddy didn't want them to have a relationship and she was the one he was closest to, at least she had been when he got here.

Max's assistant, Mandy, had been given a bedroom on the same floor as her. The woman was never called at night; Tally wasn't sure if Max ever called her at all. That lack of trust, the lack of a connection, had upset Mandy, who wanted influence. At least, that's what Sean had told her. Mandy did her best not to talk to Tally at all.

"This is an important lesson for both of you," Teddy said. "Miss Taylor, you have until the end of the day to move your things out of the house."

She gasped and closed her mouth over the tattoo on the back of Max's shoulder to keep herself from sobbing. "No fucking way," Max said. "If she goes, I go."

Teddy's pitying humor only brought more shame. "I don't think so," Teddy said.

"Well, I fucking do," Max said.

Teddy took a breath and wore a haughty look that made her nervous. "I think you'll change your mind when you find out she spent last night with another man," he said. Tally couldn't have been more shocked. Max's silence was conspicuous. "That's right, I'm sure he's still in her bed. Voices were heard in her room through the night; sounds, you understand, grunts and moans. Go check for yourself. I'm sure he's still there, unless she snuck him out before coming here."

Max said nothing and Tally couldn't even argue. She had spent the night with a man, three of them actually. There had been talking, and the noises were probably the guys telling stories or roughhousing.

Even if she were to break her friends' confidence and her promise to them, it wouldn't matter, she'd broken the rules by having them here whether she had sex with them or not.

Mandy had to be the one who'd betrayed the visit. She was in a prime position to be listening through walls.

Teddy carried on, "We tried to check her room, but the spare key is missing. She is forbidden from bringing strangers to this house. Even if you defend her now, you can't defend that behavior," he said and tipped up his chin before turning away.

"It was me," Max said. Tally's arms sank in the water, though his arm remained behind her, keeping her close. "You can't fire her because she spent the night with me, in her room. I'm no stranger and she didn't sneak me in. It was me."

Teddy turned back, all stuttering shock. "You… you what?"

"Yeah, this wasn't an accident," Max said. She recognized that determination in his voice, he was daring the other man to contradict him. "You think this is the first time I've been intimate with Miss Taylor? I've been pursuing her. Get it? I'm the one chasing her fucking tail."

"You're… you've taken her as your mistress?"

She knew Max didn't know what that meant in this family. "That's right. That's what rich fucks do, right? They pick a girl and hound her until she gives it up. Just making you proud."

But Teddy didn't look proud, he looked confused and

angry. "Very well, I will see to it," he said and turned to storm out of the room.

She stood in the water behind Max, wondering what was in his mind. "Lover—"

"Whoever he is, get rid of him," Max said, his voice deeper and colder than she'd ever heard it. "Don't ever do that to me again."

His arm fell, and he strode away. Cutting through the water, he swam to the edge and lifted himself out. Marching out of the room without looking back, Max was beyond angry. Anger she would know how to deal with, but she'd hurt him; there was no way to fix that because she couldn't offer the truth.

Teddy fired her. Max saved her. But she couldn't slip back into her usual role, she had to go to her bedroom and pack it up. Then it would be a waiting game to see if she had somewhere to sleep tonight or not.

EIGHTEEN

SHE SAT WITH THE LAWYERS for over two hours.

Tally didn't have a lawyer of her own, but even if she had, it wouldn't have made any difference. The Stretton lawyers were thorough and their contracts airtight. Though she tried to argue a couple of points, nobody budged and nothing was changed for her.

Tally was told to spend the day packing her possessions and as much as she wanted to linger and put off the inevitable, she had an appointment that she was loathed to keep. Once her things were moved to Max's suite, she had to go back to SC and have a meeting with Teddy, which wasn't a fun experience.

Teddy had been ready to terminate her employment, but Tally had argued to keep her job. After some back and forth, Teddy had acquiesced, if she agreed to some additional guidelines. If those were not met, she would be terminated immediately and permanently. She had to agree.

Her fight was gone by the time she left his office; her body and mind were exhausted. Descending in the elevator, she got a call from Robbie.

"Rob," she said, having forgotten about her

commitment to the guys. "You needed me at the shop today. I'm sorry, I forgot. I can be there in fifteen minutes."

"No, that's cool," he said with an edge of worry in his voice. "It's actually... uh..."

Leaving the elevator, Tally crossed the SC lobby to head through the glass doors and out to the street. "What's wrong?"

"Max is at Fitzpatrick's," Robbie said. "He's drinking... a lot... and he seems really pissed. Did something happen?"

Something was an understatement. "I'll be there," she said, hailing a cab and jumping in to give the address. "Just try to distract him, keep him as sober as you can."

"Oh, kay, that won't be easy, man's on a mission."

Sighing, she was too tired to deal with this. "I know," she said. "I know, just... do your best."

She hung up and moved forward to ask the driver to speed up, but it still seemed to take forever for her to get there. She had the money ready to give the driver before they even stopped. Tossing it at him, she leaped out, and dashed into Fitzpatrick's.

It was only early evening, but there were a dozen or so folks dotted around. Trey was at the bar opposite a hunched Max who was flanked by Robbie and Ryan.

Tally went straight over to them. "Thanks, guys," she said. "Can you give us a minute?"

The friends backed off; their concern prevented them from spending any time greeting her. She picked up the lid of the tequila bottle and began to screw it on, but Max snatched it away before she secured it. His head was bowed, but he turned it slowly to glare up at her with cold, sinister eyes that verged on disgust.

"I fucking love you," he spat the words like they were foul.

"I know," she said and tried to reach for his hair, but he stood and swatted her arm away.

Lunging forward, he pinned her against the bar, his arms wide and straight on either side of her. "I still fucking love you. You treat me like a fucking asshole and I still fucking love you. What the fuck does that say about me?"

Lifting her cupped hands, she wanted to touch him, but didn't want to upset him, so she let them just hover. "Baby, I—"

"Don't fucking touch me," he snarled and pushed away from the bar to side-step and snatch up the tequila bottle again.

He pulled off the cap, swearing at it in the process as he tossed it away behind the bar. Tally had seen Max drink a lot, like a lot, a lot, and she had never once seen him drunk. He'd been wild, sure, happy, maybe even tipsy, but blind drunk? Never. She'd wondered once if he was immune to the effects of alcohol because it seemed like he could drink as much as he wanted and never lose control.

This moment was disproving that theory

Throwing the bottle back, he began to gulp from it. "Max," she said, touching his back.

Yanking the bottle from his mouth, he thrust it at her. "Drink."

"I don't want to drink," she said, hating herself for putting him through this pain.

He was so angry and so hurt. All he wanted to do was take the pain away, which was why he was drinking.

He pushed the bottle against her body. "Drink," he demanded, shoving it against her breast. When she didn't take it, he leaned down to growl in her ear. "I'm gonna get you good and wasted so I can take you out back and fuck you dirty, that's what you fucking want, isn't it? You want cock, all the fucking time."

Leaning back, tears streaked her face as she laid her hand on his. "Baby—"

"Stop it!" he shouted, shoving her hand away again. "I don't want your fucking sympathy; I want you fucking drunk."

She took the bottle, but put it on the bar without drinking. "No."

He grabbed her chin. "Two cocks in one night," he said, bowing down to get in her face. "That what you want, baby? How about two at the same time? That's even better, right?" He stepped back and opened his arms, raising his voice to the room. "Bet we'll get some takers in here. Any cocks around here for my girl to ride?"

Robbie and Ryan came back, worried about their friend. When they tried to push his arms down to calm him, he shrugged them off.

Max intensified his focus on her. "Why the fuck did you come to my room, huh? If you had one on the hook? Why the fuck did you sneak into my room to wait for me?"

"I told you I didn't come to your room for sex," she said, so full of her own sorrow that she couldn't stop her tears. "That just… it just happened."

"Yeah," he spat. "Always does with you. You play the fucking good girl so fucking well. You're a perfect little angel with a pussy so tight a guy would think you're untouched. You train that bitch to do that? Huh? Just to screw with us?"

"Max," she whispered her despair, now she was hurt, sorry, and embarrassed. "Please."

"Fuck you," he said and lunged past her to grab the bottle back.

As Max gulped down the liquor, Robbie and Ryan came closer to her. "You fucked around on him?" Ryan asked, wearing an expression like she'd cheated on him too.

"What happened?" Robbie asked.

Max dragged the bottle from his mouth. "I'll tell you what the fuck happened," Max said. "Bitch came to my room and got fucked good, right there against the goddamn wall. Then she snuck off to the cock she had locked in her room. Yeah, she had a fucking dude right there in her fucking room, in the fucking house I'll inherit."

"You had a guy in your room?" Ryan asked her; Tally didn't like his judgment. "But you had sex with Max?"

Opening her mouth, she inhaled and tried to think of how she could explain herself. "When was this?" Robbie asked.

"Last fucking night," Max said, slugging more liquor. "I was fucking her in the pool this morning when Stretton walks in and tells me she's been up all night at it with some bastard… Sean, right? It was fucking Sean, wasn't it?"

"What? No! No, I told you, Sean's my friend."

"Someone in your room?" Robbie asked, his eyes narrowing. "Wait a fucking minute! This is about last night? Are you shitting me?"

Leaping forward, Tally pressed her fingers to Robbie's lips. "Don't," she whispered. "Not while he's like this."

She almost didn't want to look at Max. Tally hoped he was too liquored up to be listening. But she wasn't that lucky. Turning her head to him, she saw only confusion on his face.

Robbie pulled her hand down. "Why didn't you tell us you had sex with him last night? You didn't even tell us you saw him."

"It wasn't important. I did what you needed to be done. The sex was... for me," Tally said, rubbing her shoulder. It had been a helluva long day. "I told you Max and I were through and we were, but... seeing him, it screwed with my head. I couldn't announce to the three of you that I slipped and fell onto Max's cock again, could I? Besides, you guys were all freaked enough about your mess, I couldn't tell you that Max had seen me. I promised I wouldn't tell him... and I didn't." A surge of her own anger made her sink back onto her heels. "It's Mandy, the new assistant, Teddy and Blair give her brownie points when she brings them secrets."

Max grabbed her arm and pulled her around to examine her face. For the longest time, he just inspected her then he shoved the liquor bottle onto the bar. "What are you talking about?" he asked and began to scrutinize his friends.

"It was us," Robbie confessed. "Me, Ryan, and Bobby, we were in her room last night."

"Robbie," she said and tried to reach for him, but he marched to Max.

"We needed the lock-up key to raid the back-up fund because Lucas heard you were in the money and he called in his chit. That's it. That's all that happened. She didn't cheat on you," Robbie sneered.

"I don't want any of you fighting," she said. "Please don't look at Max that way. He had no way to know."

Bobby came closer and she saw the moment Max noticed his bruises. He scrubbed a hand over his mouth. "That was five years ago he gave us that money for the garage," he murmured. "We've fixed up every one of his crew's cars since and he's calling in the chit? That chit's long fucking paid."

"Doesn't fucking matter," Robbie said. "It's done. He's been paid and we're all square again. We told Tally not to tell you because we didn't want to fuck up your cushy new life and because we promised your mom we wouldn't take anything from Stretton when we went to her looking for the key."

Max was still absorbing this, and she didn't know all the details, but was glad to see Robbie breathe out some of his annoyance. "Now my work is done, I'm going to go," Tally said.

Ryan gave her a hug. "Stay and have a drink," Robbie said. "We owe you one… we probably owe you a million."

She shook her head. "Thanks, guys. I'll come to the garage tomorrow for the books and I'll be back on Saturday for the poker. But today, I'm beat."

Robbie kissed her cheek and she reached over the bar to Trey who took her hand to give her a squeeze as they went in opposite directions. "Don't let Max drink any more," she said.

Without missing a step, Trey let her go and swiped the tequila bottle off the bar to stow it beneath.

Heading to the street, she glanced at the conspicuous limo parked outside. There was no way she was getting in that, so she started looking for a cab.

The limo door opened, and the new driver hired for Max stepped out. "Miss Taylor?"

"Yes," she said, watching him button his jacket.

"I want to assure you that I am discreet."

"I know," she said, though she didn't really know; Mandy had put her off the new people. "Mr. Flynn is still inside."

He took a hesitant step toward her. "But I understand…"

The tone he used made her curious, and she was riled enough to reach the verge of offense. "You understand what?"

"You'll be taking up position as Mr. Flynn's mistress."

Rolling her lips into her mouth, Tally figured it didn't take long for news to travel. "Could be," she said. The paperwork was signed, but God only knew what was left of their relationship after today. "But you know what that means, don't you? I'm not his wife."

"I understand," he said. "But I assume there will be times when you are riding with him."

"Times," she said. "And this is not one of them… what's your name?"

"George."

"I'm tired, George. I'm not in the mood to read between any lines," she said. "If you're telling me you won't listen when we're having sex in the back of the car, I appreciate that, but it's really not something that worries me." A cab approached. She stepped farther into the street and held up her hand to stop it. Opening her arms, she smiled and shrugged. "I'm officially a whore now, I signed the paperwork this afternoon that proves it." Tally opened the back door of the cab. "We whores don't worry about things like dignity."

Sliding into the back of the cab before he could say anything else, she exhaled. This had been a fraught day and now she had to go back to the Stretton Estate and make herself irresistible to Max. Except there was no way she was going to get gussied up. Before there was more sex, there had to be some talking. They had to get a few things straightened out, number one being how he could dragoon her into this role without even understanding what he'd done.

WHEN THE SUITE DOOR opened later, Tally stopped writing and looked up. Max came in and stopped inside the door, tossing it into the frame behind him. "I went looking for you in your room," he said, "they said you lived with me now."

"Yep," she said, feeling no sympathy for how disheveled he looked.

Yes, she could cut him some slack for thinking the worst of her when she didn't give him any denial or story to the contrary. But she didn't give him any leeway for going out to get blind drunk; that was all him.

"I spoke to the guys," he said. "Got the full story."

"Yep."

Although he was unsteady on his feet, he came over, and dropped onto the couch. Taking a breath, he flopped back, opening his arms wide. "This has been a crazy day."

"Yep," she said and lifted her eyes to his.

Max let his head fall to the side and his eyes open just enough to meet hers. "You hate me?"

"Little bit," she said and returned to her list.

He grumbled. "You should, I'm a prick."

His breathing was shallow, and he looked exhausted. Cutting him some slack, Tally thought about how she'd feel if she'd believed that Max had slept with Anika between bouts of having sex with her.

Sighing, Tally folded her arms on the table. "We have a lot to talk about," she said. "Everything's happened quickly and I'm not sure you understand what's going on."

His smile was pained and flashed for only a second, while his eyes remained closed. "Baby, you're in my fucking room, and you're not running away from me. You're official." His smile was more genuine and wider. "I don't know what the fuck happened. But I like it."

"You swore at me," she said. "You called me a bitch."

His smile fell, and he cracked open an eye. Considering her for a second, he slid off the couch to sit at the coffee table with her.

Gathering up her hand in both of his, he pressed his lips to the back of her fingers. "I'm sorry, baby. I'm so sorry... I thought I lost you. I was crazy. I need you, you know I do. Without you, I... didn't know who I was." Okay, so the liquor was loosening his tongue too. "I wanted to kill the bastard, that's why I couldn't ask who it was. If I'd had a name, I would've killed him with my bare hands. I love you."

"Don't," she said, pulling her hand away. "Don't say that to me when you're apologizing. Only say that when you mean it, not when you have to."

"I mean it, baby," he said and leaned in to kiss her, but all Tally tasted was liquor.

Pushing up from the table, she pulled him to his feet. "You're getting in the shower and then you're getting some sleep," she said, helping him toward the bedroom. "I need you to sober up."

"So we can talk?" he asked, shoving the bedroom door harder than he needed to.

"Yes," she said, struggling under the weight of his arm. "Will you be okay in the shower?"

He rubbed his face in her hair. "You gonna join me if I say no?"

"I'll help you if you need help," she said and pushed him to the wall of the shower room when they got there so she could turn on the water. "But don't ask me for sex, of any variety."

"Why not?" he mumbled as he struggled out of his clothes.

She watched him stumble into the stall and be startled by the pressure of the water. "Because I'm no longer allowed to say no," she whispered to herself.

NINETEEN

SLEEPING IN THIS HUGE BED with Max was odd. Not because it wasn't comfortable, it was, but it just didn't feel quite right to be in such contrived surroundings with a man she knew as anything but contrived.

It was dark out, and close to three AM, but she wasn't sleeping. She'd been too worried about Max and his drunkenness. She could tell he was far gone because he started to snore, and every time she tried to put him on his side, he returned to his back. Tally wasn't strong enough to force him anywhere, so she stayed up to make sure he didn't aspirate.

Thinking about her life, she tried to trace it back to a point before all this started, before Max, before the accident that killed Laura, when she was going through the motions of each day, following the rules and… Tally was fixated on the idea of happiness. Was she happy back then when she was oblivious to Max's existence? Oblivious to what love was? What incredible, dynamite sex was? She smiled; if nothing else, he'd opened her eyes to that.

"That's a sexy smile."

The sound of his voice made her roll to her side to see that he was facing her, his eyes drowsy, but definitely open.

"How do you feel?" she asked, pressing her hand to his shoulder to support him, though he didn't seem to need it. "How's your head?"

Brushing her palm upward over his forehead, she pushed his head back, worrying that he'd have a killer headache.

"I opened my eyes and the first thing I saw was you," he said, pulling her over the bed into his arms. "I found my happiness again." Kissing her shoulder, he moved to her neck and his hands moved over her breasts. "Why didn't we do this sooner? Why didn't we just do it from the start?"

Because she'd made it clear to him that this life would make her unhappy; that was why she couldn't stop thinking about happiness. Maybe she could make herself happy here, constrained by contracts and rules instead of just being a woman in love... but she doubted it given the rules she'd had to agree to.

"Max, how do you feel about abortion?"

He stopped kissing. A minute passed before he rose to settle his serious gaze on her. "Why are you asking about that?" His hand opened on her belly. "Are you...? Are you pregnant? Did you have an abortion?"

She pushed his hand away from her stomach. "I had to sign a piece of paper today that said if I got pregnant, I'd have an abortion or sign all my parental rights over to the Strettons... I don't know why but I keep thinking about that. I'm not pregnant, I have no intentions of being pregnant. But I had to sign a piece of paper saying that if I ever did get pregnant with your child, I should deny his parentage... It pisses me off."

"It pisses me off," he said and sat up to glare. "Who the fuck made you sign that? Why the fuck did you sign it? Our kid is our kid, I'd never fucking deny him or want you to either."

"You told Teddy to make me your mistress." Tally wasn't ready to tell Max that the strict rules attached to the mistress role had been put into place after Teddy's affair with Cindy. The pregnancy that had arisen from that affair, and produced Max, had made Teddy vigilant. "That's what I meant earlier when I said I don't think you understand what's going on. The Strettons are strict about this. I'm not your girlfriend. They make mistresses sign non-disclosure agreements, airtight confidentiality agreements. I have to submit to all Stretton rules. We have to sign to say that we will submit any time we're paged. We are subject not only to the man in our lives but to their wives as well. If you get married, I have to do anything and everything your wife tells me to. You can have me fired for refusing a sex act. Mistresses don't eat dinner at the family table. We can go on trips with you; but are not to go to social events unless specifically invited."

"Well you're specifically invited, to them all," he said, his anger becoming bluster. "Baby, I—"

"The rules and clauses are endless."

"I'd never have let you sign that," he said, clasping her cheek. "If I'd known—"

"I didn't have much choice," she said. "You bailed me out and made that declaration in front of Teddy right after he caught us having sex. I didn't have an out. It was sign or be on the street."

Max took a minute to think. "How do you get out of it? I mean, how do we void it?"

"It's only a six-month contract," she said. "It's designed to be renewed with the same terms." Inhaling, she took his hand from her face to link their fingers. "I won't be renewing it, Max. I love you, but… I can't love you to a strict set of guidelines. What we had was organic, now it's… I don't know what it is, but it's not the same."

"Six months," he said. "You're telling me you'll leave me after six months."

"Unless it turns out this is an amazing way to live that suits us both." Which she knew it wouldn't be because she couldn't imagine anything worse than being told how to love Max. "Yeah. That time will give me a chance to find a new job and somewhere to live."

Worry made him squeeze her tighter. "Wait, okay, will you give me a chance to think about this? I don't want to lose you. I can't lose you."

Shifting to her knees, she leaned forward to hold him.

"I won't bring it up again, I promise. I won't keep reminding you of our end date. But I need to be honest with you now. I'll make the most of this. I'll do my duty. But I won't be employed as your whore forever, I just won't do it."

Pulling back, he ran his hands into her hair. "Let me figure this out, okay? Don't do anything rash. Let me… try."

"Six months," she said, and leaned in to kiss him. "You have me for six months."

Tally had become the one thing she'd never wanted to be: a whore. It wasn't as simple as sex for the pleasure of it anymore. The last thing she wanted to do was resent Max or second guess herself when it came to their intimacy.

Being his mistress meant they could share a bed, but they were not free, and he couldn't possibly understand that until he lived it. Everything their relationship was now was dictated by Teddy Stretton. The man might be responsible for giving her a roof over her head and a job. But she didn't want him to be responsible for telling her how to love.

Max didn't get it yet, and maybe he wouldn't ever get it. They were a contract. Bound together by words on a page. Tally hated it. Just like in the back of that limo on the way to the Walker Benefit when she hadn't felt like she was sitting with her Max, she didn't feel right in this bed.

With him, surrendered to him, she'd forget the clauses that compelled her to be there. But, in the night, and in her quiet moments, she'd always remember that just because her chains were invisible didn't mean they weren't there.

She wanted to be with Max Flynn. She loved her Max Flynn. But the man Teddy was turning him into wasn't the same man. By the time his father was through with him, Tally doubted she'd recognize the man who'd taken his place.

BY THE TIME the next morning came, Max was over his hangover and Tally was trying to be more optimistic. Really, she was trying her damndest.

"So I've figured it out," Max declared, appearing at the door of the walk-in closet.

Tally was sitting on a stool, putting on her thigh-highs. She'd got showered while Max was downstairs at breakfast. It took some time to make him understand that she couldn't go to breakfast with him. She wasn't family, they weren't married; she wasn't allowed at the breakfast table.

Tally sat up to look at him, and he looked just so proud of himself that she smiled. "Figured out what, baby?"

Chalking yesterday up to insanity, she'd relaxed when he kissed her awake. Sex in his new bed wasn't as weird as she thought it might be. Max was still Max when he was touching her and kissing her. The thread count didn't matter when he was sliding himself into her, and just being under him again helped her gain some perspective. They were together again, that was at least something to be grateful for… For now, at least.

Slipping his hands into his pockets, he propped a shoulder on the doorframe. "I want you to forget about the contract." She shook her head, not following how he could think it was that simple. "You said it says you have to follow my orders, right?" She nodded. "So I'm telling you we're going to forget it exists. I'm telling you to argue with me. To contradict me. You have one rule to follow."

Leaving her perch, she went to her drawer… That she even had a drawer in here was nuts, but there it was, along with a bunch of others, and clothes on rails that belonged to her too.

"One rule?" she asked, selecting the bra that matched her underwear.

Coming over to her, he pulled her around to get her focus on him. "I want you to treat me like your Max, at all times, you understand?"

That request just proved that he was ignorant to their predicament. "Ma—"

"You're going to keep me honest. I told you I was dying. Before you, I… I was losing myself in this bullshit. I didn't have a fucking clue who I was or what I was doing. I can't forget who I am; I don't want to forget. I've tried to be what they want me to be and it made me crazy. They accept me, or they don't really want me, you know? I need you to treat me just like you did before I came here. We're going to carry on our relationship exactly as it was before, just like it was at my apartment. Get it?"

Dubious, she examined his features. "Max, I'm not allowed to—"

He touched her lips. "The best part about this is, you can't argue with me. I don't want you cutting me any slack, I don't want you calling me 'sir' or thinking of me as your boss. You think of me as your Max, you treat me the same as before. You want to send me out to three stores for bagels, just bat those lashes at me and suck my dick like you did at the apartment."

Exhaling a laugh, she let her head fall to his chest. What did she have to lose? If she was out of here in six months anyway, she'd rather forget the money and the Stretton name and just be his girlfriend. If he wanted her to act entitled to him, then she would. It would be more fun than bowing down, and like he said, he'd just given her an order.

"Okay," she murmured, and he scooped up her head to look her in the eye.

"Yeah? A hundred percent, I don't want you to do anything different and I'll know if you do. I know my girl. I belong to you and you don't think about the family or the job, you just own me, okay? You're the boss. I follow your orders, your wishes. You call all the shots." Own him, she could handle that and maybe he'd learn a lesson about himself in the process. She nodded. "Okay." He kissed her. "Get dressed and I'll call George to take us into the office together."

And that statement presented her first task. Tensing her hand on his arm, she drew him back. His eyes asked why, and she was hesitant, but eventually took a breath and decided to rip off the Band-Aid.

"Can I ask you something?"

"Anything, Boss."

He was stroking the sides of her neck, touching her styled hair as he gazed at her lips. In short, he was thinking about sex. She'd told him to get rid of that tell, turned out he hadn't taken her advice.

But as long as he was using that look on her, she

wasn't going to complain. "Why do you use a driver?"

His brows lowered. "Why do I…? What do you mean?"

"I understand you need the car and the driver for events, when you're going somewhere social with a date when you'll be drinking or if you're having a meeting with several people in the car. But… there's a whole fleet of cars in the garage out there. I never understood why you didn't drive yourself anywhere. You always said you loved to drive, that's why you became a mechanic. I know it's not… traditional for the Stretton family. But really, I can't understand why you would get some guy to drive you into the office every day. Aren't you bored out of your wits in the back?" She sighed. "It doesn't matter, I… I just always thought you could use the time alone at the start and end of each day doing something that you love."

His gaze grew more distant and she tensed, worrying that maybe her Max had changed more than she thought. If he got mad and they ended up arguing, this whole experience would be unbearable. More than that, if Max couldn't take her voicing her opinion, it would mean Stretton had him and there was nothing of her Max left.

"Shit," he exhaled and smiled. Grabbing her face, he lunged down and kissed her hard. "God, baby, you're absolutely fucking right! There's no reason for me not to drive in and out of the office myself every day… And that frees up George for you, he can drive you anywhere you want to go."

She hadn't meant for him to make that leap and began to panic. "Oh, I—"

"No, that's fucking decided," he said, running a finger down her jaw. "George will be with you all day, every day, okay? Stretton says I get a budget for you anyway, how crazy is that?"

Yeah, and another thing that made her feel sick. "For dates and jewelry," she said. "You have a budget to take care of a mistress for trips and clothes and stuff."

"Good," he said and read her panic. "Not in the way you're thinking, 'cause we're forgetting the contract, but I can buy you decent gifts, expensive gifts…" She didn't get it, but he was trying to tell her something. "Gifts that will be worth something at hock if…"

This didn't work out. It was sweet that he was thinking about that; he wanted to give her security. "I wouldn't sell anything you bought me."

"I'm telling you that if you have to, I want you to. I want you to be safe, always."

And when they came from nowhere, from the bottom of society, it was always in the back of their minds that they could end up back there.

Tally nodded. "Okay."

"Great, now let's go pick a car and I'll drive you in to work," he said and kissed her. "You're working for me already, baby. How did I survive without you?"

How would they survive the next six months? That's what she wanted to know. Being without him was tough, but at least she had nothing but happy memories of their time together.

She'd do as he asked. But by the time this contract was over, would they still feel the way they had that Monday in his apartment when they'd said goodbye? She hoped so. But, somehow, Tally knew it wasn't going to be that easy.

TWENTY

IT WAS THE NEXT WEEKEND that Tally got the first major shock of her career as a mistress. Max was going somewhere with some corporate guys, a male-only excursion, and she expected to sit in alone. Except Blair and Kimmy invited her to dinner. Which was… unexpected.

She was dubious about going but wanted to know what they wanted. They weren't extending the invitation out of the kindness of their hearts. Anyway, it wasn't like she was in a position to refuse. Max was going out with Teddy, and her services weren't needed by either man.

During the awkward limo ride out of the Stretton Estate, Tally was ignored. Although it was rude of the other two women in the car not to address her, she'd rather be ignored than be expected to engage in polite small talk or any interrogation about her relationship with Max.

After fifteen minutes on the road, Tally was wondering if she was allowed to drink alcohol given that she wasn't technically working for Teddy. Although she was probably considered on call for Max, he could still have sex with her if she was drunk. So as long as she got back to the right bed…

A bang startled all of them and the car swerved causing all of them to scream and brace, but before her life could start flashing before her eyes, the limo came to a lurching halt.

"Are you okay?" Tally asked, leaning across to Kimmy who had to be the most scared. Her mother had died in a car accident, in a limo accident at that.

Kimmy just nodded, though Tally wasn't sure she was aware of what she was feeling. But Blair put an arm around her, acting, at least, like she was going to be human about the experience.

So Tally got out to see what was going on. "What's wrong, George?" she asked, wrapping her arms around herself to rub some heat into them as she approached the driver who was standing by the front passenger side of the car.

"Flat tire, ma'am," he said and had his phone to his ear.

Great. How did that happen? They were on a road in the middle of nowhere, in the dark and cold, without another vehicle in sight.

"Can you change it?" she asked.

He paled and shifted then shook his head. "I'm not insured to do it."

Not insured, sure, she rolled her eyes. Turning his back, he spoke into the phone. Both Blair and Kimmy got out of the vehicle and started to complain about the cold.

"What's going on?" Blair asked.

"Flat," Tally said.

George hung up the phone. "Roadside will be here in an hour… maybe two." The women moaned. "We're not a priority, no one is in immediate danger."

"This is unacceptable," Blair said. "We'll freeze to death and Kimmy does not need to be abandoned out here with a wrecked car. Do you understand how insensitive that is?"

Blair continued to shout at George and Kimmy began to cry. Tally went to the tire to look at it. Could she change it? She could try, but she'd never done it before, she couldn't even drive one of these beasts. Taking her phone from her clutch, she dialed and wandered to the back of the car, away from the others.

"Miss me already?" Max asked when he picked up the phone.

"You know how when you said I should treat you like my Max and I should forget about the family and the money and stuff?"

"Yeah?"

Leaning against the trunk, she squinted. "Does that extend into roadside assistance?"

He got serious. "Where are you? What happened? Are you hurt?"

"No," she said. "Everyone is fine. We got a flat. But the actual roadside assistance won't be out for another hour, which you know means two or more. George says he's not insured to do it." Glancing back, Tally made sure everyone was out of earshot. "That's what he says, I think he doesn't know how to do it."

Max laughed. "I can track your phone," he said. "I'll be there in ten."

Relief made her exhale a smile, then she felt that anxiety again. "Are you sure? I know you're not going out for a while, but if it will be weird…"

"Are you crazy?" he asked. "I'm already in the car. I've been desperate for an excuse to get my hands dirty."

Somehow, she'd known that. "You know there is a garage full of cars that could probably use tune-ups, and you're rich now…" Rich enough that Stretton paid him an allowance every month and gave him an expense account. The allowance was healthy enough, it was more than he probably earned in a year before meeting his father. But it was a clear signal, he wasn't given full access to all accounts; she guessed he still had to prove his loyalty. "You could buy yourself a beat up… something… and fix it up."

When it took him so long to answer, she looked down at the phone to check the line hadn't disconnected.

"I love you, baby," he said.

So he liked that suggestion. She smiled and closed her eyes. Sometimes she wanted to ask him to leave it all. If he told Stretton to go to hell, then maybe they could just go back to how things were. She should be able to call him about a car issue without worrying how Blair and Kimmy would react.

Tally could've called Robbie or any of the guys, but they were much further away, and she didn't know what they were up to tonight. Max would want to be her knight in shining armor; he'd probably be offended if she bypassed him to ask one of his friends for help.

"I want you to get off the phone and drive safe," she said. "Concentrate on the road. I'll see you soon."

"You won't say it in front of other people," he said, sounding pissed. "And you won't let me say it in front of them either."

The couple of times he'd almost declared his feelings in earshot of others, she'd sealed her fingers on his lips. "Because they think this is sex," she said. "Love is… more complicated. Your father and the others are already dubious about the influence they think I have over you. I don't doubt that's what tonight is about… I think they want to probe into what we have."

"You know if you want to walk out, just walk out and we'll deal with whatever happens," he said.

Yes, he'd reassured her many times that he'd always pick her over Stretton, and every time he did, she told him not to talk that way.

"It won't come to that," she said. "It's a dinner. I can dodge questions and if they ask me something I don't want to answer, I'll just say that."

"Good girl."

"Now get off the phone," she said, hearing the noise of his car in the background. "I'll see you soon, hero."

Her teasing made him groan. "Might drag you into the woods for a little gratitude."

She laughed. "Yeah, I don't think so, not with your sister a few feet away."

"Sister," he said. "Half-sister, and she doesn't even feel like that." He'd had real trouble connecting with Kimmy. "I don't think the girl even likes me."

"Doesn't sound like you're too wild about her," she

said. "But, seriously, Max, we'll talk about this later, okay? Just drive safe."

They disconnected, and she tucked the phone away, taking time to bolster herself before turning to stride back to her party. "Who was that?" Blair asked.

"Max," Tally said. He was going to show up in a minute, so it wasn't like there was any point in lying. "He's going to help us out."

For maybe twenty seconds, Blair, Kimmy, and even George stared at her like she'd grown an extra head. "You called the Stretton heir to come here and change our tire?" Blair asked.

"No, I called the man I'm sleeping with," she said because as crude as it might sound, she couldn't use the word boyfriend. "Trust me, he knows what he's doing. He's not going to get hurt."

"I didn't…" Kimmy was over her trauma, now she was just a bundle of stuttering confusion. Calling Max at least saved her from thinking about her mom's death. "How does Max know how to change a tire?"

"He used to own a garage," she said, watching Blair walk away. Tally folded her arms and propped a hip on the car. "You know, Max is actually an interesting guy when you take the time to talk to him."

Kimmy sneered. "You're his mistress, not his wife, you don't really know anything about him."

Kimmy turned to flounce off after Blair. Watching her go, Tally wondered if that's what Teddy had told Laura through the years when he had affairs, and if Kimmy had heard her parents arguing about it. As brilliant as Teddy was in business, he'd never been fulfilled in love. Tally thought he loved Laura but couldn't understand how he could and then sleep with other women.

"Are we going to lose our jobs for this?" George asked, coming closer.

It was nice to have a friend. Most of the others at the house had shut her out since she'd become Max's mistress. There was a strict "us" and "them" divide among employees and those who crossed it never crossed back.

"Max won't fire us," she said, and when he blanched, she patted his arm. "This wasn't your fault and I think my phone call is going to be the highlight of the night, take solace in that."

An engine faded up, and she smiled when she heard his speed. He'd say he was worried about her and wanted to get to the scene fast, but she knew he also liked to let loose on long, straight roads like this.

Kimmy and Blair were back with them by the time Max pulled up and got out. "Having some trouble?" Max asked, walking around the car to check the tires.

"You don't have to do this," Blair said. "It was ridiculous of Tallulah to phone you."

Max stopped by the flat tire, looked at it for three seconds, and then turned to toss her a set of car keys. Tally only just managed to catch them. "Get in my car, stay warm," he said.

"No," she said. Passing off the keys to a flabbergasted Kimmy, Tally strode to his side and nudged him with her hip. "Teach me."

He drew his eyes from the tire to her, the corner of his mouth rising as he did. "For real?" he asked, and she nodded. Turning to face her, he folded his arms over his broad chest. "Tell me, Tal, baby, when do you think you're going to need to change a tire?"

She opened her hands at the flat beside them. "I find myself in that very situation tonight."

"You'd have changed this yourself?" he asked, tipping his chin toward it.

"If I knew how," she said and had to smile when she read the amused pride that grew in his expression.

"You know, baby, I believe you would've given this a fucking shot if you had to."

"If it wasn't so cold," she said.

Max took off his jacket and wrapped it around her. "You don't even drive a car. You're ever in one that gets a flat, you call me, just like you did tonight."

"What if you're in Boca Raton?"

His grin flared. "Why would I be in—" Cutting

himself off, he shook his head. "Never mind. If I'm not around… call Robbie."

"Call Robbie," she said at the same time he did, and they shared a smile.

For a second, Tally had forgotten they weren't alone. Recalling that they had an audience made her clear her throat and squirm. This kind of familiarity should be reserved for when they were in private.

A flash of curiosity crossed his face as he noticed her mood shift, then he looked up to the others behind her. "The rest of you go and sit in my car. I'll be done in five."

The others trotted off to do as they were told. Tally didn't go with them. Max started to move toward the rear of the car, she stepped backwards, out of his path. "Not going to put your foot down and send me away?"

"Nope," he said, opening the trunk. " 'Cause you're the boss around here and if you want me to talk you through it, that's what I'll do." She smiled but wondered if her being assertive had really been the thing to break through and silence his objections when he peeked over the trunk lid at her. "Plus, seeing me do shit like this makes you horny."

Trying to deny it would be insane, but she did try to subdue her smile so he wouldn't know how right he was. But Max knew her, and her moods, especially her carnal ones, and saw right through her attempt to be reserved. Both of them ended up forgetting about the cold as they stared through the night at each other.

Calling Max when she was in trouble had immediately made her feel safer. Blair and Kimmy would take news of this back to Teddy, and as much as that concerned her, Tally knew this night would serve as a test. Would the family let Max run his own relationship with his mistress or was daddy going to step in?

TWENTY-ONE

THE ANSWER TO THAT QUESTION came swiftly; the next day to be exact. Tally had been called into Teddy's office before, but never like this. Usually, if he had a task for her, he'd send an email or have his assistant call, but there were always some details about the reason for the summons, even if they were vague.

If he wanted to have a discussion or ask something, he'd usually do it at the estate, either in the morning before he went to work or after he was home. The only reason she was ever called to the office was to transport files or for function arrangements. Neither was on the agenda that day.

Tally had never been summoned to his Stretton Chemicals office in the middle of the day by three simple words in the subject line of an otherwise blank email: Get Here Now.

That's how they'd been written, each with a capital letter, and somehow each conveying his displeasure.

She'd been naïve to think she'd get away with it. Max had somehow convinced her that if they just pretended to be them, it would work out, and the other people in his family wouldn't notice their level of intimacy. But what had happened last night was the perfect example of how they couldn't just ignore the mistress contract.

Max wanted them to be them; it was a lovely, romantic notion. But they weren't them anymore and would never be them again. Not like they had been. It was almost pointless for her to even show up at the meeting with Teddy at Stretton. Tally knew what it was going to be about and its likely outcome.

The email had come through while she was lying in bed with Max after he'd showed up at the house and stolen her upstairs for a little afternoon delight. She'd been watching Max sleep, and after reading Teddy's request she'd gotten dressed and tiptoed out of their bedroom.

Grateful that they'd had the chance to enjoy each other before she'd received her orders, Tally had peeked at Max one more time before closing the bedroom door. All the while she wondered if she'd ever see him again and how he'd handle it if Teddy had to give him the news that she'd been let go.

The situation got more dire when she found Pierre waiting for her at the bottom of the stairs in the Estate lobby. Tally had slowed when she'd seen how pale her once dear friend was, and what was left of her hope seeped away.

The journey to Stretton Chemicals seemed shorter than it ever had before. But that could've been due to the ominous silence that hung between her and Pierre, or her own sinking dread that she'd crossed the line for the final time.

Pierre dropped her off at the main SC entrance, and for a brief moment she considered bolting for a brief moment, but knew that wouldn't change anything. So she'd gone inside and up to the executive floor. It was a journey she'd done countless times, but it had never filled her with such trepidation.

Left waiting outside Teddy's corporate office, clutching her purse, Tally figured that although it was nerve-wracking, the time gave her a chance to reflect on how the hell she'd gotten to this point in her life and her career… which seemed to be over.

For almost every minute Tally sat there, she wished

Teddy would hurry up and just call her in to get the tongue lashing, and potential firing, over with. Except as soon as the door opened and Teddy's newest assistant came out, Tally wanted to send her straight back inside and delay the inevitable.

Unfortunately, she didn't have magic powers that would make that happen. "You can go in," the assistant said, doing her the courtesy of looking contrite.

But this situation wasn't the youngster's fault; Tally wasn't going to shoot the messenger. Inhaling and resigning herself to her fate, she swung herself up, out of her chair, and began that long final walk, wondering if death row inmates felt the same way on their journey to the electric chair.

Theodore Stretton's office was large and intimidating at the best of times, decorated in a traditional style, it was a classic example of Teddy's belief in his own importance.

The man did nothing to reassure her as she crossed the thick pile carpet and ascended the two stairs to the second level which held his desk.

Usually, she'd stand next to the desk to get instructions and then leave again without giving the encounter much thought. But this time, she didn't know what to do. So she just loitered, waiting for Teddy to look up.

It was a good ninety seconds before he did, and even when he looked at her, he considered her for thirty seconds before opening his hand toward the chair opposite his desk.

"I think we both know why you're here," Teddy said.

She scurried over to the seat and sat down. "Yes, sir."

"What you did, it…" He sort of smiled as he scoffed out a laugh, but it was one of incredulity. "You know you had no right to do that. Your behavior… it's completely over the line. I know you think you have some claim to my son. But you know that's an illusion. You're a vessel for his use, that's what you agreed to."

Meaning she wasn't allowed to have opinions and wasn't meant to put ideas in Max's head, much less take the liberty of making demands on his time. "I know."

"He's… protective of you. He doesn't understand how this world works."

The condescension in his tone almost made her lip curl, but then she remembered it was her role here to be meek and apologetic. This wasn't Max who'd encourage her to stand up, this was Teddy who wanted her to bow down.

"Sir—"

"There was a time when I thought you could be useful to him… and to me. But the Walker Benefit switched me on to your influence over him. At first, I was dubious. Blair thought maybe you could be used to our advantage. But…" Slowly, he began to shake his head and peer at her like he didn't recognize her. "I'm not sure you are who I thought you were, Tallulah. You've changed."

It was her impulse to argue that point, but the moment her lips parted, she took a silent breath and closed them again.

When she'd first gone to find Max, she'd been Teddy's minion. There to do his bidding. She'd cared more about making sure he was happy and that her job was secure, and less about who Max was or how this experience would change his life.

Tally had been naïve. She'd thought anyone being told they were going to live in a fancy house and have almost unlimited access to funds would be the thrill of a lifetime. Max had barely blinked.

He hadn't cared about the money and had no desire to change, though he had. And he'd changed her; his love for her had changed her. Max had done nothing but encourage her to be who she was, and somehow, she'd ended up pushing him into a life that changed the very essence of who he was.

The weight of her head was almost too much for her to hold. She began to retreat into herself as it fell. Tally had nothing to be proud of here. She wasn't the only one in a no-win situation. Max should have everything this life could offer. It was only his ties to her, his love for her, holding him back.

"Max is a powerful man," she said, but this wasn't his fault. His only sin was falling in love with her.

"He's a Stretton," Teddy said like he was somehow responsible for the man Max was, when she knew that couldn't be further from the truth.

Tally loved the man who'd taken her earring to pay for their drinks. She loved the man who'd fed her beer and chips and pulled her into his lap to watch a ballgame. Her love was for the man who'd slid his finger into her in a dark, crowded nightclub and whispered dirty words in her ear.

All she kept thinking about was the back of the limo the night of the Walker Benefit and how she'd tried to put space between them. But she'd given up on being sensible when being with him just felt too good.

The heartache she'd been avoiding hit her hard now. Some corner of her must have always believed that there would be a way for her and Max to come back together. But this brief time at his side as his mistress had proved that was impossible. She couldn't be with Max. He couldn't be with her.

Their relationship. Their love. It was over.

"I'll pack my things and be out of the house before you return," she murmured.

Teddy scoffed. "If I thought my son would let that go by, I wouldn't have bothered with this meeting. I'd have had you turfed out the moment Blair told me what happened."

So he hadn't found out from Max last night, he'd found out from Blair today. That was telling and proved that whether he realized it or not, Max had known to be discreet. He knew that Teddy would only accept so much from their relationship and that being themselves together would never be permitted.

That awareness in itself should be enough to show Max they couldn't flout the rules and be together as they wanted to be. But he was pigheaded and wouldn't give up on her like he should. Even if it meant losing each other, Max had to see that this life could offer him so much more than she ever could.

Tally had once told him they would grow to resent each other if they struggled through and shunned Stretton's money. Now, she feared, they'd come to resent each other if they were forced to live together with it.

But Teddy was right. If Tally thought she could make Max see it was better for her to leave, then she would walk out the door and never see him again. But he wouldn't make it that easy on either of them.

"He has to learn for himself," Tally murmured. "He has to know that we can never be…" But there was no end to that sentence, it was a sentence in itself. "That we can never be."

"Exactly," he said. "I don't know why he's infatuated with you. But he is."

The subtext was that Teddy would never allow her to be part of the family, but she wasn't naïve to that fact and was actually pleased he hadn't said it aloud, because it would just be embarrassing for both of them.

To have the Stretton heir marry a former employee would be a scandal that Teddy just wouldn't tolerate given how he valued his reputation.

Not that Tally wanted to marry Max Stretton. A life dictated by Teddy would be tolerable for a while, but if they wanted to live on their own, it wouldn't be allowed. To have children would mean signing over parental decisions to Teddy who liked to be in control of everything and everyone.

Living in the Estate forever, raising their children there, neither of them would be happy, and they'd end up taking it out on each other.

The hardest part was knowing that Max was losing who he was. The man she loved, the one she'd fallen for so hard, would fade away. He'd learn to bow to Teddy and would eventually marry a woman he liked and let his father dictate how his grandchildren should be raised.

Tally would be long gone by then. Without the Strettons she had no idea what her life would be. All she could think about was Max's life and her wonderful, powerful, incredible Max Flynn slipping away.

"What do you suggest?" she asked, knowing that Teddy would already have a plan.

"Embrace the life," he said. "We'll move you into your own suite of rooms. You'll visit him at night to allow him access to your body. But you won't sleep with him and will limit all other contact. It won't take him long to see that this isn't a life for you."

It wasn't a life for her, but she didn't like how much that pleased Teddy. He might think her compliance was something to do with allegiance to him, it wasn't. Tally knew that both she and Max would change if they were forced into this life. If she wasn't sure she could love the man he'd become, then she wasn't sure he'd be able to love the woman she would grow into.

The only thing worse than losing Max was thinking he could ever look into her eyes and not feel for her the way he did now... or the way he had when they were wrapped in each other in his apartment.

Rising to her feet, Tally wasn't going to wait to be dismissed when he'd said all she needed to hear. Teddy hadn't expected her to stand, but he leaped up after she was on her feet.

"I'll go and pack. Just tell me where you need me to go."

Teddy smiled and rocked back on his heels. "Good girl, Tallulah. This family has been good to you. I would hate for you to forget that."

"I won't forget what this family gave me," she said because if it wasn't for them, she'd never have met Max. The relationship might be doomed, but she'd never regret those precious moments when she'd been happy with him. "I assume if Max releases me from my contract, you'll allow me to terminate all connection to the Strettons. My mistress duties and my employment."

"Yes. With immediate effect."

Nodding once, she turned to head for the door. Max would see it. Yes, he would. But he'd hate her by then. Losing him once was bad enough, now she had to do it again, and this time it would be for good.

TEDDY WASTED NO TIME in assigning her space in the house. So after learning that Max had returned to the office, Tally got to work packing her things and moving them. She had taken everything of hers from Max's suite, and had decided it would be best to wait for him there to let him know what was going on. But he arrived before her and must have got back to his room while she was in her new space, arranging her things.

Because it was while she was walking down the hallway, back toward his suite that Max came out through the door she'd been heading for. Tally didn't expect him to be back from the office already. The sight of his rigid form and his face set in anger made her stall.

"What the fuck is this shit?" Max asked when he caught sight of her. "All of your shit's gone from our room."

Though she hadn't expected to see him yet, she had known this confrontation was inevitable. Grateful for small mercies, she was pleased it was taking place outside the suite rather than within it.

"I was just coming to talk to you."

But he wasn't in the mood to be accommodating. She could tell by looking at him that he was gearing up for a fight, which was the last thing they needed. "Oh, this shit will be good," he said, folding his arms and widening his stance. "Come on, give me the bullshit."

Stopping in front of him, she kept a respectful distance, something neither of them usually did. "You can have sex with me any time you want," she said, catching her fist in her opposite palm and giving it a squeeze. "But I won't be sleeping in your room anymore."

"What the fuck is—"

"I tried to tell you that there would be resistance to us and you wouldn't listen," she said, doing her best not to raise her voice.

This corridor turned into perpendicular corridors at either end. Anyone could loiter just around the corner out of sight and hear every word.

"So this is him... this is Stretton because of last night?" he said, like he was amping up to do something. "Because you called me, he thinks he can take you away from me?"

While Teddy might have instigated this change, Tally had always known it would come to this. "No, this is me."

His brows twitched, like he couldn't quite figure that

out. "You don't want to be with me? Is that what you're trying to sell? 'Cause I won't believe it."

Sometimes he just couldn't see what was right in front of his face. It infuriated her that she had to keep repeating herself. "I told you it would be like this, Max. I told you."

He snatched her hand. "Then grab whatever shit you need, we're getting out of here."

Tugging her hand back, she wanted to scream out loud. "It's not as simple as that! God, Max! Why do you make me spell it out every time! You're bound by the contracts you signed at SC. Just like I am. We're in this now. There is no getting out."

"Then we should be together," he argued. "If we're here and stuck, we should be stuck together."

And that broke her heart. Her hands fell to her sides. "We are, Max," she murmured. "We're stuck… together. We're not together because we want to be, we're together because we have to be; because a piece of paper dictates everything about us… I'm your mistress. Your whore. I'm not the Tallulah you fell in love with; I'm a body to warm your bed for as long as you need me."

Softening, he moved in close, sliding a hand to her face. "Baby, it could never be like that between us… You need some distance, I'll respect that. But don't let them punish us for being us."

Pushing his hand from her face, she stepped away. Just the fact that he didn't pursue her told her that they'd changed him already. Her Max wouldn't let her push him away, he'd pick her up or pin her to something, but this guy was just, there, a shadow of the dynamic man he'd once been.

"It is gone, Max. We tried it your way, we tried to ignore the rules, but they caught up with us… This is it now, the best we'll ever have."

"I love you, Tal," he said.

She began to back away. "And I'll cherish that love forever," she said. The pain in her chest made her eyes narrow. "But don't say that to me again here. I don't want to hear those words from the lips of Max Stretton… Coming to you at night, sharing my body with you, that's not love… not like we had. So don't say it anymore, Max. Use me for pleasure, but don't ask me for anything else. If you ever loved me, give me at least that dignity."

Turning around to walk away from him was one of the hardest things she'd ever done. It was possibly harder than losing him the first time.

She'd go to him when she had to. She'd do her duty. But her heart was in Max Flynn's apartment and she wouldn't let anyone confuse that for this.

Tally was a good girl, or she would be until her contract was up. By then, they would have nothing left.

TWENTY-TWO

MAX HAD THOUGHT that her sparkle was gone. But it wasn't gone at all. He was watching her, and she was more vibrant than she'd been in weeks. The sparkle wasn't gone; it just wasn't for him anymore.

Inside the lobby of the Stretton fucking Chemicals building that had become the bane of his goddamn life, he was looking through the glass front to the coffee cart on the curb outside.

He hadn't meant to spy; he wasn't some creepy fucking perv. All he'd wanted was some coffee and a minute of fucking peace without projections and potential ROIs being thrown in his face.

All the work was bullshit. In the first weeks, he'd wanted to jack it in every second. Hoping he was making her proud was the only thing that kept him from telling Teddy to go fuck himself or putting one of Stretton's minions through the wall.

Getting her back, having her in his bed again had been a dream. But he hadn't been able to keep her there.

Curling his fingers into fists, he watched her take a bite from the muffin that the Sean fucker offered her mouth.

Sean touched her lip, probably collecting some crumbs that he then sucked onto his own tongue.

She was glittering. Laughing and chattering. Happy.

She didn't come to him every night. In fact, she had come to him less and less over the last month. After telling him not to love her and walking away from him in the hallway outside his suite, a gulf had grown between them. Every day he hoped something would change, that it would get better, but he was realizing now that a month was a long time and things weren't going to get better. Any time he tried to tell her how he felt, she'd put a hand to his mouth or kiss him. She didn't want to hear it.

That stuck in his craw. Who had the fucking right to tell him not to love her? She was his fucking dream, his life, his woman.

But he had to ask himself. If she was his, why was she out there connecting with another man on a level deeper than he'd had her at in weeks?

It had been days since she'd come to his room. Maybe as much as a week. He missed her, craved her, but it wasn't the same. He couldn't fucking figure it out, couldn't figure out what had changed or why she was so cold towards him.

"You're a lucky man," Teddy said. Glancing away from his view of what was going on in the street beyond those thick glass doors, Max saw Teddy coming up at his side, taking in the same scene he'd been observing. "She's a vision."

"If that woman belonged to me, I would be," he murmured. "But that's not the woman who comes to me."

Teddy sighed a sound that could have been disappointment. But Max was too focused on Tally touching Sean's face with her delicate fingertips that had once been reserved for him.

A hand landed on his shoulder and he recoiled, almost lashing out at its owner and causing Teddy to hold up both hands and step back.

Much as he didn't like it, Max had gotten used to the way these soft, business bastards liked to pat each other on the back and fondle each other's balls. It was all about sucking up. Brown nosing wasn't something he'd ever been good at, but most of the time he was on the receiving end, not that he gave a fuck about who was basically offering to suck his cock week to week.

Turning back to his vision, his frown got deeper. The thing he'd cared about more than anything was out there. But she was so different to the woman who'd been getting into bed with him that he almost couldn't remember what it was like to taste her.

His Tally was vivacious and voracious. She'd been a wet dream every minute even in the early days when she'd been meek and unsure… when she was sober anyway. Drunk she was a wildcat and always had been.

That wildcat, who he could see glimpses of out there with Sean, wasn't accessible to him anymore. He wanted her back. Goddamnit, all he wanted to do was make his woman proud.

"It's not for everyone," Teddy said. "This life puts pressure on us all. Some people aren't cut out for it, even if their role is minor."

Tally could handle pressure; she could handle anything if she had the drive to do it. And her role wasn't minor, not her role in his life. Even when they weren't next to each other she was his driving force.

This fucker, his father and all his cronies owed Max's presence to the woman out there. He couldn't figure out, if he was supposed to be so great, why they weren't more grateful to her.

"She's more than you'll ever understand," Max hissed the words.

Each day he could get through if he just did the task set in front of him… and remembered not to swear. Other than that, he felt like himself. He was being himself. So why was she pulling away from him?

"Do you know what this affair showed me?" Teddy asked, patting him again. "From the very beginning, it made me see that you have foresight. Tallulah Taylor is efficient and, yes, she is attractive. But she doesn't have the blow away beauty or flashy figure that we come across so frequently. I had no idea she could be so mesmerizing…" He leaned in closer. "Maybe if I had, I'd have taken her to my own bed, long before you found her."

Throwing Teddy's arm from his shoulder, Max spun around fast, his fist balled, ready to swing. "You—"

"Now, we don't want to make a show in the lobby, do we, son?" Teddy said, taking a step back and raising his hands.

There was a time when Max would have hit him just for calling him son. Where had that instinct gone? When had he stopped feeling like he should stand up for himself and for Tally?

It hit him hard when he realized that he *wasn't* the same person anymore. He wasn't himself. They had changed him, and he hadn't even seen it coming. Figuring that out helped him to figure Tally out. She'd told him she didn't want a rich, influential man. At the time, he'd been damn sure he'd never be like these fuckers she'd been talking about. But now… he didn't know who the hell he was.

"She deserves more."

The probing glint in Teddy's eye was almost curious. "You cared about her."

Max almost laughed right in his face. He didn't know how it wasn't obvious to every schmuck he walked by that she was his whole world and the only thing that mattered. Tally was all that he had left of what he'd once been. Without her, he'd be lost.

The air around him seemed to get thinner. He pulled at his tie. His tie! When the fuck did putting on a tie every day become his normal and why the fuck had he let it happen?

"You have no idea," Max growled.

Teddy exhaled and became sympathetic. "That's a shame. A real shame, son. I'm sorry."

"Sorry?" Max said and leaped forward. "If you even think about taking her from me—"

"Me?" Teddy said, all innocence as he laid a hand on his chest. "No, of course not, son, but… you know this life is eating her up. You can see it from here." Moving in a quarter turn, he opened his hand to the vision of Tally and Sean still out there laughing together. "That's the woman she's supposed to be. Free and joyous. Living the way she is, at your mercy, waiting for your call every minute, unable to make decisions for herself… that's not who she is… It pains me to know how she'll come to resent you. How she'll never be able to love you like this."

Resent him. Funny, that was exactly the line that Tally had tried to sell him. Max hadn't believed it then and didn't want to believe it now. But he couldn't say that he didn't believe it. From the minute she'd come into his life, that tempting pouty mouth and her red-riding-hood eyes had snagged him. He knew that hook wouldn't ever go anywhere, and he had thought she felt the same about him.

Guess not.

It wasn't fair to judge her, she'd probably seen the changes in him that he'd missed. He wasn't the Max she'd fallen in love with anymore. Just like she'd foreseen, he was a different man. In the back of that limo that time she'd cried because he wasn't in his dirty jeans and scuffed-to-fuck jacket, she'd wailed about how she didn't like him in the tux with the smooth jaw.

But he hadn't listened. He'd listened, but he hadn't heard her. Because while he was trying to tell her everything would be fine if they just pretended to ignore all the changes, she'd been screaming at him that the changes were shattering what they'd built.

He hadn't talked to any of his friends since the Fitzpatrick's debacle. Couldn't remember the last time he'd watched a ballgame or listened to a band play live in a club. He sure hadn't spent a weekend locked up with his girl or gone trawling for the bagels she liked just to make her happy.

"You could cut the crap and get rid of the damn contract," Max said, snapping a glare to his father.

"I could," Teddy said, slipping a hand in his pocket. "But would it make a difference? This is your life now, son. You, here, with me, building the business. This is your future… You're not the man you were when you and Tallulah met… It seems to me she's faced that reality… Why are you refusing to do the same?"

Because facing that reality meant admitting that

Tallulah had been right all along. She'd been straight with him, he couldn't deny that. She'd told him that she didn't want to be with one of the beanpole crew and he'd become one of them.

Starched and upright, he still followed her rules and played up the bored and mean thing; most of the time because he *was* bored. But she'd told him to embrace this life for all the street rats out there who would kill for a chance like this.

For the first time in his life, Max had prospects. He didn't have to worry about money and he had respect everywhere he went, even when he didn't deserve it.

The cost for that was more than just his old life and friendships, those things were carrying on without him. Even though he missed them, they were still there, and weren't suffering without him. The cost for his security was Tally's happiness. It was her. She was the cost.

By keeping her in his bed and in his life, he was being selfish in letting her pay that price. That wasn't what her man should do, her man should protect her. He should sacrifice for her. Max could take the burden from her and pay the price himself... by giving her the freedom she wanted.

Admitting to himself that there was a chance she didn't want to be with him anymore was difficult. It fucking tore him up. But his girl was hurting, and the Max he was wouldn't ever have tolerated that.

Aware now of the truth of where they were, he vowed to use the next time he saw her as a test. If he could see her smile, feel her warmth the way he used to, he'd fight to keep them together. But if that light was gone, and he couldn't see anything of the sparkle she'd once exuded for him, he'd have to let her go.

TWENTY-THREE

TALLY DIDN'T EVEN BOTHER to do anything fancy with her hair or her makeup. She knew that she was supposed to splurge on expensive lingerie and arrange herself in a seductive pose, but she wasn't good at performing like that.

So, instead, she walked through the house in her long robe and went into Max's room without caring that anyone who passed her knew where she was going and why. There wasn't any point in trying to pretend this was a relationship or that there was affection between them… Tally wasn't even sure there was respect anymore.

Other mistresses, Teddy's mistresses, played it coy and simpered. But it just wasn't in Tally to be that frivolous and shallow for the sake of it.

When she went into Max's bedroom, she could hear the shower running from beyond the closet. Unfastening her robe to hang it on the back of the door, Tally took the small tube from her pocket and crossed to slip into the bed, tucking the tube under her pillow as she did.

Lying there beneath his sheets, she thought about the paperwork she had to finish and how eager she was to get it done so she could get an early night. This had been a long week for her; she'd taken on more household duties and that involved more administrative stuff, but she was happy with the routine that allowed her to avoid the office.

This was just another part of that routine. She could really have done without having to do this today, but it had been a week since she'd last come to his room, and she didn't want anyone to have cause to say that she wasn't fulfilling her duty.

Movement by the closet made her turn her head on the pillow; she was pleased to see Max come out in only a towel. Good. They didn't have to deal with the removal of clothes and that stuff which just took up more time.

"Come over here," she said, shifting up the bed a little and stuffing the pillow under her head.

He started around the bed to head for his side. "I didn't know you were visiting today."

She pushed onto her elbows. "If it's inconvenient, I can leave," she said, pointing a finger toward the door and sort of hoping he'd dismiss her, so she could get on with her work.

"It's not inconvenient."

He said the last word in a weird voice, but she chose to ignore it. His mood was irrelevant, all she had to do was let him get it on. The sooner he did. The sooner she could split.

"Good," she said, pulling back the covers on his side. "Get in."

Wearing a smile, he dropped the towel and slid in beside her. "You're eager."

Rolling toward her, he tried to scoop a hand to the side of her face, but she shook it away and pushed it down. "You don't need to kiss me."

"I don't need—"

"No," she said, dropping onto her back.

"Oh... kay," he said and laid a hand on her belly, sliding it down toward—

"You don't need to do that either," she said, moving his hand away and picking up the covers to check that he was erect. "You're hard, just stick it in."

His hand rose toward her only to fall onto his leg. "What?"

"You're erect," she said and opened her legs. "Just put it in me."

"I'm hard because you're naked and you're hot… and I missed you." He tried to comb his fingers into her hair, but she swatted his hand away. His frustration didn't come out in a growl, but he did grit his teeth. "What about you? You wet for me, baby?"

"You know the friction will cause that," she said, sliding her hand up under the pillow beneath her head. "But just in case…"

Tally was about to pop the cap off the tube when he grabbed it from her. "Lube?" he snapped, glaring at the item he found so offensive. "Are you fucking kidding me? Since when do I need lube to fuck you?"

He launched it across the room.

The dramatics didn't impress her. "You don't need it," she said and dropped a hand to her pubis so she could rub her clit. "If it's that upsetting to you, just give me a minute."

Closing her eyes, she stimulated herself, trying to encourage the natural juice he seemed to need. One demand clashed with another and she was frustrated. It wasn't just enough that she showed up anymore, she had to be primed too.

"Don't you fucking do that," he said, grabbing her hand away from its task. "Open your fucking eyes, look at me."

Doing as she was told, she couldn't change the blank expression on her face. At least, not until he tried to take her fingers to his mouth.

Sneering, Tally recoiled, pulling her hand away. "Don't do that."

"Taste you? Since fucking when—"

"Look, Max, can you do the teenage tantrum later? I'm here. We're here. Just put it in. Have your way. And get it the hell over with!"

Letting her go, he sat up. Drawing his knees higher, he rested an elbow on one and scooped a hand through his hair. This was… odd. Tally hadn't meant to annoy him. The last thing she had time to do was coddle his hurt feelings.

"This isn't right," he muttered after a minute of saying nothing at all.

Still behind him, she sat up, holding the sheet to her chest. "Want me to jerk you off?"

Pushing her lips to one side, she was trying to think of how she could best ensure he was sated without having to deal with any drama. It was impossible for her to feel anything around him anymore. This was her duty. A task to be completed. While she still had affection for him, it didn't help her to give in to those softer feelings, not when he wasn't really hers anymore.

Twisting around, there was a glare in his eye when he grumbled, "Would you listen to yourself?"

"What?" she asked. "I'll blow you if you prefer." Though she'd kind of rather not, it might be the best way to get him to the finish. But he didn't seem moved and she was growing impatient. "If it's my ass you want, just do it..." Her attention drifted to the window. "I've suffered every other indignity."

He moved so fast when he flew out of the bed that she almost gasped. "How the fuck can you talk like that to me?"

"What?" she asked, crossing her legs beneath the sheet. "You can do whatever you want. I'm basically your wank sock."

"That's what you think you are?" he asked, standing facing the bed. "My sex toy?"

"Yep," she said, unable to even think about a smile as she flopped onto the bed and let her head roll in the direction of the closet.

Seemed like her paperwork was going to keep her up all night. She'd just have to lay here and wait until he decided what he wanted.

The deep well of nothingness inside her only grew when she was here. The chasm between who she was and who she wanted to be increased. Her fingertips touched her hair and she let them move within it.

She was drifting on her own thoughts when the sheet was suddenly whipped away from her body. Her head rolled and she was shocked to see Max standing at the end of the bed, looking at her body.

"Close your eyes, Boss," he said.

But she didn't. Squeezing her legs tight together, she had a sense of what he was thinking, but she grabbed the edge of the sheet and pulled it over her again. "This isn't what it used to be."

"Why not? Why isn't it the same?"

"Because if I give myself to you like I let myself be with him, I won't be able to endure this anymore."

Sitting on the end of the bed, he tried to touch her ankle, but she withdrew, curling her legs up toward her body. "Him?" he said. "You mean me."

She swallowed. "I mean who you were. The Max I still love."

His chin moved toward the window. "That's not who I am anymore."

No, it wasn't, and it was progress that she didn't have to be the one to tell him that. Coming to terms with who he was would help him to better fit in and find his place in this new world.

"No, it's not." Sitting up, Tally was wondering what he wanted from her. "So… you want a blowjob, or…"

"I don't want to fuck you."

There was a time those words would have ripped at her guts. This time, she got a surge of excitement and leaped off the bed. "Good, I have work to do, and I'm sure you do too, so…"

Dashing across the room, she grabbed her robe and pulled it on. She was tying the belt when he uttered his next words.

"You're fired."

The length of fabric in her fingers fell when they loosened, and her head slowly rose. She wasn't sure she'd heard him right and had to take a second just to process the words. Slowly, she turned around to look at him.

Creeping a step closer, Tally peered at the man seated on the edge of the bed, the one she didn't recognize as hers anymore. "What?"

"Your services are no longer required, Tallulah…" Raising his attention, he locked his eyes on hers. "You can go."

The last thing she'd expected was to be freed from the life that she'd come to loathe. Once upon a time, she'd have given anything to be with Max. But she'd always known it would never happen. The man she loved didn't live here. Teddy wouldn't let him be him, and he wouldn't let her treat Max like anything less than the heir he was.

Being intimate with him had been incredible at the start when she'd mistaken it for what they had before. But it wasn't. Never had it been starker than when she'd had to creep out of his bed, while still wracked with the effects of orgasm, quivering through after-shocks, and having to leave the room.

Tally couldn't have a boyfriend, or love a man, who she wasn't allowed to talk to or rely on. This wasn't a real relationship. It was an illusion and he was freeing her from it.

"I can…" A smile burst to her face in time with her gasp of joy. "Oh my God." Tally let a squeal of delight leave her lips, but she took both hands up to cover her mouth. "Thank you, Max! Oh my God, thank you."

Rushing over to him, she put both arms around his neck to hold him. Being free of the contract meant never seeing him again. But she'd had to come to terms with giving up the man she loved weeks ago.

"If this was what you wanted, why didn't you just tell me?"

Easing back, she looked him in the eye. Letting her go meant giving up the last part of himself, and that couldn't be easy. A world of possibility lay before him and he'd embrace that in time. But it couldn't be easy for him to hear how she was happy with the idea of leaving him.

"We both held on longer than we should have," she said, touching his face. "But this is the only way this could have ended… There was never any other way."

He'd stopped fighting her. Somehow, he knew it was time because he didn't even try to change her mind or disagree with her. "What do you need from me?"

Backing away, she knew this was it. The last moment

she'd share with Max… her Max or this one. "Nothing," she said, continuing to move in reverse. "This gift is the best you can give me."

Turning around, she opened the door, but he spoke again before she left. "The Strettons were your whole world until I became one of them… now they're your worst enemy."

"Only because they took the man I love from me," she said to her shoulder without looking at him before leaving the bedroom to cross the living room.

It hurt.

To be free was everything she'd wanted for weeks and now that it was happening she couldn't consolidate the joy with the pain. Max was gone. Her Max was no longer an option for her or any woman. But this was hard, harder than she'd let herself think it would be.

"I changed my mind."

The sound of his voice made her spin around. Max was coming toward her, stalking across the room. "You won't let me leave?"

Crouching down, he didn't miss a beat when he scooped her up and rushed her back against the wall. "I do want to fuck you," he growled and plunged his tongue into her mouth.

There was no option to say no to his kiss. Her head was trapped between him and the wall. Hooking a hand around her thigh inside her robe, he didn't give her the option to refuse sex either.

But she didn't want to say no. This man was more hers than any she'd slept with since signing that damn contract. Now she was free, he was letting her go, and he was trying his damndest to be the man he'd once been to satisfy her.

The strength of his thrusts and the entitlement in those possessive hands reminded her of the Max who'd wanted her so bad he hadn't been able to refuse her.

This Max was her Max. Sure. Arrogant. Determined. This was the Max who hadn't cared about Teddy's rules or insulting anyone. This Max wanted her. All of her, and in these final few seconds they shared, she was going to give herself to him again, one last time.

NEITHER OF THEM had said a word after they'd both come. Max had let her feet drift to the floor and then he'd stepped away. Just like the first night, when they'd done it in roughly the same spot, and like the old days, as soon as they were done, she bolted.

It was poetic really that their relationship ended the way it had begun with sex against the wall and her running for the hills the moment it was over.

She packed the essentials that totaled all she'd accumulated in life, into two suitcases, and left the Stretton Estate for the last time.

Without anywhere to go, and with nowhere to belong, Tally didn't think too hard about where she was headed.

She'd been to Fitzpatrick's in the last month, though she refused to talk about Max. But she'd never brought all her worldly possessions with her before. So the moment she pulled her cases to a halt and climbed up onto a stool, a peace settled over the place.

"Tequila," she said without even looking at Trey who was on the other side of the bar. He went to retrieve the bottle and a glass and came back a few seconds later. "Leave the bottle."

Slipping a hand into her pocket, she pulled out a diamond to match the one Max had given the bartender on their first night here.

"Put your money away, MG," Trey said, pushing the diamond back toward her.

An ironic smile slid to her lips, but she picked up the glass and tossed back the measure. "Just G now, Trey," she said, pouring more liquor into her glass. "Just G with nowhere to go, no one to turn to, no roof over her head." Throwing the next measure back into her throat, she was less careful about pouring the third. "No man. No job. No home... I'm really doing a good job of life."

A posse of bodies crowded in around the back of her

and she didn't need to look up to know the guys were closing in. "What happened?" Robbie asked, sliding onto the stool next to hers.

"Got fired," she said and drank more booze.

It probably wasn't smart for her to get drunk when she had no idea where she was going to spend the night. But if she ended up under a table in Fitzpatrick's, she was sure someone would throw a coat over her or something.

"No! I don't fucking believe it. I don't believe Max would let that—"

She snorted. "He was the one who did it." The guys were all mumbling their objections and disbelief, but she waved a loose hand over her shoulder. "It's okay, it's fine. It's what I wanted. It's for the best."

"For the best to be out on the street?" Ryan asked.

"She's not on the street," Robbie said. "She's here. We've got her." Tally was sipping her drink when she turned her eyes to him. "You can work with us at the garage. You do the books anyway, you can come answer phones or something until you get on your feet."

Ryan laughed. "Yeah, maybe we'll actually show up to work if there's someone there booking in jobs and ordering parts."

"I'll need a motel or something," she said. "I won't intrude on any of you."

"Rob lives like a slob, you'd end up with a disease if you stayed at his place," Ryan said.

She managed to broaden her smile. Filling her glass again, Tally gave herself a mental pat on the back. Coming here had been a good idea; the guys were helping her to relax. Robbie was digging in his pocket and she sighed into her glass after drinking.

This was good. The alcohol. The atmosphere. The people. Slapping a hand on the bar, Robbie slid it away to reveal there was a key beneath it. "Good thing I've got an apartment on standby for her."

"An apartment," she said, looping the keychain through her thumb to pick it up. "What are you..." Clarity made her whip around. "This is Max's key."

"No, it's your key," Robbie said, putting an arm around her. "You need a place to stay and it's sitting there empty. I know it might be weird, but we'll air the place out, help you unpack. You can make it yours." Examining the key, she couldn't help but feel trepidation. "It's not like he's coming back... is it?"

No, it wasn't. Robbie was right that it would be weird. But Max's place was the only place that had been close to home other than the Stretton Estate and she wouldn't ever go back there. It wasn't like Tally had a lot of options. Max's place was empty, so she guessed it wouldn't hurt to stay there, at least for a while, until she could figure something else out.

Her Max hadn't wronged her, neither had Max Stretton, not really, they just weren't compatible. Coming to terms with life without Max was going to take time, and if she could hold onto some thread of the love they'd once had, she wasn't going to pass that chance up.

TWENTY-FOUR

"I DON'T GET HOW there can be a sex contract," Robbie said.

Sitting in a sort of circle in the living room around a bunch of wood and cardboard, Tally and the guys were trying to figure out how to build the bookcase she'd bought. She'd started to garner a collection of books and there was space behind the front door for some shelves, so she figured this piece of furniture was as good a start as any in making the place more her own.

During her days at the garage when she wasn't doing her paperwork or answering calls, the guys didn't mind her reading. It brought her comfort and that was in short supply these days.

"It wasn't a sex contract," she said. "I guess it's more like a prenup… but without the nup… It's a pre-affair contract, I guess, with NDA and all that."

It had been almost a month since she'd left the Stretton Estate and she was just beginning to feel like life could maybe go on.

Most days she still thought of Max or things they'd done together. Living in his apartment was a constant reminder of him and their relationship. But she had changed up some things and the place was much cleaner than it ever had been when he lived here alone. Each day, it was beginning to feel a little more like hers and a little less like his.

"Sounds like a sex contract," Bobby said.

The coffee table was under the window and the couch pushed back to give them more room to work.

Sliding up onto the armchair she'd once shared with Max, Tally was on instructions duty. The guys were sure they knew what they were doing, but she was going to keep an eye on things and direct them as best she could without being too obvious about it.

After all these weeks, she was only just getting to a place where she could talk about Max. At first, it had been happy memories and reminiscing. But the guys had started to ask about what had happened while he was there and why they had decided not to be together.

Explaining the mistress contract was mortifying, but it was nice to see their reactions because they were in support of her position. Her relationship with Max had been so great precisely because it was so organic and not forced or contrived; contorted by rules and regulations and boundaries.

But the guys were still trying to figure it out.

"It's not a sex contract," she said. "Well, yeah, I mean, it's something like that. But it's not explicit. And there's no exchange for cash. I wasn't paid to be his mistress. Things were unusual in my situation because I was already an employee. I was paid to be the family liaison, the same as I always was. The mistress contract was just implication and suggestion."

"I don't get it," Bobby muttered, confusing himself with a pile of screws, but glancing up at her to indicate she was the one confusing him.

"Okay," she said, pulling her legs up to fold them under her. "It said that I was required to 'perform duties' for the Stretton heir as dictated by him. It didn't say what, but I knew what it meant. A similar thing would be written into any employment contract because employers like to cover their asses if they have to assign different responsibilities. The mistress contract laid out the hierarchy, stating I was ultimately answerable to Teddy."

"So he could hire and fire you," Robbie said, laying out shelves, though he paused to scowl. "Doesn't that mean he could've asked you to… you know?"

"Have sex with him?" she asked and shrugged. "I don't know. I tried not to think about it… I wouldn't have done it though."

"But you slept with Max."

"Because I loved Max," she said, folding the instructions and thinking she'd need to go get the tools she'd found under the bed. When she lifted her chin, all the guys were looking at her. "What?"

"Loved?" Robbie asked, his head tilting. "I think that's the first time I've ever heard you use the past tense."

"You don't love Max anymore?" Bobby asked, almost like a bereft child.

Tally knew that they missed him and knew that there were times all of them used her as a crutch to the man who they'd taken for granted while he'd been their friend. It wasn't their fault that Max's life had changed so much. It wasn't Max's fault either. It was just one of those things. But their nostalgia about the old days bound them all together in the difficult times.

"I'll never stop loving the Max that we knew," she said. "The Max that he was the day you guys found out about Stretton… But you guys understand better than anyone else why it's important for me to let go of that… of what we had."

None of the guys appeared happy about it and she wasn't either. But it was what it was and there wasn't a thing any of them could do about it.

Getting off the couch, Tally went into the bedroom to pull the toolbox from under the bed. Falling to her butt, she let the heavy thing move on its momentum another few inches and tossed her hair back only to see…

His tee-shirt. There snagged under one of the bottom corners of the heavy box was one of Max's tee-shirts. Tally wasn't sure she wanted to touch it. This was one of the reasons she hadn't gone snooping. Most of the drawers were empty because he'd taken his clothes with him. She'd aired the room out, trying to get rid of his lingering scent because she just couldn't handle living with the torture of it.

Reaching forward, she was about to touch the fabric when a thud next door made her head rise. It sounded almost like the front door closing, but she couldn't believe it was. All the guys were here, and they were going out for dinner after building the bookcase, so she didn't know why any of them would leave.

Unless someone had got bad news.

Leaping to her feet, worrying about her friends, Tally was on her way to the bedroom door when the sound of his voice stopped her in her tracks.

"…I'm asking why you're here."

That was Max. She recognized the tone, though he was far more deliberate in his speech than she'd ever heard him before. The Stretton conditioning was beginning to pay off… from Teddy's point of view anyway.

"Us? What are *you* doing here?" Ryan asked.

"Yeah," Robbie leaped in to back up his buddy. "Who the fuck are you, anyway? What's with the suit?"

She smiled. His friends wouldn't be used to seeing him groomed. She'd lived with him while he'd been like that and never gotten used to it.

"It's clothes. Look at the state of what you're wearing," Max said, and though she couldn't see him, she could hear his disgust.

Teddy was in that room. Not physically, he wouldn't reduce himself to coming to a place like this. But Teddy was there in Max. Tally had never heard him sound more like his father.

Back in the day, Max wouldn't have noticed what any other person was wearing, much less judged them for it.

"It's sick, isn't it?" Bobby said, but he wasn't agreeing with Max.

"So which one of you screwed up enough to take advantage of this place being empty?" Max asked, and the judgment in his voice made her stomach roil.

No swearing, no twang of slang or laziness to his

words. Before Stretton, Max would have given his last to these guys and wouldn't have cared if he woke up to find them all sleeping on his floor. He'd have let them all move in and would never have considered it sponging or screwing up.

"You're a real bastard, you know… didn't take long, did it? What a fuck."

This could quickly descend into a fight and Tally didn't want that. The friendship group had only pleasant memories of their buddy, well, mostly. All of that could be undone with one swing and then her Max truly would be gone.

"Just tell me which one of you screwed up—"

Tally stepped out of the bedroom. "I did."

He didn't look like him. He didn't even look like the man who she'd left at the Stretton Estate a month ago. With his hair slicked and his face smooth, there wasn't an eyelash out of place or a single stray brow hair.

The scowl on his face looked different too, but it faded to shock when he saw her. "Tallulah."

Any of the guys who weren't on their feet before were up now. "Go back in the bedroom, G," Robbie said.

Sucking in a breath, Tally slid her hands into her back jeans pockets. "It's okay. We knew this would happen eventually."

Max still paid rent on this apartment, although he probably didn't notice the money leaving his account. Just like he wouldn't have noticed Robbie making a deposit into his bank account every month; a deposit that was from her to replace the rent that he was paying.

There was no way Max still used his old accounts. He probably hadn't opened a statement or even a banking app for months. Back in his old life, he'd been aware of every cent, or the lack of them, now each one meant little to him because they were surrounded by so many dollars.

"Want me to call Trey?" Robbie asked.

She shook her head. "I'll do it…" Tally eyed the door. "Will you guys…"

"You sure?" Robbie asked.

Bobby and Mark came over to kiss her, Ryan lurked by Robbie, but when she smiled and nodded, both came over to kiss her before the four shuffled toward the door past Max.

"Prick," Mark grumbled as he went past.

All four went out and the door closed. The living room was a mess with the pieces of the bookcase laid out on the floor, but she wouldn't have any way to transport that, so it would have to stay where it lay.

"Can I have a half hour to pack up?" she asked and gestured at the floor. "Not that, you can burn that; I just need to pack clothes and stuff."

"I didn't say you had to leave," Max said.

No, but she wasn't going to make this any more awkward for either of them. "The only reason you'd have to be here is if you're giving up the lease," she said. "This wasn't supposed to be a long-term solution for me anyway, I got lazy… It won't take long…" She took a backwards step, then paused. "I have a box of your stuff, I… I don't guess any of it is important, but, you know, it felt wrong to throw it out."

"I don't need any of that stuff," he said, undoing the button on his jacket and pulling at his tie to loosen it. "I don't need anything."

"Oh… okay," she said, figuring that would've been the case, but she didn't expect him to be so abrupt about it. A lot could change in a month and he was a prime example of that. "Then just give me a minute… please."

Turning around, she was going to head into the bedroom and was trying to prioritize what she'd need to grab. As though their conversation wasn't done, he surprised her by talking. "You look good." She paused but didn't turn around. "This place looks good… Better than it ever did when I was here."

Moving to face him, she was still wary. "I clean."

His eyes kept moving around the apartment. "Must be what it is."

"Have you talked to Benny?"

He looked sort of blank and that just intrigued her. Tally couldn't figure out why he'd be so out of it. "Hmm? Who?"

"The landlord," she said. "I can call him. We're paid up until the end of the month, so that should give you time to clear out anything you need… Robbie couldn't remember if the furniture came with the place or not…"

Max's attention was still drifting. "Hmm?"

"The furniture," she said. "Did the apartment come furnished?"

"Uh… yeah, I… I think so."

Much as it wasn't her place and she was sort of reluctant to, she asked, "Are you okay?"

"Am I okay?" he murmured, wandering toward the kitchen, but stopping before he entered it to turn and wander back toward the door. "Am I okay…"

Taking a backwards step, she pointed over her shoulder. "I'm just going to—"

"My friends don't recognize me… My girl fucked off and left me… I've got targets I couldn't give a damn about… Women without souls throwing themselves at me… And I'm being commanded by an organ grinder who asks me to do a different damn dance every day…"

His pace had increased as he strode a path from the door to the end of the breakfast bar and back. But it was the urgency and tension in his tone that made her think he might be on the cusp of some kind of breakdown or explosion.

"I'll just—"

"Who the fuck am I, Tal?" he asked, stopping to open his arms wide at his sides. "Who the fuck am I?"

"You… You're Max Stretton."

A wry, unimpressed smile twisted his lips. His arms fell. "Yeah, that's who the fuck I am… And when the fuck did that happen, huh? When the fuck did I decide it was okay to let some fuck who I never gave a damn about dictate my entire fucking life?" Raising a pointed finger, tension worked his jaw. "I never gave a damn fuck about money, or investments, or maximizing profit. But every fucking day, I trot into that damned glass crypt emblazoned with the name of the fucker who abandoned me and my mom, never gave a damn fuck about either of us. But every day I show up and perform like his dutiful little slave."

"The life you have is one of privilege," she said. "It's not to be sneered at. Of course it comes with some responsibility, sir."

The word just sort of slipped out, but it made his whole expression and demeanor change. She'd thought he was tense before, but that was nothing to how his body clenched when he leaped toward her.

"You remember what the fuck I told you about calling me that?"

"Things have changed," she said, annoyed and frustrated that he seemed to have regressed in his understanding. "You know that. You know that things aren't the same in your life as they used to be. They're not the same with the guys, here in the apartment, with us. You're a different man. A new man. You have so much potential and—"

"Goddamnit, Tallulah!" he shouted so loud that she thought she saw plaster crumble from the ceiling. "I liked the man I was. I liked my friends, my life… being with my girl."

"So what, Max?" she asked. "You're just going to give up everything you've worked for?"

His tone became a growl. "Everything in my life was just fine before I heard the name Stretton."

"Before I showed up," she said. "That's what you're saying. Everything was fine before I came into your life and ruined everything."

Loosening to contrition, he started toward her, rounding the couch and closing the space between them. "You know that's not it," he said and tried to touch her face, but she pushed his hand away. "Tally, you know how I feel about you. You coming into my life, us meeting, it changed my perspective on everything. There's nothing I wouldn't do for you… Baby, I'm sorry."

His fingertips touched her jaw and she closed her eyes. Resenting the tear that streaked her cheek, Tally couldn't imagine a worse place for him to be touching her. In this apartment, which they'd shared as a place of love, Tally could feel connected to him. But this Max, in this moment, could ruin all that.

"Don't," she whispered.

"Baby," he murmured again and eased her chin up to

lower his mouth to hers.

Their lips barely met before she put both hands on his chest and pushed him back. "What do you think? Sex will make you feel better?" she asked, letting the burn of her tears become anger. "How dare you come in here and think you can use me like that! You think you can fuck me and then fuck off without giving a damn about what it will do to me? Do you know how hard I've worked here? How impossible it's been to move on from us? But you don't care about that, do you?"

"I can look after you," he said and smiled. "With you here, it's great. Stretton doesn't have to know. No one does. We can be us again, Tal. Right here."

She couldn't believe that he looked so relaxed and easy about the idea. "My God," she whispered. "Your daddy would be proud." His smile dropped. "I will not be your mistress. How many ways do you want me to say it? For one thing, Strettons aren't allowed mistresses who don't sign a contract. If we start up again, I guess that means the one we had will become valid again, I don't know. The six months aren't up. I won't live like that. I won't be with a man I can't respect, a man who doesn't respect me."

"Tally, I respect you."

"If you did, you wouldn't have ever used the phrase 'I can look after you' with me. How dare you, Max? Jesus, it's no wonder the guys don't recognize you. I don't recognize you… You're damn sure not the man I fell in love with. If the man I fell in love with was here, and he heard anyone saying that to me, he'd put his damn fist through their teeth… You should be ashamed of yourself, Max. I always knew that hiding under Teddy's wing would change you, but I didn't ever think it would turn you into this… If you want to kick me out of this apartment, kick me out. But if you're here looking for pity or sympathy or my self-respect, you can get the fuck out of here and never come back."

Saying the words sent a barb of terror and pain right through her chest. She could feel the agony in her heart and in her spine, and the sensation spread throughout her. Tally didn't want to hate him. She had tried so hard not to judge him for the life he had or the man he had to become to fit into it. But she'd always wanted to believe her Max was still in there.

Just the suggestion that she'd want to be a kept woman, a secret kept woman, made her sick. That Max could think she'd even consider it proved to her just how far he'd come and it wasn't a change that pleased her.

Without another word, or even a flinch of expression, Max turned around and walked out.

Letting go of her held breath, Tally yelped in pain and sank down onto the floor, clasping both hands over her mouth. Max was gone, her Max, gone in every way. The heartache that she'd held at bay hit her all at once and she bent forward, pressing her face into her hands against the carpet.

Max had asked who he was, but Tally wasn't all that sure she knew who she was anymore either. Her heart hurt, and her future was uncertain. Any comfort she'd taken in knowing Max was out there in the world and happy dwindled.

Their relationship was over, the respect was gone, and Tally had never felt more alone.

TWENTY-FIVE

COMING BACK FROM THE GARAGE, Tally was looking forward to collapsing on the couch and ordering some greasy Chinese food. Tired and achy, she attributed her low mood and exhaustion to what had happened with Max yesterday.

If that was what was causing it, she had to shake it off, but telling herself to get over it, wasn't as easy as actually getting over it.

Taking her key from her pocket, she slid it into the lock, and threw her weight behind the door that had liked to stick in the frame for as long as she'd known it. But as she burst through into the apartment, she was startled to see the TV on.

She might have thought maybe she left it on that morning, but she only ever watched the news in the morning, and the TV appeared to be on some sports round-up, something. Still watching it and creeping closer, she dumped her purse on the floor and was about to reach for the remote on the end table when she was startled by the sound of a male belch from the kitchen.

Turning, she didn't know who to expect because she'd just left the guys at the garage and knew they were planning to go out for food and then to Fitzpatrick's because they'd invited her to go along with them. But Tally was too tired to be social tonight.

There was no way any of them could've got there before her, but…

Max appeared at the end of the breakfast bar, tipping beer into his throat. He gulped down what appeared to be most of the bottle before lowering it and rubbing a hand on his bare belly. All he was wearing was a pair of jeans, his hair was tousled, and his jaw rough. It almost felt like she'd stumbled back in time.

"Hey, Boss," he said. "Want a beer?" In a stupor, she just let her head move side to side. "You earn us lots of green today, baby?"

"Did I…"

He frowned. "I'm starved… What you cooking?"

"I…" She hadn't planned to cook at all, but… Tally dropped her keys onto the end table and tried to shake off her surprise. "What are you doing here?"

"I live here," he said, passing the bistro table and leaping over the back of the couch to slouch on it with his legs stretched toward her. "Throw me the remote, baby, huh?"

"Max, you don't live here. I live here. And I told you yesterday, if you want me to go—"

"No, I don't want you to go," he said. "We live here. Maybe that's a better way to say it… Yeah, we live here." Crunching up, he doubled himself to grab the remote and then lay back down, sliding a hand behind his head. He patted his stomach. "Come lay down, baby. We can order pizza. Make out… I'll let you pick the movie."

"Max…"

"That's my name," he said, his eyes locked on the television as he surfed the channels. "There's some shit on these days, right?"

"Max," she said, going over to bend down to shove his feet from the couch so she could sit down. "What are you doing here?"

"I'm moving back in."

Tally didn't know if she should be shocked or

terrified. "What? No! You can't… I mean, your father will never accept you living here. It doesn't even make sense."

"You know what doesn't make sense?" he asked, pushing up so he was positioned in the corner of the couch facing her. "You."

"I… what? Me?"

"Yesterday, in here, the guys were protective of you. They protected you from me. And the way you smiled at them when they kissed you goodbye… You're happy here."

"Yes, I am," she said, folding her arms, determined not to feel guilty about it. "I am happy, Max. I won't apologize for that."

"You used to be happy with me… Were you ever happier than when you were with me, here, in this apartment? Before I moved to the Estate and all that bullshit. Were you happy with me? With… your Max?"

"You know I was," she said because she wouldn't apologize for that either.

He raised his arms and then let them flop to the couch again. "Here I am. Every damn thing you said yesterday was right. No one tells it straight like you do. Thank you for speaking to me the way you did. I do deserve to be punched in the face." He sneered at himself. "I can take care of you. What the fuck is that? I can take care of you and I will, but I'll do it from right here with you."

Shaking her head, Tally stood up. "No," she said, "you can't live here and work there. You can't do it."

Sitting up straighter, he didn't take his eyes off her. "I have never been more miserable than I was at that place. Never. And you were right about us too, we were unhappy there, living with rules, under his orders. No fucking way I'll do it again. I'm your guy, Tal. Nothing is more important to me than that. No one tells you how to be with me, how we should be together. No amount of money is worth being without you. What we have, what we're going to have, is priceless. I want this life, no other life. It took coming back here and seeing my life, seeing the guys hanging out, you coming from the bedroom, putting your mark on the place… It took all that for me to see… this is my life. This is the life I should have. This is where I belong. I belong with you and I'm tired of trying to fit in somewhere I hate… I don't want to be the guy you can't love anymore. Tal, I can't be that guy."

Swallowing, she could feel her lips begin to crack. It was insane and overwhelming and unexpected. Max was talking about them being them again, about them being together again.

"If you're here, you can't work there," she said.

"I know."

"He'll disinherit you. You won't get a cent."

Bobbing his head, he clasped his hands on his lap. "I know that too."

"You're… you're giving it up? You can't do that."

"I can. I have. I will. I do."

He was so relaxed and at peace that it made her nervous. The simple smile on his face was the most content she'd seen him in months. "Max… Have you told him? Have you told Teddy you plan to walk away?"

"Nah," he said, like it was no big deal. "I've got more important people in my life to look after first. He'll get the message… I'm going to talk to the guys, make it up to them, get my job back at the garage. Times might be tough sometimes, but we've been apart, Tal, nothing can be worse than that. We couldn't make it through the Stretton shit. We deserve to give ourselves a shot doing it this way. We have a chance to make it. We're happy here; we were never happy there."

The idea of him giving up the money and the lifestyle was almost more than she could fathom. Max was a man of his word and she expected since he'd signed on with his father that nothing would break that promise. But he loved her too, and she guessed he was at war with the loyalty he felt towards her.

For a second, she let herself drift on the notion of them being together here, building a life together, it was seductive.

But reality struck her hard and she tensed. "No," she said. "We can't be together. You have to go."

A frown crept to his face. "Tal, why are you fighting

me? I'm telling you it's over with them. Fuck the money. This is what I want."

But she shook her head and backed away a step. "It doesn't matter. We can't. You have to leave. Please leave."

Standing up, he tried to come toward her, but she backed away. Just the aura she had around her seemed to be enough to tell him that she was serious, and he stopped.

"Tallulah, I love you. This is what I want."

"I don't care, Max. I want you to go… And if you won't, I will."

She didn't have a damn clue where she'd go. She couldn't stay with any of the guys; Max would track her down. Her only source of income was with them, if she lost that…

"Baby," he said. "You don't love me? Remember what it was like before Stretton. That's what it's going to be… You're going to love me again. I'll fight for you, baby. Whatever it takes, I'll show you I can be the guy you fell in love with… I brought all my shit back from the house. My shit, not that crap he put me in. I'm back. Me…" He opened his arms. "I swear, you'll never have to see me in a suit again, not ever…" He smiled. "Least until we get married… unless you want to do that on a tropical beach somewhere or some shit."

Closing her eyes, her chin dropped and moved to the side. It was like a dream. Max was here, offering her exactly the future she'd fantasized about, and she was having to reject it.

"We can't be together," she said, trying to garner all the strength she could. "I can't be with you."

"Why not?" he snapped. "Why the fuck not? There's no damn good reason—are you seeing someone else? That it? Some other guy that you—"

"No!"

"I'll take the fucker down, Tal, whoever he is—"

"I'm pregnant."

She hadn't meant to blurt it out. The moment the words left her lips, she curled them into her mouth and silenced herself. The frown on his face stayed in place as he searched her, but after a few seconds, his attention slipped down to her stomach.

"You're… you're… It's mine?"

Pushing her shoulders back, she pulled on her determination. "I won't answer that."

Trying to walk away seemed like the best option, but she only got a few steps before he grabbed her upper arms and pulled her in front of him.

"Tally—"

"Please," she whispered. "Please, don't make me say it… He'll make me abort and I… I can't, Max. I can't. I won't do it… I won't kill our child."

"Oh my God," he exhaled. "Were you going to tell me?"

History really had repeated itself this time. "No," she said. "At least, not until it was too late for him to force me into anything… I hadn't decided whether to tell you after that or not."

Scooping a hand onto her cheek, he brushed away her tears. "Tal, I would never want you to give up our kid." His lips curled. "Baby, this is amazing. Oh my fucking God, this is great!"

There was real exuberance in his embrace when he pulled her forward into his arms, which only told her he didn't have a clue what it really meant.

"I wonder if this is how your mom felt." His arms loosened. "She must have been so scared that your father would take you away from her."

Easing back, he bent his knees to get to her level. "Baby, no one will break up our family."

"I'll deny it," she asserted. "If he asks me, I don't care if he thinks I'm a whore. I'm having our baby, Max."

Widening his smile, he cupped her head, stroking her cheeks with his thumbs. "I'd kill for you, Tal, and for our kid," he murmured. "I won't ever let anyone take our child away."

It was obvious that he didn't understand her fear. "The mistress rules, they were all put in place after Teddy's affair with your mom. He didn't ever want to be in the same position again. That's why he got me to sign those contracts; he didn't want you in that position either. He didn't want you trapped by obligation… It might sound crazy, Max, I've only known a week, but…" Pressing her hands to her abdomen, she let her fingers alternate. "I love this little one. I'll do whatever it takes to protect him. I'll sacrifice anything I have to."

She'd expected him to read between the lines and know that meant him. As soon as he did, Tally thought his smile would drop and that maybe he'd get angry. Instead, he surprised her by swooping forward to sweep her feet from under her.

"And that's why I love you," he said, carrying her toward the bedroom. "You're one determined chick. You'd go to war for our family and I'll be right there at your side, fighting with you. It's you and me, Boss."

Kicking the bedroom door out of the way, he carried her to the bed and laid her down, bowing to kiss her lips before moving to the end of the bed. With a knee between her feet, he unzipped one of her boots and then the other, pulling each off to drop them onto the floor.

"Max," she said when he crawled up the bed on his knees, between her legs, pushing her skirt up out of the way. "I can't let this happen… You can't give up your life."

"This is my life," he said, bowing down to kiss her lower abdomen. "I love you. I love our family."

She wanted to remind him how insane it was to give up a billion-dollar lifestyle for a ten-dollar one, but his breath on her stomach made her laugh and she brought her hands around to his head.

"You only just found out," she said. "You can't love him or her already."

With his mouth still on her stomach, Max let his eyes rise to hers. "You ignore your momma, Junior. Daddy's home and he's not going anywhere."

He really looked so happy, and it made her sigh. Her Max was here. That man there, gazing up at her with his mischievous, adoring eyes, was the same man who'd shared this bed with her before.

"Are you sure? I can't… I can't lose you again, Max… We can't trust you and be hurt by you… Our child, Max…

Your father will want me to kill him or give him up… I can't, I… I won't."

Rising to prop his fists on the bed on either side of her waist, Max met her eyes. "Tallulah Taylor, I'm going to marry you before this baby is born. We're going to have junior, then we're going to have another, and another, and as many as you want… No one will hurt my children or my wife. No one. I don't give a fuck about Stretton, I never did. Everything I did, I did to make you proud. Somewhere along the way, I forgot that, and I let you slip away… Nothing is going to break us up again. The guy can sue us. We'll live in a goddamn box on the street, I don't care. As long as I lie with you every night, and our kids are surrounded by love, he can go fuck himself."

Trying to subdue her smile wasn't easy, but he was so sure. Tally had always pushed him towards Stretton, at first because it was her job, and then because she thought it was the key to his happiness. But she'd seen him smile more since she got back from work than she had the whole time she was his mistress at the Stretton Estate.

"You know, if you're going to be a father, you'll have to learn to curse less."

"Whatever you want, Boss," he said, lowering slowly to brush his lips on hers. "You're gonna rule us all."

The slip back to his old speech patterns made her shiver and she slid her hands onto his cheeks as he deepened the kiss. Opening her mouth, she sucked his tongue deep into her mouth and her legs began to coil around his.

Before she could let them tighten, he reared up high on his knees and grabbed the edges of her shirt to rip it open. "You never answered my question, baby," he said, pulling her arms out of her shirt and tugging at her bra to get it off.

"What question?"

"You gonna marry me?"

"If we're going to be Flynns, I will," she said, unbuckling his belt and pulling open the buttons of his jeans. "I never want the name Stretton. I will never let my children have it either… I always planned on our little one being a Flynn."

"Baby, I never changed my name, and I never will.

This is the Flynn house."

He started to bend again, but she put her hands on his abs to stop him. "He's not evil, you know, your father, he's… misguided and stubborn and conceited… But he's not evil."

"You're minimizing."

Licking her lips, she couldn't hide the apprehension in her swallow. "I'm afraid, Max."

Stroking her hair from her face, he lay down over her, letting his weight comfort her as much as the soothing motion of his hand. "The only thing he can give us is money… Does that mean something to you? Is that something you want for our child?"

Maybe it was her pregnancy, or maybe it was sharing this bed with him again, but her selfish side flared enough to let her tell the truth. "I'd rather he have his daddy… The money never meant anything to me."

She didn't even like it when he tried to buy her things when she was living as his mistress. Max kissed her. "Then that's what he'll have… Trust me, baby. I'm back and I'm not going anywhere."

Resting her hands on his cheeks, she looked into him. "Promise me, Max. You, me, and junior. I need to know you're sure. This is a huge decision."

And one she'd never thought for a second that he'd make with the allure of the life Teddy Stretton was offering as an alternative.

"I only know who I am when I'm with you," he said. "I can't be without you, Tal… I can't."

Trusting him, she breathed out her tension and pulled him down to join their mouths. Wrapping her arms around him, she wanted to pull him close, but he slithered down her body and began to kiss her breasts, then her stomach. Taking extra care to stroke her there, she felt his lips move against her skin. Although she couldn't hear what he was saying, it was pretty obvious he was having a conversation with their child.

Finding out she was pregnant the previous week had been a shock. Tally hadn't wanted history to repeat itself. More than three decades ago, Cindy, Max's mom, had found herself alone with a child, probably terrified that Teddy would steal him away. Tally had always known Max wouldn't harm their child. She couldn't believe that Teddy would ever get his hooks into Max so deep that he'd consider it. But she didn't trust the patriarch.

Even in her wildest dreams, Tally couldn't have imagined having this. Max, the father of her child, cupping his mouth against her abdomen, whispering words of love. He kept on doing that, though his other hand managed to pull down the zip of her skirt while he spoke.

And when he slid an arm under her to raise her hips, she let him pull her skirt off, and his jeans weren't slow to follow. "You can't just come back like nothing happened and slide straight back into—" Grabbing the lace in both hands at her hip, he tore through it and then ducked down to kiss her. Her body responded in the way it had when she'd first lay down on this bed under his command. Refusing him was futile, this was the man she loved; he was back with her. "Never mind."

"Open those legs for me, Boss, I'm hungry for your pussy. The sweet girl needs to be worshiped, and I've got the tongue to do it."

He was already tracing his mouth toward her center, and her lips curled as her legs parted. Losing her fingers in his hair, she recalled the first time he'd said those words to her. "It's been a while since you…"

Tally swallowed her words when his tongue flicked over her clit. Max was back. Her Max, and she wasn't going to let him go again. Sacrificing for herself was one thing, but giving him up now meant sacrificing him for their child too.

They would have to face Teddy at some point; there would be no avoiding it, Teddy wouldn't just let his son and heir vanish without a trace. But Tally had to trust that Max wouldn't let anyone harm their child. They were a family now, and theirs wouldn't be fragmented, it would be sacred.

TWENTY-SIX

TALLY DIDN'T MEAN FOR THEM to lock themselves in the apartment for two days, but they did. Sharing a bed had turned into sharing food, and then there was making out, which ended up with them in bed together again.

Talking about the baby and their plans for the future, she was infused with a sense of optimism like she hadn't had before Max came back into her life.

Max hadn't wanted to go out, he'd wanted to stay in with her and junior, who he spoke about like the baby was already here. Tally hadn't noticed when she'd come back from work that Max had built her bookcase, but it turned out he was a pro at carpentry and was already planning a whole bunch of furniture for the nursery, which would just be in the corner of their bedroom.

Money was alright at the moment. Max hadn't withdrawn anything that had been in his original accounts, as she'd suspected, so they had what he'd accumulated in there, and that included some of what Teddy had paid him. Having come from nothing, Max was always preparing for a rainy day.

"Four is a good number," Max said, his weight resting across her shoulders through the arm he had draped there.

They were walking down the street towards Fitzpatrick's. "It's not your uterus. I'm not committing to any more than one until I get through this experience first. I promise I will have your baby, Max. This baby. After that, I make no promises."

Turning his face down, he buried his mouth in her hair. "You've gotta face reality, baby," he said. "I knocked you up without even trying. Fact, you were trying not to get knocked up, but my guys just wouldn't take no for an answer."

More than a few times, his level of virility had been brought up during their joking around in the last couple of days, mainly by him.

Tally nudged his ribs. "You'll just have to start using a condom, for double protection."

"Okay."

She didn't expect such immediate acceptance. As they stopped outside Fitzpatrick's, she looked up at him. "Really?"

"Boss, it's done now," he said. "I got the next nine months bareback, by the time you push this little guy out, you'll have forgotten all about this conversation..." Bowing forward to kiss her, she noted the curl in his lips. "And you're gonna love him so much, you'll be begging for number two."

He reached over her to grab the door handle. "Then Daddy better hurry up and get a damn job. If Mommy is pushing out all these babies, she can't be working shifts in a bar... unless you're going to stay home and breastfeed."

"Don't worry, baby. I've got it all figured out."

Didn't take him long to get that cocky attitude back. There had been a real transformation in him over the last couple of days. Turned out that you could take the guy out of the hood, but the hood didn't go far. He hadn't shaved, hadn't washed his hair or thought about styling it. He'd been as attentive with her as he always had been, but still managed to drink beer, watch sports, and let her do all the cooking.

Being with him felt right. Living with him was what she was supposed to be doing. Giving up what he had for her and their child still baffled her mind. He could have had a jet-setting lifestyle and a different model every day of the week. She wouldn't have pursued him or asked for a cent, she'd have raised her child and let him live his life.

History would have repeated.

But any time she tried to bring up the possibilities he was shunning he'd kiss her and change the subject. His tension over the issue was palpable, and as much as she didn't want to have a full-blown argument about it, she didn't want him to resent her for what he'd given up.

The truth was, she didn't think he even registered the fortune he'd sacrificed. He was so casual about it. But that was Max. He was happy with her, in their apartment, planning their future. Being him again meant so much to him, she could just sense his anxiety and aggravation seeping away, and in her selfishness, she was thrilled to have her Max back.

"Whatever happens in here," she said, laying a hand on his chest as he started to open the door. "We're going to be okay."

"Damn right," he said and bent to kiss her head.

Pulling open the door, Max laid a hand on her shoulder when she turned to stride in first with him at her back. Those at the bar saw her, they smiled and seemed ready to speak, but when they registered who was behind her, those smiles faltered.

"What's going on?" Robbie asked, sliding off his stool to come toward her. Ryan, Mark, Tomas, and Bobby moved in behind him. "You okay, G?"

"Haven't times changed," Max said and took her shoulders to move her aside. "Anyone want to take a swing, I'm open."

Tally wasn't going to have them brawling, especially not when she was supposed to be behind the bar. Working here was her second job, she only took a shift or two a week, and helped Trey out when he needed it. But, as an employee, it was her responsibility to make sure there was no violence.

Leaping in front of him, she opened her arms to block Max. "No, we are not going to fight."

"We will fight if they keep going with this G shit," Max said because she'd explained the abbreviated nickname. "It's MG."

All the guys dropped their scowls to look at her. "It

is," she said. "We're back together."

"Wait a second," Robbie said. "I thought he was the asshole who fired you… got you to sign that weird sex contract."

Although she wanted to groan, she didn't. "It wasn't a sex contract and I told you that I wanted out. He only gave me what I wanted." Reaching behind her, she threaded her fingers through his and brought it around to her stomach. "He was a prisoner there too and only did what he did because he thought it was what made me happy… But we've talked and… we're going to do this."

The guys all switched their focus to her stomach. "You told him?" Ryan asked.

"Whoa, wait," Max said, putting his other arm around her shoulders. "You told them?"

"They would have noticed," she said, thinking about her belly looking more and more pregnant as the months progressed. "And I work with them every day. I knew I'd need their support."

"Yeah," Robbie said. "We said she could bring the kid to the garage if she wanted. We're gonna look after her. She doesn't need you bailing her out."

"No, I need her bailing me out," Max said. "You guys have a right to be pissed, I was an asshole. But I gotta say it straight, I was messed up. That life, everyone said I should want it, but it's a crock of shit. There's nothing there for me. So you know what? I'm sorry if I fucked it up for every guy on the street who'd kill to have that chance. But the way I see it, you all should be more jealous of what I've got with my girl… And I can't give that up."

"Hold up," Ryan said. "You're giving it up… You're… coming home?"

Inhaling, Max breathed out and nodded. "Yeah, it's over, man. I choose this. I choose Tal… Might not be easy and we'll have to deal with Stretton's shit, but he's nothing here now. This woman is all I care about."

For a second, the guys all considered him, and then they looked to her again. "You happy, Tal?"

Nodding, she widened her smile. "We've got him

back, Rob," she said. "This is the life he wants, I'm sure of it." Rubbing Max's arm that was around her throat, she tilted her head to rest her cheek against it. "It's selfish, I know. But… I want him back. I need him."

Drawing in a long breath, Robbie folded his arms and glanced back at his posse. "Well, why the fuck didn't you say so?"

The guys all moved forward, jeering and patting Max, welcoming him like a returning hero. Figuring it was safe to leave them, Tally squeezed out of the group and went to her place behind the bar. If she wasn't able to drink anyway, it made sense to be pouring the drinks rather than on the other side of the bar watching others getting drunk.

She was slicing fruit when the gang of guys came back to the bar and they seemed to be making plans for Max's return to the garage.

"You'll need money, right?" Robbie asked. "Are you gonna buy a house? Man, you just come back to the neighborhood and then you're leaving again."

"Tal doesn't want to," Max said, sliding onto the stool he'd occupied the first night she'd met him there.

Everyone looked at her. "We're only having one child right now, and it doesn't make sense to leave our support network. There are some bigger apartments on the edge of the neighborhood that are a bit nicer, if we decide we need to move. But while it's just the three of us and the baby is little, I'd prefer to stay where we are."

"Gives us time to plan the wedding," Max said.

That did make her groan as all the guys perked up and began to declare their congratulations. "I told you we would just go to the courthouse for that," Tally said. "I don't want a fancy ceremony. We get it done, come back here, order some pizza, and then have a honeymoon at home."

Max winked at her and then sort of puffed out his chest as he scanned the guys. "I got myself a good one, huh?"

"Low maintenance, that's for sure," Robbie said. "You don't want the big dress and all that shit?"

After her life with the Stretton's, Tally had been to enough fancy occasions to last her a lifetime. She wanted to enjoy her wedding day and constant reminders of how her life used to be and the invisible shackles she'd lived in wouldn't make it a fun day for her.

"I want my man," she said, putting a bottle of tequila on the bar and a bunch of shot glasses. "And I want my friends… that's all I need…" Max began to pour out the shots. "Though, it would be nice if my man was gainfully employed."

"Don't worry, Boss, we got it all figured out," Max said. "I'll be back in there Monday."

"Another guy on the schedule for you to order around," Ryan said and leaned toward Max. "She's really damn good at barking orders, whipping us into shape."

"What do you think she's like in bed?" Max muttered, so she threw a lemon at him, but he caught it and put it on the bar.

"Don't you forget it, baby," she said, mimicking his use of the pet name. The guys raised their glasses and downed their drinks together, slamming the glasses to the bar as they finished. Max started to pour again. "I want to get laid tonight, Flynn."

Pausing, he raised his amused eyes to hers and the guys burst out laughing. Tally just smiled.

"We scheduling sex? I want it in the morning, tomorrow, probably for the next fifty, sixty years."

"I'm saying," she said, taking the bottle from Max to hand it to Robbie. "I don't care if their pee-pees work after midnight or not, but yours has a shift to pull."

"He'll be up to it, Sugar, don't you worry about that."

Trey came upstairs from the cellar and dumped a crate of beer on the counter. "What's going on?" Coming over, he curved an arm around her waist and dipped to kiss her cheek. "Thought this guy was history."

"When the fuck did I become *this guy* around here?"

"Around the time you started to wear a real Rolex," Ryan said, reaching around Robbie to pull at Max's sleeve. "Let's see it."

"Left all that shit at the old man's place," Max said.

At the apartment, Tally had shown Max all the jewelry

she had that they could hock if they needed to make ends meet. Max had had a bunch of nice accessories and suits, but had left everything at the Estate, bringing back only what he'd taken from his apartment in the first place. He didn't want anything from the man who'd almost cost him everything, that's what Max had told her. And he didn't want his father to accuse him of theft and get him in trouble with the cops once he found out Max was shunning his Stretton heritage.

"There's gotta be a damn fortune there," Bobby said.

Max raised his glass to her as she took the lemon from in front of him. "See that beauty there," he said. "She's my fortune." He downed the shot and then propped an elbow on the bar to turn toward his friends. "Now, how many asses I gotta kick for getting too close to my lady without my eyes on… Who made a move?"

Leaning over, she laid a hand on his wrist. "Go earn some money at the pool and poker tables," she said. "Kick the asses after you take their money."

Sliding his arm back, he picked up her hand to kiss the back. "That's why you're the boss, baby."

Max started to move away with his friends who were walking toward the back of the room, but she tightened her grip to stall him. Waiting a few seconds, Tally let the guys get some distance. "I'll come find you on my break… There's this alley out back…"

The corner of his mouth rose. "Can't wait."

Letting him go, she watched him disappear into the darkness at the back of the room. His friends had accepted him back and it was such a relief. Their life was coming together and she could almost envision how incredible it would be, or it could be. But they hadn't faced Teddy yet and until they did, they wouldn't be free.

TWENTY-SEVEN

WAKING UP IN MAX'S ARMS was still a dream. Tally wasn't sure how long it would take her to get used to it, but having lost him, she knew never to take it for granted.

On her back, she opened her eyes to find him on his side beside her, his head on her shoulder, hand on her belly. He was stroking her with such care and tenderness, she immediately smiled.

"I hope you're this attentive when he's up screaming his head off at two AM."

Shifting back, Max kissed her cheek and kept his head on her pillow. "Are you happy, Boss?"

His hand was still on her belly and the soothing caress was enough to make her eyes sink shut. "It feels normal," she said on a content sigh. "I can't believe how fast it's become just... normal."

"I lost who I was. Being back home with my girl, doesn't take long to remember what I loved about this life."

His attitude helped, but hers was transformed too. While being a mistress, she'd known they had no future, that they were controlled by Teddy, so she could never relax. Tally had always known she couldn't be with a man she couldn't rely on. But Max wasn't a Stretton superior anymore, he'd become who he'd been for his whole life; the Max she loved.

It probably shouldn't have been a surprise that being away from Teddy's scrutiny and back in his natural habitat, Max had relaxed back into his old rhythm.

Rolling toward him, she combed her fingers into his hair and drew him close for a kiss. "I am happy, Max Flynn. You make me happy. I love you."

"I've been lying here waiting for you to wake up forever," he said, scooping a hand around her face to pull it under his.

"Wow, you're civilized now," she said, parting her legs when he moved over the top of her. "You never used to wait."

"Never wake a pregnant woman," he said, trailing kisses down her jaw. "That's what I was told last night… I'll be all animal again soon as this kid is out of you."

Opening her arms, Tally stretched them upward to drape them around Max's neck. "You put this kid in me, Buster, so that's the last time I better hear you complain."

"I don't think you heard me complain, Mrs. Flynn," he said, taking his mouth to hers.

But she pushed deeper into the pillow to get some space so she could search his gaze. "Uh, what?"

"Just trying it out," he said. "I like it."

His bliss rubbed off on her. It was so relaxed and cozy there in their bed that it was easy to be seduced by it. "Me too."

Pulling his mouth back to hers, Tally tilted her head to welcome his kiss and enjoyed the lazy pace of their good morning greeting.

She was so lost in the delight of their kiss that it took her a minute to register the sound coming from the other room. Banging on the front door made both her and Max break free of the kiss.

"The guys said they'd come over," she said, skimming her hands over his face and shoulders in a soothing motion when she saw how his frown deepened.

"They wouldn't knock like that." He kissed her. "Stay

here."

Leaping out of bed, he began to get dressed and she rose onto her elbows. "Maybe they're messing around," she said. "Think they're being funny."

"Yeah, hilarious," he said. "If it's them, I'll still put my fist through their faces."

"Max," she droned. "Please, don't fight…" But she could see the look of anger on his face. "You're going to be a father. What if junior was here and this happened?"

Tally pushed the covers away from her body to lie back down and rest both hands on her stomach. Pausing, Max looked at her for a second before seeming to forget the knocking to come and sit by her on the edge of the bed.

"If junior was here, I'd shoot the bastard," he said, bending down to kiss her, stifling her exclamation. He bounced down to kiss her belly and then strode over to the door. With the handle in his grip, he looked back at her. "Stay here, Boss."

The moment Max left the room, she flew out of bed and went straight to her underwear drawer. Tally had put on her panties and bra when she heard the raised voices. There was no way the guys were out there and if she recognized the angrier tone, which she did, the moment they'd been dreading was here.

Figuring that there wasn't time to get dressed, Tally went to the door, grabbing a robe from the back to pull it on. Closer to the door, she could hear what was being said in the living room.

"You are walking out that door with me this minute," Teddy Stretton asserted.

Tally couldn't believe it; she would never have thought that in a million years Teddy would be persuaded to come here to this neighborhood and this apartment. Losing Max must have had quite an impact on him.

"No, man, I'm not," Max said. "And unless you brought an army, you're not getting me out that door."

"You can't want this," Teddy said, his disgust apparent. "What the hell does this life have that I can't offer you?"

Taking that as her cue, Tally tightened her robe and left the bedroom, staying just by the door. Teddy was only a couple of feet inside the front door, and the moment he saw her, his disgust turned to a sneer.

"Hello, Mr. Stretton."

Her words, and probably Teddy's expression, made Max whip around. "Get back in the bedroom, Tal."

"No," she said. "I'm not ashamed of us."

"So that's it," Teddy said. "You're choosing the whore?"

Max spun around. "Don't you fucking—"

"You're as insane as your mother," Teddy spat. "This isn't a life for anyone. I can offer you anything you want. Anything at all. You'll tire of this life and then what? Then what will you be left with?"

"I haven't tired of this life in thirty-two years," Max said. "Your life bored me real quick. This is where I'm supposed to be. Where I want to be. I don't have a damn clue what you think is so good about your big-ass house and your ass kissing friends. None of what you have is real, it's shallow and sick. I don't want any part of it. You can keep it all."

Teddy laughed, a deep, disturbing humorless sound of conceit. "Stay then," he said and let his attention jump to her. "But Tallulah is still in contract."

Inhaling a slow breath, it was difficult not to show her surprise or let fear seep into her voice. "You said if Max fired me that you'd allow me to terminate my contracts. Employment and otherwise."

"Yes, but there was never any official termination of services," he said. "And I think it's obvious that my son has rescinded any implication of termination."

If it was just a matter of going back and seeing out her duties, then she would do it and just battle through the months that were left. But that was the trouble, there were months left on the contract. Her pregnancy wasn't showing now, she could conceal it. But for how long? If she got sick or had other pregnancy symptoms, Teddy would find out. Even if she hid all of those, eventually, she'd have a bump, and he wouldn't miss that.

"You bastard," she whispered.

But Teddy was smiling. "So, Tallulah, if you'll put your clothes on and—"

"No," Max said. "She's not going anywhere."

"That is not your decision," Teddy said. "Now, if you wish to come with her, son…"

"Neither of us is coming with you."

"How do you think that will work out? I have the resources to ruin you," Teddy snapped. "You think this is bad. You don't have any idea what I can put you through, put you both through. I know people who can make your life hell."

"My life was hell in your house," Max said, and she was surprised to hear the smile in his voice. "But you did me a solid, see you're not the only one who knows people now. I got damn close to a few people at those fancy parties, people like the DA."

Tally didn't know where this was going, but Teddy was a little more in the know, though he was taken aback. "I don't see why I—"

"See, baby," Max said, over his shoulder without taking his attention from Teddy. "All that shit with the flush talk and the Abacus stuff intrigued me enough to pay attention. They weren't archiving, they were hiding evidence, shredding files at the office and replacing them with dummy files in the house archive… It's all money laundering for their illegal operations."

"Max!" Teddy exclaimed.

"I know, it's okay," he said. "It's just how the business works, I get it, and I don't really care. Most of the stuff you do is legit, who cares if you make a little extra on the side with the wrong kind of people in shitty corners of the world… People you're not supposed to trade with. Who do you think would care about that? I could probably ask the DA for advice, might even know someone at the FBI… or maybe Homeland would be more interested."

Tally couldn't believe it. Stretton Chemicals did create some unsavory and dangerous things, chemicals in industrial quantities that no one should want to fall into the wrong hands. But money was alluring, and she guessed that pull was too tempting for Teddy to resist.

"You can't do this to your own father."

"My own father almost cost me the only damn thing in this world that's worth anything to me," Max said. "Then you come to our house threatening it again."

"You won't get a cent," Teddy hissed. "I can't believe you would give up billions… for this."

"For her," Max said. "Tallulah is my fortune… You're completely worthless."

Teddy began to shake his head. "I can't understand it."

"Yeah," Max said, with an odd strain of pity. " 'Cause I guess you've never been in love… not with anything but the money."

Opening his arms, Teddy dropped them in a shrug. "So that's it… You threaten me, expect me to leave—"

"You threatened me, expecting me to come," Max said. "Go live your life, Teddy, let us live ours… And don't ever contact us again."

Teddy glanced over Max one more time, but his gaze lingered longer on her. "You've cost him everything."

"Then I better spend the rest of my life trying to make it up to him," she said.

Relief didn't come close to what she felt when Teddy turned around and walked out. But she breathed out and thought she might collapse to the floor if Max hadn't come rushing over to gather her into his arms.

"Are you okay?" he asked, pushing her head back and getting her hair from her face with a rough hand. "Baby?"

"Let's never do that again," she said, resting her hands on his chest. "How did you know about the illegal stuff? I didn't even know about that."

"You weren't involved in the company. That talk the night of the dinner party made me curious, so I checked it out… Didn't dig much until I lost you, then I started putting stuff together… I brought a few things that will help us prove our case if he tries to come for us."

"My God," she said, and socked his shoulder. "You might have told me we had an arsenal."

"I didn't want you to be any kind of accessory to anything. I should tell them what I know. I never participated in it, but I do know about it… that's a crime in itself."

Wrapping her arms around him, she squeezed herself close. "I knew you were a bad boy when I first laid eyes on you. You live in the grey."

"Not anymore, sweetheart," he said, holding her. "Now it's you, me, and junior, everything's black and white. Top of that list is never letting anything separate us again. What do you say we get dressed and go on down to the courthouse today?"

Tipping her head back, Tally needed to look into his eyes. "Are you sure? I mean, everything, the money, your father… You can still go back there. You can still choose that life… You can still be rich."

His mouth slanted in a half smile and he cupped her face with one hand. "Instead of happy?" Max shook his head. "Nothing could make me walk away from you, Boss. I wouldn't trade you in… not for all the money in the world."

THE END

Thank you for reading this tale!
If you can, please take the time to review.

~

Ask your local library for more Scarlett Finn novels!

~

For all things Scarlett Finn check out:

www.scarlettfinn.com